The Westerman Affair

Art & Discipline Book 1

Regina Kammer

Viridium Press

Published by Viridium Press, Friday Harbor, Washington
ISBN-13: 978-0-9910166-9-3 (paperback)
ISBN-10: 0-9910166-9-6 (paperback)
ISBN-13: 978-0-9978893-0-7 (ebook)
ISBN-10: 0-9978893-0-6 (ebook)

Dedication

Dedicated to my art history thesis adviser Professor Kathleen Cohen, a globetrotter now in that undiscovered country from whose bourn no traveler returns.

Acknowledgments

Thanks go out to my family, friends, and colleagues for their enthusiastic support of my vocation. Thanks to National Novel Writing Month for inspiring authors all around the world. Most of all, thanks to my husband for his encouragement, advice, patience, and love.

CHAPTER ONE

London, April 1880

Charles Westerman sipped his champagne and leaned against a yellow-veined marble column in the noisy and crowded foyer of Rutford House. He surveyed the guests in search of a familiar face—or, at least, an inviting one. Really, there should be halos of light above the people with whom he wanted to socialize so he could know them instantly in such a throng. Colorful waistcoats and ties—outrageous choices in evening wear—were one way to divine artistic tendencies. Unfortunately, the art world had its poseurs and sycophants, and far too many of them were there that night, hoping to blend in with authentic social Bohemians.

Viscount Creslow had done the unthinkable in establishing his first annual *Salon des Refusés d'Académie*, a pre-Season presentation of paintings not appearing in the Royal Academy's Summer Exhibition. Expecting to see radical experiments by prominent artists, or at the very least works of salacious sensuality, the crowd had descended in droves. They were not disappointed, despite the display being predominantly pencil sketches and unfinished canvases.

Charles's lips curled into a half smirk behind his drink. Lord Creslow knew how to promote his title, that was damn sure. The previously bland and stodgy viscountcy had become vibrant and popular with his latest venture. He had turned the entire ground floor of his house into a museum of sorts, with gleaming galleries and a well-stocked art library run by a staff of private registrars and curators, including—too shocking!—a woman.

Charles chuckled to himself. He wouldn't mind meeting her.

What was he thinking? He wouldn't mind meeting any *her*. He'd been far too monkish of late.

He downed the contents of his glass before availing himself of a waiter's passing tray to restock his void.

No, that was not true. He had his standards as far as women were concerned. A thrilling mind, for one. Allure and charm. Although too much of any of that could be dangerous. His last lover had claimed to be a Russian countess, Ekatarina Krozinsky, yet, it turned out, in reality was Catherine, the youngest daughter of Lord Mayberry, a woman prone to flights of fancy. She had been "sent down to take the country air," which Charles understood to mean she had been dispatched to a sanitarium.

Such a shame. She had been quite the satisfying little piece in bed.

The crowd parted ever so slightly, affording him a view of a woman. Despite a spray of lace from her hat shadowing her face, she seemed vaguely familiar. An artist's model, perhaps? She had striking features one might find appealing if one painted or sculpted portraits. She wore a dress in the latest sheath style, robin's-egg blue trimmed with chocolate brown, the cut and colors accentuating her feminine attributes quite admirably. She moved with a slightly seductive air, gracefully swooshing her skirts as she turned to talk to those around her. She had attracted a small gathering of intrigued men and shocked women, all guffawing and giggling at whatever story she told. She exuded confidence and laughed easily, qualities most of Queen Victoria's female subjects should surely eschew.

Precisely the type of woman Charles had been looking for.

"I am surprised to see you here, brother."

Charles turned to the voice slightly below his left shoulder. Despite her stature, Francesca always commanded his undivided attention.

"And good evening to you, Frannie."

She ignored his feigned churlishness. "Darling, you've not called on me since your return. How are you faring?" She slipped her arm through his. "I heard about your Ekatarina."

Theirs was an easy association mostly solidified after Francesca's husband's death. Her three children had been too young for a mother to lean on emotionally, so Charles had made sure he was by her side when she needed support. The touch of gray in Francesca's blonde hair was the only hint of her having endured a strain to her heart and psyche. Otherwise her attractive features—that, for better or worse, ran in their family—remained unmarred. She wore a lemon-yellow dress that suited her so much more than the drab stages of mourning. The spectrum from black to a dull grayish lilac had been simply draining on her complexion and had taken the life out of her soft blue eyes.

"As well as can be expected, I suppose." Charles glanced back at the vivacious woman holding court on the other side of the room as Francesca tugged him in the opposite direction.

"Papa wants to know if you've found another woman. Someone you've set your sights on."

Maybe after he'd met the woman in blue and brown. "No."

"He's worried you ran off to Scotland to brood. He wants to you to get over the Ekatarina incident as quickly as possible."

"How kind," he said a little too acerbically. "More like he wants distance between the incident and his family name. Although, as I'm the only one of our lot with any reputation, it is my prerogative to tarnish the name Westerman as I see fit."

Francesca scowled.

He patted her hand. "And I didn't go to Scotland to brood, Frannie. I went there to paint."

"Well, perhaps you could make a public display of having a mended heart by paying attention to some of the ladies present? It's not a grand ball at a duke's, but there are not just a few rather handsome women here tonight." She pointed unobtrusively to a young woman standing with a matronly chaperon. "She's pretty. The one in pink over there."

"Ah. Yes. She *is* pretty, isn't she?" remarked Charles. "And crushingly dull, I might add. I've already forgotten her name."

"Perhaps she's merely shy."

"She is most definitely not shy and most definitely boring. It was a rather painful twenty minutes of my life." Charles glanced at his empty glass. "I need another drink." He waved to a waiter.

"Mr. Westerman." A familiar melodic voice came from behind. *Annalee?* Charles's cock responded favorably.

He turned around to face the speaker. Annalee Brockhurst was as beautiful as he had remembered. She wore a gold evening gown in the Grecian style, the folds and pleats embracing the curves of her body like a lover's arms. Atop her gleaming blonde hair sat a golden laurel-wreath headdress. Her cornflower-blue eyes shone like gemstones amidst the ensemble.

The crowd around them slipped away.

He smothered a small surge of desire threatening to spark into flame. "Miss Brockhurst," he exclaimed at the same moment he realized she was no longer "Miss" anything. He took her hand briefly and gave a slight bow. "How are you? I must admit I did not expect to see you here."

"I've returned to London somewhat permanently. Just in time for the art world's latest spectacle." She smiled politely. "How was Scotland?"

"Bleak." *Without you to distract me.* "But productive." Probably because he had lacked such distractions.

"Bleak? I imagine your landscapes must all look the same, then."

He chortled and sipped from his newly acquired champagne flute. "And your husband? Is he here tonight?" He should look away to endure the disappointing answer, but he simply could not divert his gaze from her lovely visage.

Her smile thinned. "Ah, no. I never did marry the gentleman in question. There was…a bit of scandal surrounding him from which, it seems, I needed to be spared."

Charles almost choked on his drink. Not that he was unsettled by the hint of scandal, because that seemed to follow the young lady. The implication of the failed engagement was that Miss Brockhurst was unattached. "I offer my condolences."

"Charles, I think an introduction would be polite."

Francesca's tone was chiding. Miss Brockhurst's presence had, once again, distracted him from the world around them.

"Francesca, may I introduce Miss Annalee Brockhurst." Charles extended his palm. "Miss Brockhurst, may I introduce my sister, Mrs. George Burridge."

"How lovely to meet you, Mrs. Burridge." Annalee offered her hand. "Mr. Westerman has spoken fondly of you."

Francesca's eyes widened. "He has?"

Annalee blushed. In any other woman such an affectation would be demure. "Yes. I knew Mr. Westerman in the Île-de-France when he painted several murals at my father's country home last year."

"Ah, of course," remarked Francesca. "I recall his spring sojourn to Paris."

"Oh dear," Annalee suddenly exclaimed. "I apologize, but I must fly. I see my aunt and uncle looking for me." She bowed to Francesca. "I'm glad to have met you, Mrs. Burridge." She offered her hand to Charles. "I hope to see much more of you, Mr. Westerman, now that we both are returned to London."

The tips of his fingers tingled when he touched her. "Yes, Miss Brockhurst. I hope to see more of you, as well." *Much, much more.* He bowed. She left in a froth of billowing gold.

"Charles," Francesca hissed. "Who, pray tell, was that?" She shot him a perturbed look.

Charles shifted uncomfortably. "Remember when I returned from France last year and didn't want to talk about something?"

Francesca lifted a brow.

He grabbed another passing glass of champagne and took a deep swallow. "She's the something."

Francesca gripped his forearm before he could finish the contents of his flute. "Tell me now," she said through clenched teeth.

"She's the daughter of Lawrence Brockhurst. When I met her last year, she had been engaged to a young man for a year or so, I believe. That did not seem to stop her from—how shall I put this?—'flirting' with me." Charles surreptitiously looked around. "Frannie, I was indiscreet, I admit. You see how beautiful she is. It was very difficult to rebuff her."

"Charles," Francesca scolded.

"And I only flirted back," he lied. Every encounter had worked him up to a fantasy of fucking Annalee fast and hard, while she'd seemed to relish causing him such physical distress. "It appears she is now unattached."

Francesca tilted her chin. "Charles, how old is Miss Brockhurst?"

"She's twenty-two, I believe."

"Oh, all of that." Francesca shook her head.

"Yes I do know she is half my age…or younger—"

"Charles, she's half your age and a flirt."

"And Ekatarina was thirty-five and a lunatic."

Francesca sighed.

He leaned in. "She's a charming girl, Frannie, you'll see."

"Yes, Charles." Francesca relented with exasperation. "Don't you have artist friends here to distract you?"

"It seems they are outnumbered by the fawners and flatterers. I'm having a devil of a time trying to find them. I had thought if I stayed in one place, perhaps they'd find me."

Francesca patted his arm. "Well, darling, I will leave you to your distractions, old and new, and seek out some of my own."

Charles flashed her an encouraging smile. His freedom in his own love life had emboldened her of late. Widowers and bachelors abounded in the art world. Seeing his sister once again happy in a man's company would be heartwarming.

She smiled back. "Being the sister of the celebrated Charles Westerman has its perquisites." She took her leave with a flounce of her skirts.

One old distraction continued to plague Charles. *Annalee Brockhurst.* If only there were a way to get her in a dark, secluded corner, up against a wall, his hands gripping her butt as he slammed inside—

A very boisterous and masculine laugh brought Charles back to the present, subduing the ache in his cock. A fragrant crowd had gathered around the artwork immediately behind him. He turned to see the spectators gawking at garish pastel studies of a woman's breasts. An equally garishly attired man gesticulated nearby, describing how the artist tried to get the female form "just right," how the delicate shading of white and yellow added such depth of realism that a man could just reach out and touch the soft globes.

Good God. Had the windbag just said that out loud?

Charles let out an exhalation and caught a glimpse of the woman in blue and brown still entertaining her own clique, albeit they had somewhat thinned out. Surely she was not as ridiculous a lecturer?

Did he really want to find out if she would shatter his fantasies?

Women. He needed to get away from them.

Well there was one place in Creslow's ad hoc museum that would be quiet.

Charles shook his head at the breast-gazers and slunk off to the art library.

Rosamund Chambers, the Viscountess Threxton, was having a splendid time waxing philosophic regarding the lack of male nudes amongst the sketches displayed on the walls of Lord Creslow's brilliant amateur gallery when Margaret Longacre—wearing a color one might consider a little too orange for her skin tone—joined her enrapt audience. While Rosamund considered Margaret a friend, the latter was something of a complainer and, consequently, a bore. Now the grande dame had decided to insert her meddlesome—although somewhat interesting—comments into the discourse. Her droning platitudes repelled those more interested in light conversation, which, it seemed, was most of the crowd in attendance. Minutes later, Rosamund and Margaret stood alone, Margaret jabbering away, Rosamund praying for an escape.

Rosamund glanced around while she nodded in assent to whatever it was Margaret was saying. Unfortunately, Jeremy was nowhere to be seen, having left her over an hour ago to chase "a flutter of beauty heading down the corridor." She did appreciate her husband's discretion in pursuing his affairs, and was quite used to being introduced to his *amoureuse du jour*. Rosamund had recently espied her own flutter of beauty—an attractive blond man with a woman who looked as if she could be his sister. Perhaps that was wishful thinking. And now Margaret's weighty presence had distracted her long enough that the man was nowhere to be seen.

If he were a wise man, he would be escorting his relative away from the lewd studies of female body parts to view the unfinished landscapes in the next room.

"Really, Rosamund," Margaret rambled, "my dear Viscountess, you should be far more concerned with the abysmal showing of women artists rather than the preponderance of female subjects. If this is truly to be a *Salon des Refusés*—"

Margaret's accent was impeccable.

"Then Viscount Creslow should have approached the Society of British Women Artists." Margaret's pitch went up an octave as her voice boomed louder. "Of course, if the viscount wants to be utterly *outré* and shock the Academy, then he should find a woman artist who sketches male nudes. With all this display of female flesh—"

"I quite agree, Margaret." She really did. Still, agreement was the only way one could interrupt what was quickly becoming a tirade. "And I will do my best to make such notions known to my uncle for next year's Salon."

Margaret stared wide-eyed as if stunned she had finally swayed someone to her side. "Why thank you, Rosamund. I very much appreciate your assistance."

"I'm happy to oblige, Margaret." Rosamund whipped her head to the right, hoping her feigned attempt at recognition was dramatic enough to be considered credible. "Oh, I beg your pardon, but I've just seen a client of my husband's and I promised I would follow up on his assessment of the commission." She smiled her most saccharine smile. "You understand, Margaret, don't you? It *is* an art exhibition, and my husband is a working artist. We must make the most of our opportunities to garner business."

Margaret's cheeks colored, veiny and red. "Of course, my dear Viscountess."

Rosamund took off as quickly as propriety would allow, but with enough swiftness that left no time for Margaret to rescind on her acquiescence and start conversation anew.

Rosamund strode with purpose down one of the corridors covered with row upon row of figure studies in oil, her husband's work standing out as the more palatable to the modern taste. She knew none of the gawkers—the middle class had turned out in droves to the *gratis* event. But she had to find someone somewhere to chat with or she'd insult Margaret. Her tedious friend had the ability to cut a person from certain fashionable circles. For that reason she was tolerated.

The half-open door to the art library was her salvation. Rosamund ducked in. All around the room, rich mahogany shelves were lined with the gilt-decorated spines of leather tomes. A few scholarly chaps were scattered about, perusing books while seated at gleaming oak tables. Others thumbed through etchings or architectural plans housed in long, shallow drawers. Marble busts of learned men lined the shelf above the bookcases. Rosamund smiled. Lord Creslow, or, rather, Uncle Bradley, had never been a scholar, had actually railed against "tutors and dons," yet now he was the proud owner of a true gentleman's scholarly library.

She lifted and tucked up her veil. Just a few minutes in the comfortable, peaceful room, long enough for Margaret to think she was meeting with a patron, and then Rosamund would rejoin the unlearned masses.

The susurration of silk induced Charles to look up from leafing through Creslow's landscape architecture plans. He couldn't believe his luck. The woman dressed in robin's-egg blue and chocolate brown had just walked into the library. She glanced around, then moved to the bookshelves, drawing a finger along the spines, alternately nodding or shaking her head with a wry smile. She walked down the row until she was right next to him, the flounce at her rear eye-level from his position bent over the drawer. He straightened, the action drawing her attention.

She smiled, the expression slowly transforming from a superficial mask to startlement curling her luscious lips and brightening her light-brown eyes. She held out her hand, exuding a natural sensuality that mesmerized Charles until the need to breathe forced him to respond.

He took her hand in his, the warmth from the touch shooting straight to his crotch. He bent his head and hovered, wanting desperately to touch his lips to the tips of her delicate fingers bejeweled with gemstone rings but naked at the end of her sheer lace half gloves.

He released her, too soon really, as she too seemed to want to linger. "Madam, I see you've discovered Lord Creslow's library."

"As have you, my good sir," she responded casually. She glanced down at the drawer he had just closed, level with his burgeoning erection. "And might I find you in those drawers, or—"she waved her hand at the bookcases "—on these shelves?"

She was good. She'd guessed him for an artist. He chuckled quietly. "Ah, no, I fear not."

"But really you should exhibit. For your career."

Charles returned her gaze. The fine lines on her face revealed she was older, perhaps almost his age. She was an exotic beauty, with a subdued flirtatiousness that was enchantingly attractive. The smoldering spark of lust ignited. "I'm grateful for your concern. But you needn't worry. I'll be showing at the Summer Exhibition."

And that was just a drop in the bucket. He was riding a wave of professional notice. Some Grand Prize winners eventually fell into utter obscurity. However, he had works spread throughout Europe—

He cringed. Peacocking his own accomplishments would get him nowhere with this woman. She was far more sophisticated than his usual fare.

She turned, a move so graceful and sensual he simply stared. "And what will you be showing?"

"Sorry?"

There was that sly smile again, tinged with cool awareness of his physical state. "At the Summer Exhibition."

"Landscapes."

"Landscapes?" she said with a modicum of surprise. "In oil?"

"Yes."

"How colorful." Her gaze took him in from head to toe, lingering about halfway. "And do you employ an assistant?"

"An assistant?"

"To mix your pigments? Stretch your canvases? Clean your brushes?" Her voice deepened ever so slightly. "Really, there is so much an assistant can do for you." Her intonation was positively seductive.

She was teasing him. Lusciously teasing him. He leaned in a hair's breadth. "Madam, let me explain something." He kept his tone low with just a hint of sultriness. "When a client commissions my services, he expects me to do the work. I am an artist, not a manufacturer."

She blushed to the roots of her golden-brown hair, the coloring provocative, not demure. "Of course, sir. I did not mean to insult."

"No insult has been taken."

The crack of a snort drew their attention away. A balding man with his hands on his copious belly had made use of a leather club chair and footstool as a bed. His overly loud yet peace-inspiring presence had emptied the library and seemed to keep newcomers at bay.

Charles was virtually alone with his newfound object of desire.

Should they introduce themselves? That's what one did at these sorts of events, wasn't it? She could be the daughter of a famous art collector, or the wife—

Yes, of course. She could be a wife. In that case, if she asked his name, he would offer. But he would follow her lead in the matter.

One should never seduce a wife unless one were absolutely certain she wanted to be seduced. Wives who wanted seduction were often married to men who wanted their wives to be seduced. It made for a happier marriage all around. One did not need to know details such as names.

Well, that was all well and good in theory. He'd never actually been with a married woman. The closest he'd ever gotten was with Annalee during her engagement.

His temptress sauntered away from the bookcase. "And what brings you to Viscount Creslow's inaugural exhibition?"

He watched but did not follow her. "I have friends here, both on the walls and in the galleries."

She glanced back, that smile playing upon her lips again, teasing, inviting. "How droll you are."

He chortled. "Dare I ask you the same question?"

"You mean, am I a denizen of the art world, or merely a flatterer looking to advance my circumstances?"

"Those embedded in the art world are always looking for opportunities to advance their cause."

She laughed softly. "Spoken like a true cognoscente."

Charles shook his head in disgust. "You don't want to know."

She tilted her chin and pursed her lips as she studied him, providing him the opportunity to study back. Her bone structure gave her face angles and planes that would make her a marvelous model for one inclined to portraiture. She held herself gracefully, as if posing for a full-length figural painting, seemingly knowing exactly which assets a man might find most appealing. Her body could easily tempt him away from dispassionate landscapes in more ways than one.

She couldn't possibly be a model, though. Her accent and knowledge implied a cultured, educated, aristocratic background.

She held out her left hand. "Maybe I do."

Desire smoldered in his groin. Before him was an invitation from which he did not want to—no, *could not* extract himself. Her magnetic draw was too powerful, and he too willing to be pulled right in. Perhaps he was too suggestible, his need for female companionship too easily quashing his reason.

And yet, his reason weighed in, there was something about her that was different from all the others. She understood his mind as well as his body.

He stepped toward her, perhaps too eagerly, taking her hand in his. Her warmth further drew out his utter need. The slow burn inside burst into a conflagration of desire, spiking heat to his cock. He flushed, half in mortification, half in lustfulness.

He skimmed the pads of his fingers over her hand, over the lace and rings, letting the sensuousness of the intimacy feed him. He stopped his explorations at her fourth finger and looked down. A gold band glittered under the delicate lace. He hesitated.

"It appears the fact of my husband is more important to you than it is to me."

Her eyes held sincerity, her smile held promise. He parted his lips, an excited breath escaping in a rush. Her gaze fell to his mouth, her tongue traveling slowly to wet her lips as if tempted with a treat. She closed the remaining space between them, raised herself on tiptoe, and brushed her lips against his.

The world around him faded as the fire of passion took hold. He grasped her to him, startled by his desperation for her touch. He plunged his tongue into the depths of her willing mouth, tangling, exploring, tasting. He cradled her head, the froth of lace on her hat rough under his palm. He shifted his stance, spreading his legs, his arm wrapped around her waist as he pressed his crotch against her skirts. She clung to him as she fell supple in his arms.

He broke from the kiss, traversing his mouth down her neck, flicking his tongue under the lace of her high collar.

Her breaths puffed quietly. "Sir," she murmured, "shall we take this conversation somewhere more private?"

He continued his kisses across her shoulder to her bosom tightly bound in exquisite silk brocade. "Where do you suggest?"

"There's an office behind that bookcase." She pointed to shelves heavily laden with leather tomes.

"An office?" He barely understood her words.

"The librarian's office. The bookcase closes out the world."

That was precisely what he wanted. To shut out the world and have her for himself. "Show me."

She glanced around before heading to the secret doorway. They were still alone with the snorer, his exertions resonating like a hundred men sawing in unison.

She fussed behind some books, shifting them along a shelf to reveal a latch folded flush with the wood. She lifted the bolt and pulled slightly.

The dim light of the library revealed a small office behind.

He gestured to the doorway. "After you."

She disappeared into the office. A light flared. A lamp.

He followed.

She closed the door. The inside appeared as a proper door, oak with inset panels and guilloche trim.

Suddenly he was as nervous as a schoolboy in the headmaster's office.

He glanced up the wall toward the ceiling. Two metal grilles with geometric designs offered air—and possibly a way for someone to overhear what was going on in the librarian's secret abode.

She followed his gaze. "Don't worry. I know this house intimately. No one can hear." She gave him a once-over and raised an eyebrow. "Although perhaps there will be nothing to hear."

Anxiety had slackened his arousal. "Madam, unfettered lust goads me to do something I've not done in far too long." It had been almost a year since Ekatarina. In Scotland, there had not even been a shepherdess to keep him company.

"I'm not holding you back." She casually unhooked the draping flounce wrapped around her hips, loosening the tight gown.

"No." Quite the opposite. She was prodding him forward.

She cupped his crotch. His cock sprang to life under the heat of her palm. She held his gaze as she licked her lips slowly, provocatively, while massaging his erection.

Good God. She was not innocent of fellatio, an Englishman's most secret desire. Did she suck her husband's prick? Did the man even deserve such a wife?

He stilled under her ministrations, waiting, hoping she would get down on her knees and unbutton his fly. He grew harder by the second, wanting to close his eyes and just feel her, but the sight of her lust-filled expression was excessively irresistible.

She let out a little mewling moan.

He could stand it no longer.

He turned her around and bent her over the desk. With one hand he tossed up her skirts, tearing at the fly of his trousers and drawers with the other. He threw off his jacket and waistcoat, unbuttoned his braces, and pulled out his too-eager cock.

Before him, arrayed in the finest French silk and lace, were the most marvelous buttocks. He pressed his crotch against her as he smoothed both palms down the curves of the cheeks.

"Magnificent," he breathed.

"I am delighted my backside pleases." She wriggled against him.

Her teasing spurred him to swat her gently. "It sets my imagination on fire." He slid his hand through the slit of her drawers. "What else may please me?" He found her sex, sticky and plump. She wanted him as much as he needed her. He glided his middle finger inside her and was greeted by a clench and a moan. He moved to her clitoris, the bud slippery under his fingers. He stroked the hardened nub as she rolled her hips in encouragement.

This was a fantasy beyond fantasy. "Madam, I do not wish to pull out," he intoned in a gravelly whisper.

"Sir, I do not want you to," she said between excited breaths.

So she used some prophylactic. His anxieties eased a little.

He grabbed his cock, the head glistening with arousal, and shoved in.

His senses exploded.

He had forgotten what it felt like to be inside a woman, the welcoming warmth enveloping him, radiating into his stones, the suctioning slickness enticing, nay *urging* him to continue. And this particular woman rocked her hips in a determined rhythm, commanding him to pleasure her.

The force of her passion undid him.

His knees weakened. He slumped forward to get his bearings, continuing to drive into her not from conscious control toward a glorious culmination, but from a base masculine impulse surging forth in an uncontrollable tumult. He clutched at her hand flat on the desk, the wedding band under her lace glove galling, repelling, reminding him of her undeserving husband, while her French fragrance flared his nostrils, the scent ensnaring him, compelling him to stay the course.

Instinct took over, tamping down lingering qualms, pushing him forward to climax.

She came with a powerful contraction. His inexorable release ensued immediately.

He bent over her, utterly spent, his heart pounding up his throat to his head. He sucked in breaths, trying to calm his physical body, while wave after wave of gratification inundated his mind.

She sighed, then squirmed under him with a gentle groan of protest.

He pushed back, breaking contact, grabbing his handkerchief in time to prevent a stain.

Calmly, as if getting fucked over a large oak desk were commonplace, his office paramour righted herself, reattaching the flounce, pushing down then fluffing up her skirts, turning this way and that to survey the state of her dress.

"Madam, your gown is unscathed." He gazed at her. "And you look delightfully refreshed."

She beamed. "Thank you." Her lips twisted into a smirk. "And you, sir, look positively disheveled."

Damn. He tugged his waistcoat into place, then grabbed his discarded jacket.

As a wife might, she helped his arms through the sleeves, fussed with his collar and tie, then smoothed back his hair. "A touch of gray I hadn't noticed before. Your blond hair hides such effects of age." She brushed the lapels of his jacket. "Of course, I am assuming you to be of such an age." She lifted a brow. "I hope *I* am not the cause of a sudden shock of silver."

He chuckled. "I assure you, madam, others hold that honor."

She smiled broadly. "And now, I shall leave you. Give me a few moments." She sashayed around him and scurried away in a sensual swoosh of silk skirts.

Charles stared into the emptiness of the office for quite some time, until a snort followed by a vociferous yawn resounded in the library, shaking him from his reverie.

He'd give the lady a few more minutes to move through the galleries while he perused the library shelves. He'd hardly know how to act should he encounter her again.

Good God. What if she were attending the Salon with her husband?

CHAPTER TWO

Rosamund exhaled in relief. Her sojourn to the library had resulted in quite the unexpected—and refreshing—diversion.

She straightened her gloves as she sauntered down the corridor, sidelong glances ensuring no one she knew had seen her. The attractive blond man had satisfied her in more ways than he probably knew. While his admiration of her bum had roused her, his little swat had positively inflamed her. The spot still burned deliciously.

She had done similarly for him. He had needed to be with a woman, that was obvious. Perhaps he had not had a fuck in some time, or perhaps she reminded him of someone he desired.

Perhaps they would find themselves together soon. She would, most likely, see him at one of the many events surrounding the Summer Exhibition.

She'd ask him his name then.

Rosamund laughed softly as she searched for Jeremy amongst the new faces in the ever-changing crowd. Surely her husband was finished with whatever dalliance he had hoped to have?

She spied him gabbing with an older man, smiling and nodding with affected politeness. A client or potential client, dressed exquisitely, which meant he had money and vanity enough to commission a portrait. Jeremy would complain that the exuberant whiskers on the man would be difficult to paint, but then he would put himself into his work and do a marvelous job. He always did. He was exceedingly talented. It was too bad he didn't realize it himself.

She caught his eye. If Jeremy wanted her to meet the potential sitter, he would wave her over. Otherwise, he would end his conversation. He did the latter with an exchange of calling cards, then rushed toward her.

"Darling." He took both her hands in his and kissed her cheeks, his beard tickling the lingering flush on her skin.

"Good news?"

Jeremy grinned. "That man wants to pay for the privilege of having me paint him."

"A fine use of his money."

He draped an arm around her shoulder. "I never expected gaining notoriety as a professional portraitist would feel so good." He arced over her. "Let me buy you jewels," he murmured. "Please. I want to."

"Of course, darling husband. And what will you give your mistress?"

"No one compares to you, my love."

"What about the distraction you had earlier?"

"Ha!" he snorted. "That little confection I ran after was none other than the daughter of Edward Burne-Jones."

Rosamund hid her astonishment behind her hand. "Oh, my. And just how far did you pursue your suit?"

"Good God, Rosie!" Jeremy hissed. "Not at all! She's bloody fourteen years old. She was dressed in some outlandish Renaissance costume—"

"Much like a Burne-Jones painting."

"Precisely. It made her quite attractive from afar. There were other potential suitors as equally shocked and deceived as I. Surely her mother had not intended for such keen interest. It was most distasteful. I'll need a long draught of cognac when we get home." He puffed an exhalation and collected himself before offering her a provocative uplift of a brow. "And you? Did you meet anyone interesting?"

"I did."

Satisfaction tugged on Jeremy's lips. "Oh? Do tell."

"Unfortunately, I did not get his name."

"At least tell me it's not the man who's just promised to pay me heaps of money." Jeremy grinned. "Is it?"

She laughed. Jeremy made her laugh easily. "Don't worry, darling husband. Your commission is safe. I don't think I could abide those whiskers."

Jeremy scrubbed a hand over his well-trimmed beard. "Ugh, painting those is going to be—"

He stopped and gaped at something in the distance. Rosamund followed his stare. The object of his attention, the actress Lisette LaFleur, was stunningly beautiful in her froth of lavender skirts swirling dramatically with every step, distracting an observer momentarily from the display of far too much of her bosom. In keeping with her profession, her lips were painted a vivacious red. The crowd parted as she strode forward confidently, flashing a smile for Jeremy's benefit.

She arrived amidst an aroma of roses and champagne. "Lord Jeremy, I have just heard you are to exhibit at the Royal Academy." She held out her hand for a kiss. "Congratulations." She gave a slight nod in Rosamund's direction.

Rosamund hated that Lisette called her husband "Lord Jeremy" and not "Lord Threxton." She did it to affect an air of intimacy, yet the false designation sounded silly. Especially when it was said with her excited, high-pitched voice. Not to say Rosamund didn't like Lisette. She liked the girl—sometimes. Lisette was always engaged in something fascinating and *au courant*.

Jeremy kissed the air over the proffered hand. "Thank you, Miss LaFleur. I am quite ecstatic myself. It is an honor to be included in the Summer Exhibition."

Lisette insinuated herself alongside Jeremy, a position that highlighted the fact she was quite a bit taller than Rosamund. Her height and hair, the same black as Jeremy's, made her appear more well-matched with the viscount. "My lord," she said with too sultry an air, "I need a painter for my next show. I'm doing Shakespeare's *Tempest*." She stood erect and placed her palm on her half-bared breast. "'O brave new world that hath such people in it,'" she quoted. "I'm playing multiple parts. We had to rewrite it a little so I could do so. I'm on stage almost every minute."

"Sounds intriguing," remarked Jeremy.

"I need someone to create my sets. Oh, you could do that, couldn't you, Lord Jeremy? I mean, it shouldn't really be all that difficult." Lisette batted her violet eyes, her expression hovering between seduction and begging.

"Well, I *do* have to prepare for the Exhibition," he reminded her.

"But the actors will help. We're all just one happy family. I would love for you to join our family. I already have a gob of ideas."

The fine lines around Jeremy's eyes softened, the sign he was acquiescing. "I can at least take a look at your plans and the stage."

"Perhaps sit in on some of our rehearsals, as well?" Lisette looked pleadingly through her long lashes.

"Yes, I suppose." Jeremy glanced at Rosamund. She tried not to convey her annoyance too conspicuously.

"Where do you plan to perform?" he asked.

"Oh, it's just a little place. I'll send you the information. You have a card, do you not? You should have a card, a great artist like you."

Jeremy beamed at Lisette's estimation of his talents as he handed her his card. Rosamund held her head steady to keep it from shaking in disgust.

Lisette wrapped Jeremy's hand with both of hers. "It will be so much fun! And to have a real artist paint our scenery! Oh, that would be too much. Too much!" She leaned in as if to kiss his cheek, but instead only kissed the air. "Well, I must be off to make my rounds."

Jeremy sighed as she waltzed away.

"I really don't care if you sleep with her, darling." Rosamund said harshly. "But don't let her coerce you with flattery."

"Coerce? Oh, Rosie, no. You're reading her wrong. She's a sweet girl."

"And very pretty."

"Yes, she is very pretty." Jeremy did not equivocate. "Darling, don't be jealous. She's got suitors aplenty. Young and handsome, they are. What on earth would she want with a forty-year-old married man?"

"What any flirtatious girl would want with a rich and talented handsome man, my dear." Rosamund stood on tiptoe. "And, love, you're forty-two. As am I," she whispered in his ear. "I suppose her childlike exuberance has affected you."

Jeremy gazed at his wife. "Perhaps you are correct." He snaked his arm about her waist. "We should make the most of it."

Rosamund pressed herself against him as much as she could without drawing attention. "That sounds like 'fun'." She sidestepped out of his embrace. "But, darling, we are in public."

His eyes twinkled. "Quite."

He was incorrigible. Ever since they had chosen a new path in their marriage, Jeremy had been emboldened to be more overt in his demonstrations of affection, as if the gestures were meant to convey a possessiveness counter to their unique open arrangement.

She glared at him before easing into a smile, a smile she unintentionally turned on the attractive gentleman coming toward them.

The very same gentleman with whom she had just enjoyed a carnal indulgence. The spot on her rump burned anew.

"Westerman!" Jeremy bellowed with a wave.

Westerman? Rosamund chilled. *Charles* Westerman? *The* Charles Westerman? It couldn't possibly be.

Mr. Westerman approached. His gaze flashed to Rosamund, one eyebrow slightly lifted as if in query. Rosamund maintained a veneer of composure as best she could.

Jeremy shook the man's hand and gave a little slap on his shoulder. "It's been a long time. We've missed you at the club. So glad you could come to our little soirée."

Mr. Westerman's half smile conveyed a touch of bewilderment. "Threxton," he greeted. "I wouldn't have missed it for the world. But now I hear you've been accepted to the Summer Exhibition anyway."

"Yes, yes. Still one needs all the exposure one can get when one is just starting out as a professional."

Rosamund cleared her throat. "Jeremy, darling. Introductions?"

"What? You two haven't met?"

"Not formally," Mr. Westerman said with a nonchalant air.

"Ah, yes. I quite forget sometimes Rosie's not allowed at the club, and you've yet to accept an invitation to dinner." Jeremy chuckled. "Rosamund, I would like you to meet Charles Westerman, Britain's eminent landscape painter." He turned to Mr. Westerman. "Westerman, my wife, Rosamund Chambers, Viscountess Threxton."

Mr. Westerman blinked, his expression remaining stoic.

Rosamund held out her right hand, wanting to feel his touch again. "You're Charles Westerman? *The* Charles Westerman?"

He grasped her hand and gave it a squeeze. "The very same."

Oh, good God. Well if she had to pick an artist to sleep with, she couldn't do much better than Charles Westerman, could she?

"It is a pleasure to finally make your acquaintance, Mr. Westerman. I am a great admirer of your efforts. Your skills at evoking a sense of bucolic serenity are enviable." Rosamund flushed, hoping the pink of her cheeks would recall for Mr. Westerman the moment he had raised such a blush on her derrière.

Because that would be a very good thing, indeed.

Fucking, fucking Hell.

His *wife*? Threxton's blasted *wife*?

With great effort Charles forced himself to maintain control and not even hint at his annoyance. Or his continued attraction.

At least Lady Threxton looked as if she felt guilty about their furtive dalliance. Although, perhaps only mildly so.

He stepped forward a hair to catch a whiff of her perfume. She blushed just a touch more. It was charming.

"How was Scotland, Mr. Westerman?" Lady Threxton's mellifluous voice filled his senses with a memory of her moaning.

"Scotland?" Of course. If she thought of him as *the* Charles Westerman, she would keep up with his career. "The summer was gorgeous, the winter bleak. The prospects and colors unique."

"I'm certain you will do it justice, and it will seem as if one is standing amidst the very heather itself."

He bowed his head briefly. "Thank you, my lady."

She smiled politely, as a stranger might. "Will you be showing at the Summer Exhibition?"

She knew damn well he was. "Of course," he said smoothly, unabashedly perusing her face with curiosity. "Eight Scottish landscapes."

"Then this year will prove to be a phenomenal one." She was good, indeed.

"I'm sure there will be a number of fine artists this year, yes."

"No. I mean, specifically, you, Mr. Westerman." Lady Threxton tilted her head demurely.

He snickered. "I'm flattered you think so much of my ability."

Threxton cleared his throat as if interrupting a private conversation. "Rosamund's opinion on such matters is quite astute, Westerman. Her father is Spencer Rutford."

A frisson of alarm set every hair on end. "The art critic?" The woman he had just shagged was bleeding art aristocracy.

"The very same." She smirked. Or seemed to.

Realization descended. "Then Lord Creslow must be your uncle."

"Yes. My father's elder brother."

"Ah, so that's why—"

Charles stopped. He was about to say, "that's why you knew the library so well," but then he'd have to come up with something rather clever to cover for why he thought the lady knew the library so well.

"Why what?" Threxton asked innocently.

Charles looked at his friend. What should he say now? That's why Threxton was one of the featured artists of the event? That would seem insulting.

Not that Threxton wasn't any good—he was more than good, he was bloody brilliant. He was simply undisciplined, not having to actually work for his keep. He "dabbled in paints", as he put it. But he dabbled with quite a bit of skill. He was the best damned portraitist in London at the moment.

"That's why you sent me a personal invitation. I see it is a family affair." He turned to Lady Threxton. "You must be very proud of your husband, my lady."

She gazed up at Threxton like a newlywed bride. "Oh, I am."

She beamed, truly beamed. It was astonishing. She could fuck a stranger one minute, and the next be fawning over her husband.

And there stood Threxton completely innocent of the whole matter, thinking his wife a faithful companion, their union mutually rewarding.

And here he stood, *the* Charles Westerman, internationally renowned artist, having the most wicked thoughts about the heated cunt of his friend's wife.

Charles felt slightly sickened by his shameful behavior. Although his cock felt otherwise.

"Charles!"

Francesca's call dampened his ardor instantly. She approached from the left and slid her arm through his.

Her timing was perfect. He smiled. "Lord and Lady Threxton, may I introduce my sister, Mrs. George Burridge."

Greetings were said all around. The ladies complimented each other on their dresses.

Charles gave Francesca's arm a little squeeze, their private signal when one needed an escape. "You know, Threxton," he said, "I have not yet found your works in this spectacle. I'm certain Francesca will want to see them. Can you point the way?"

"Certainly," Threxton said excitedly.

Half a minute later Charles looked over his shoulder as he and Francesca sauntered over to the north gallery.

Lady Threxton watched as he walked away.

Jeremy sank deeper into the slipper chair in the corner of Rosamund's dressing room and ran a fingernail over the teeth of her silver-backed comb. She undressed haphazardly, as if distracted. He smothered a grin.

Something deliciously wicked had transpired that night.

Rosamund had a terribly revealing trait of blushing when she was around a man she found attractive. The normally self-controlled hauteur with which she carried herself had clearly broken down in front of Charles Westerman.

Westerman. The quintessential in artistic success. A man not to be envied but to be emulated. He wanted Rosamund, perhaps had toyed with her earlier that evening. But Jeremy? Jeremy *had* Rosamund, and had given Rosamund the power to have any man she wanted.

"Charles seemed interested."

"Charles?" Rosamund did not look up as she fiddled with her petticoat.

"Westerman. The artist."

"Oh. Yes." She was clearly feigning indifference. "Interested in what, dear?"

"You."

That caught Rosamund's attention. She had undressed down to her corset and combination, her legs already delightfully nude. She stared at him.

"Me?"

"Did he flirt with you?" He smiled lasciviously.

She shot a glare. "No." She worked at unfastening her corset.

"So you flirted with him." He knew his wife too well.

"Argh! Help me with this damn thing." She was deflecting, but she really did need help. She always did. That's what her lady's maid was for. But Jeremy had dismissed Gretchen earlier that evening.

He rose and went to his wife. "Darling, I don't care." He fussed with the stubborn hooks and eyes. "We made an agreement when Alex and Isa died—"

"Don't." She always quieted him when he brought up their children.

He stopped halfway down her corset. "All right." He continued to work on the fastenings as if nothing had stopped their conversation.

"We made an agreement that a life worth living needed to be lived." He finished and pulled off the boned garment, then regarded her. "So tell me about Charles."

"I didn't know it was him," she protested.

"Those are often the best encounters, are they not?"

She flicked her gaze up at him, biting her lower lip. "I fucked him."

Jeremy's cock stirred at the notion. "Of course you did. I could tell." He began to unbutton the combination underwear. "And how was he?"

Her lips twitched, wanting to smile. "Malleable."

What man wouldn't be in her presence?

He brushed his lips against her ear. "Have you washed since?" he murmured.

She smiled. "No."

"Then the slide through his spunk will be thoroughly enjoyable."

She closed her eyes as he divested her of the final garment of under-clothing. She stood before him utterly nude, utterly vulnerable. Utterly his.

He picked her up and carried her through the east door to the large mahogany four-poster bed that dominated the room.

Her eyes widened. She understood the implication.

This was the third bedroom, their shared bedroom. This was their domain. No other lovers were allowed. Jeremy was her primary partner. While tolerated and accepted, all others were secondary. And Jeremy was about to emphasize his claim.

He laid her down on the bed, arranging the covers and pillows so she would be comfortable. She gazed at him with a modicum of nervousness while he undressed.

He stretched his naked body over hers. "What did he do to excite you?"

She threaded her fingers through the hair on his chest, tickling him. "Initially, it was his charm. He's very charismatic."

"Initially?"

"And then when we were about to…"—she glanced away as she trailed off—"he touched me."

Intriguing. Jeremy traced along her cheekbone. "Touched you where, my love?"

"My bottom." She whispered it, as if someone might overhear such a wicked notion.

"How did he touch your bottom?"

She sucked in a breath, then exhaled sharply, the memory clearly exciting her. "A stroke." Her gaze met his. "A swat."

A bolt of lust enlivened his erection. "After which you could not possibly resist." He cupped a breast, weighing it before pinching the crinkled nipple.

She gasped, shutting her eyes briefly. "No." She opened her lids, revealing dilated pupils. "I was rendered powerless."

"What about me?" He pushed open her legs. "Can you resist me?"

Her eyes widened in awe as her brow twisted in apprehension.

"Are you ready for me?" he taunted.

"Yes. Yes. Please."

Jeremy slammed into her. Rosamund screeched with satisfaction. He had wanted to fuck her all night. Watching his wife confidently hold court amongst fawning men was thoroughly arousing. Knowing other men wanted her was simply thrilling.

Knowing another man had been inside her hours before made him harder than steel.

"You're mine, all mine," he panted, his thrusts gaining momentum.

"Yes, yes, yours," she whimpered, her head rocking against the pillow.

"No one else can have you."

"No, no one," she said deliriously.

"But they all want you. They all want to fuck you."

Her breathy moans lay hot on his shoulder. "Yes."

"So I let them."

Her first crisis fluttered around him, egging him on.

"A queue of men, all for you."

She gulped a gasp.

"Each one in their turn."

Her sudden tightness flung him to the precipice.

"Including Charles."

She exploded in climax, squeezing him, sending him over the edge. With a sharp cry, he pumped his seed deep inside. He hung poised above her for a moment while his body rode the crest of pleasure. Sated, he slumped against her heated flesh.

They stayed in their positions, panting, sweating, until he caught his breath.

"God, that was good," he sighed.

Rosamund laughed and pushed him off. She reached for a towel on the nightstand and put it between her legs.

"Are you really going to paint scenery for Lisette LaFleur?" She plopped an arm across his chest and snuggled her cheek against his shoulder. "It's beneath your talents."

"Oh, I don't know, it might be enjoyable. I've never done such a thing." Jeremy stroked her hair. "Why do you object so?"

"She's frivolous and flighty. She only wants you around so she can appear to be more legitimate." Rosamund lifted her head to look in his eyes. "You know that, Jer."

"I'll go to the theater once and see what she's all about. If she is serious that all the actors are willing to help out, then really I just need to direct the activity at first and leave the rest up to them."

"I suppose I'll let you do that, love."

"You know you really have no right to be jealous."

She sighed into his chest.

"Charles seemed rather attentive, my dear."

"Of course, he did," she protested. "You're his friend, remember? It is only polite to feign interest in the wives of one's friends."

"I think he was not feigning."

Rosamund smiled. "Really?" she asked playfully. She kissed his beard. "So, you think he's taken a fancy to me?"

"Possibly."

"Like you have possibly taken a fancy to Lisette?"

"You are impossible, woman. Tell me again why I married you?"

"Because you love me desperately and I satisfy your demanding sexual appetite."

"Hmm," Jeremy intoned skeptically. He wrapped his arms around her and hugged her close. He'd have to somehow let Westerman know he was at liberty to pursue his fancy.

But Rosamund was wrong about Lisette. Jeremy had no interest in the girl. Really, he didn't.

Charles leaned back into the curve of the tub and rested his head against the cool porcelain rim. He stared at the bathroom ceiling as hot water embraced him, buoying his tense muscles.

Bollocks.

He'd done it again.

First Annalee while she was engaged, and now the wife of a colleague.

Jesus. Maybe it was time to practice continence, become not only *the* Charles Westerman, but the *monkish* Charles Westerman.

He blew out a sputtering sigh.

Who the hell was he trying to fool?

Sweat beaded on his forehead. The water was probably too hot. Or he was agitated. If he were honest with himself, he'd acknowledge he'd done the worst possible thing in Lord Creslow's library.

And it wasn't just because Threxton had always been amiable and supportive of him down at the club—the atmosphere at the Museion was preternaturally collegial—but that Threxton was obviously in love with his wife. Whenever the man mentioned his "Rosie," it had been gushing and effusive. Odd that he never mentioned her parentage. Of course, Threxton had his own reputation to maintain. He was a bloody good painter and any success he had was not because Lady Threxton just happened to be Spencer Rutford's daughter.

Christ. Spencer fucking Rutford.

Charles closed his eyes, remembering the first time he'd read the review of his exhibition at Moulton Gallery in the Summer '78 issue of *Kallitechnis*. He had read it over and over again until he'd practically memorized every word written by Rutford:

> *The landscape offers a view so realistic one believes oneself standing amidst the trees of Hampstead Heath, a slight breeze teasing one's whiskers, only to suddenly awaken surprised to find not sod beneath one's feet, but a wooden floor in want of sanding. The perfection of Mr. Westerman's view is found in its honesty. There are no imagined flowers and bushes to pretend the park more bucolic, no fanciful paths and bridges to render the scene more palatable to bourgeois tastes. This is neither Constable's Heath of imagination and drama, nor an Impressionist canvas with a murky, prettified view.*
>
> *This is raw, unadulterated life. Not an artistic ideal of what life should look like, but, instead, the bald reality of actual appearance...*

Soon after the review was published he'd sold every damn canvas hanging at Moulton, with inquiries and commissions pouring in for more. To keep up with demand, the gallery had framed and sold his oil sketches. He'd never had so much money in his life, had never been so busy. By December he had been nominated to the Royal Academy.

His life had been a whirlwind. It had almost driven him mad. Scotland had been a necessary respite.

And now he found himself spinning into a vortex again, this time because of his damnable prick.

Lady Threxton had stirred something deep within. Something unusual. A need, a yearning hitherto unknown.

It was exciting and he wanted to explore it.

Was it her wriggling backside? Ekatarina's glorious mounds had enticed him to fuck her in the arse, a sensation so intense he came within seconds of penetration. Was the possibility of satisfying himself in that way with his new paramour driving him to distraction?

His paramour...his lover...

His Rosamund.

No! He slapped the water with his open palm, splashing heavy droplets onto the tile floor. He had to stop fantasizing about her. He'd have to forget the whole incident. It was a fling, a one-time affair. He'd probably never see Lady Threxton in such circumstances again. He'd known Threxton for a couple of years and had never had the opportunity to meet his wife. So why would the future hold anything different?

He let out a long exhalation and stared once more at the indifferent ceiling.

Well, except now he was back in London with the start of the Season looming. Parties, teas, salons. He'd be expected to make an appearance, especially as he was *the* Charles Westerman. There would be Waterhouse's post-Banquet affair attended by Royal Academy members and their wives, then the opening of the Summer Exhibition, both opportunities to see Rosamund—*Lady Threxton.*

Opportunity was not the right word. Disaster was more like it.

He grabbed his cock, left half-hard from the tangle of thoughts besieging him. He squeezed, then let go. This was not the time for masturbation. He should be abstemious, repentant. He willed his prick to the more agreeable state of flaccidness.

It was a losing battle.

His prick roused at a sudden, new thought. Annalee was unattached, was she not? Now *there* was opportunity. He hated lying to Francesca, but she would have rebuked him mercilessly had she known his dalliance with Annalee was a bit more than mere flirtation. Annalee's kisses were divine, and he'd like to do a lot more than kiss her.

He gazed at his cock, now iron hard. But this time from improper thoughts about a far more appropriate woman. Well, appropriate in her lack of a husband. She was only twenty-two, or thereabouts, and knew very little about the life and career of an artist. If he were to ever take a wife, she'd have to have a level of maturity to easily navigate the vicissitudes of the art world, to know which patron was worth the time and which exhibition was worth the effort. Annalee appreciated his canvases, most certainly, but he needed a wife who would be perspicacious enough to see his career was on course.

Someone like Lady Threxton.

Christ. Why did he have to torment himself so? He stared at his cock again, wanting so desperately to toss off. Not tonight. No, tonight was not the time for fantasy. He would wash his sins away in the bath and sleep without dreaming.

Tomorrow he would call on Miss Annalee Brockhurst.

CHAPTER THREE

Jeremy sank against the cushioned seat of the hansom cab as it wended its way through tired streets, passing squalid row houses and soot-smeared industrial buildings. He twisted his beaver hat in his hands as the driver dodged hollow-cheeked children and grimy peddlers. It was a damn good thing he took a cab and not his own carriage. Curious stares only followed them for a short while. A crest on the door would have attracted an unruly mob.

He pursed his lips, trying to smother his utter dismay. He should not have dismissed so lightly the cabbie's query "ya wanna go *there*, guv'nuh?" The address where Lisette LaFleur had requested Jeremy meet her was nowhere near London's West End theater district. Quite the opposite, in fact. It was across the Thames in Lambeth, in an area known as transpontine London. There, the cabbie had explained, playhouses showed a particular type of sensational entertainment so unique the geographic moniker "Transpontine Theatre" had become synonymous with the melodrama presented in such establishments.

The cab stopped before a wide three-story brick building sporting several cracked windows. Evidently Lisette's theater had once enjoyed some other use. Perhaps as an orphanage.

"'Ere you go, guv'nuh."

Jeremy stepped down from the cab and offered to pay double the fare if the driver would return an hour later to pick him up. The cabbie smirked and took only what was owed him, saying he'd think about the offer.

Jeremy sighed as he entered through heavy oak double doors. His footsteps on cracked and dulled hardwood planks echoed in the dim corridor. A painted sign announced *The New Delphia* with a silhouette of a man's hand pointing the way to his destination.

Inside, the theater proper looked as if it had at one time been a lecture hall, with curved rows of wooden seating forming an intimate amphitheater. Red velvet curtains hanging from a ramshackle proscenium flanked the stage. A discoloration on the boards indicated where at one time had sat a lectern.

Jeremy stood on a stair in the left aisle, ruminating a tad too long. Perhaps he should call out his presence.

Lisette poked her head out from behind stage right. She smiled buoyantly, infecting him with a broad grin.

She approached with a little skip in her step and a swish of her skirts. "Oh, Lord Jeremy, thank you so much for coming." She grasped both his hands as she stood before him, their noses at the same height. Her eyes were striking, a sort of violety blue one saw in a sunset or in a rare amethyst. A lovely distraction from the top of her dress, so dangerously low-cut it almost exposed her areolae. The effect was somewhat muted by an inset of gauzy fabric.

"You're welcome, Miss LaFleur," he said softly.

"Oh, please, you must call me Lisette." She batted her eyes with a demure sidelong look.

"If you insist, Lisette." The name rolled off his tongue as if he had spoken it a million times. "Then, please, call me Jeremy."

She wrapped her arm around his and led him down the aisle to the stage, her hips swaying perhaps more than a woman's ought. "Let me give you a tour of our humble theater."

Humble was something of an overstatement. He had already seen all there was to show off. But what there was, Lisette described with the utmost of flair and hyperbole in her rapid-fire style.

"The stage is huge, isn't it? It will be perfect for the shipwreck scene."

Jeremy had only been in a few theaters in his life, but he was certain "huge" was not a proper description. Perhaps if one were a child it might seem as thus. A very small child.

"And the boards really just need a bit of wax and varnish, don't you think?"

A bit of sanding, scraping, and nailing down, as well.

"Then with your sets it will be magnificent, like a real hidden-island paradise. Better than anything Shakespeare could have imagined."

Jeremy inspected the dingy and dull little stage. He admittedly knew nothing of stagecraft, but it would have to be quite a miracle for a small backdrop to convey the magical stormy island setting of *The Tempest*. "I've never done such a thing as stage painting before, Miss, uh, Lisette. And landscapes are really not my forte." He tried to imagine the shabby space before him decorated with scenery from presentations of the play he had seen in the past. "It will most definitely be a challenging task."

"Oh, we'll have loads of fun." Lisette squeezed his arm, pressing an abundant breast against his chest.

His cock responded favorably to her softness. "And you do know I have the Summer Exhibition to prepare for."

"Oh, yes! Of course. *The Tempest* won't open until mid-May." She faced him, letting go of his arm to take up his hand, holding it a hair's breadth from her glorious bosom, fluttering her lashes before gazing into his eyes. "I'm sure you can find a bit of time for me in your busy schedule?"

She smelled of jasmine and chocolate, two scents his nose had never before found erotic, and yet his cock was finding it otherwise. Lacking any other distractions, he could finally study her. She was an exotic beauty, with wide-set eyes, coal-black hair, and plump, full lips.

She guided his hand to curve around her side. Not at her waist, but a little higher, just under her bosom. She slowly ran her fingers along the collar of his sack jacket.

Jeremy swallowed hard. A stunner like her could have any man she wanted. Why she wanted him was unfathomable, but she clearly did.

And he wanted her.

He drew closer, staring at her mouth as he tilted his head just a little. He really should pay more mind to the fact they were in a semipublic space, that he was an up-and-coming artist who needed to avoid scandal at this point in his career. That he was perceived by the outside world as a married man in a monogamous relationship.

But lust made a man forget reason.

His lips touched Lisette's, igniting a spark in his loins, flaring through his core. He wrapped one arm around her waist and pulled her to him, deepening their union. He palmed her generous bosom, teasing a too-accessible nipple. She moaned and looped her arms around his neck. Her lips were so very soft, so supple, her body so pliable.

God, she would be so willing in his bed.

"Lisette?"

The booming bass of a man's voice filled the theater. Jeremy released her, stepping back to a more discreet distance. She blushed and adjusted her bodice.

"In the house, Malachi," she called out. "Come meet the newest member of our company."

From behind the proscenium came a very large black man, his skin a glorious color of ebony that would be a joy for any portraitist to paint. His height was made greater by his powerful build, yet softened by his exquisite taste in dress. His shirtsleeves were rolled up to his elbows, the sign he had been working at some manual task back stage. Yet his trousers and cravat were finely tailored and à la mode. He was no mere laborer.

He came to Lisette's side, she suddenly seeming so pale next to him, her curves so feminine against his bulk. Their contrasts would make for a fascinating portrait.

"Jeremy, this is Malachias Ndoye. He's our stage manager and set designer. He's also playing the part of Caliban." She gazed up at Mr. Ndoye with admiration. "Next year we'll do *Othello* and he'll play the lead to my Desdemona." The spell broken, she returned her attention to Jeremy. "And before you ask, he's from Senegal originally. Then France. But he's been in England for quite some time." Lisette turned to Mr. Ndoye. "Malachi, this is Jeremy Chambers, Viscount Threxton. He will be painting our scenery."

Jeremy thrust out his hand. "A pleasure to meet you, Mr. Ndoye."

Mr. Ndoye shook the proffered hand, his grip strong. "Yes, a pleasure indeed, my lord." His accent was vaguely French with a mixture of East London. "Please do call me Malachi. We are family here." His sweeping gesture quickly covered the small space.

"Then you must call me Jeremy." He meant it. Malachi inspired familiarity. "Set designer, eh? I'll be working directly with you, I suppose?"

"Yes. Although Lisette sings your praises as an artist, so I am certain you will have a better idea about how to proceed."

Jeremy snorted. "Ah. I see Lisette has failed to inform you I am a portraitist and not a landscape or scenery painter. I will need much direction in the matter."

"Our Lisette has a way of bringing out the best in a man." Malachi grinned. "I was a bank clerk when she discovered me."

Lisette giggled. "A stodgy City bank where real gentlemen keep their money."

Hence the clothes. Jeremy regarded the pair. "How many of these productions have you done?"

Lisette smiled. "We've only ever performed in drawing rooms. This is our first in a grand theater."

Grand being a matter of opinion.

"It will be a challenge for all of us," Malachi said. "But I am up to the task." He blew out a long exhalation. "I must resume my work behind the scenes." He bowed slightly to Jeremy. "A pleasure to meet you."

"And you."

After a flash of a smile, Malachi disappeared backstage.

Lisette tugged eagerly on Jeremy's lapels. His cock stirred anew.

He gazed into the depths of her violet eyes. He could get lost there, especially as he thrust inside her, holding her down. He would require she keep her eyes open as he took her.

He hauled her against him, a display of the dominance she should expect if they were to pursue an affair.

She licked her lips, her breath escaping in excited little puffs, the color in her cheeks a delightful pink.

He kissed her once again, this time with determination, plunging his tongue inside to command hers. Her mouth was his to plunder, like her body would be very soon.

He pulled back, but she leaned in, her arms still around his neck, wanting more.

He put a finger to her lips. "That's enough for today, darling."

She colored again, a rosy hue, and released her hold. She smiled, the glint in her eye implying she couldn't wait for next time. "We'll make a wonderful team, Lord Jeremy, don't you think?"

"I do." They would, rather. In and out of bed.

Charles stood rooted to the pavement before the Brockhurst mansion in Chelsea. His cab had pulled away over five minutes ago and he had even walked through the arched entry gate near the curb, but he was finding it difficult to go up the front steps and ring the doorbell.

Surely his qualms were ill-founded. There was really nothing untoward about his presence there. He was a good friend of Lawrence Brockhurst's. They attended the same gentlemen's club—Newbury's—for professional, middle-class men, because that was what they were. And as such, the rules were different.

Surely a middle-class man could simply visit another without an invitation? They were not subjected to social subterfuge as the aristocracy was, where an invitation had to be the "right" kind, or where one had to mingle with the proper sort in order to avoid the dreaded cut. The day-to-day existence of men not in the upper class was fairly straightforward.

But Charles had not arrived at the front door on Edith Grove to visit *Mr.* Brockhurst. No. He was there to see *Miss* Brockhurst. And the rules governing the intercourse between middle-class men did not apply to one such man and the daughter of another. Appearing at a young woman's door outside of her at-home hours was bold and forthright. It might send the wrong message.

Or the right message, as that was exactly his purpose. Charles was there to offer his suit.

The thick wheels of a delivery carriage rumbled noisily on the rough street, rousing him back to the fact of his standing at the foot of the front steps. He should have consulted Francesca. She would have given him advice, but only after she had gently berated him about pursuing one so much his junior.

Jesus. Was he doing the right thing?

What if Annalee balked? Well, at the very least, it was known they were also friends. A visit could be construed as resuming their acquaintance.

He sucked in a breath to assuage his frayed nerves and mounted the steps to the front door. His finger hovered a moment over the doorbell before he pressed it, the noise jolting him to the bald reality of what he had just done. What he could not undo.

The butler answered. The Brockhurst's *London* butler. The staff in France was entirely different.

Damn. Which meant the London household might be a bit curious about his presence there. The French servants didn't seem to care, in fact probably expected Annalee to have lovers while she was engaged.

"Yes?" the butler drawled.

"Mr. Charles Westerman to see Miss Annalee Brockhurst."

The butler's eyebrows shot up infinitesimally in muted shock. Being a celebrity artist did have its merits.

"Please." The butler opened the door a bit wider and motioned Charles inside. "Is Miss Brockhurst expecting you?"

Damn again. Did he have to ask? "I daresay not. But we did see each other last night at Lord Creslow's." Inwardly he cringed. Why he offered that tidbit of information to a servant was beyond him.

"Right." The butler inclined his head slightly. "If you would please wait in the morning room, I will fetch Miss Brockhurst."

And after Charles had been deposited in the morning room, he let out an exhalation so hard it dizzied him. He paced to get his bearings. *Christ!* He was acting like a schoolboy. He was only there to call on Annalee, perhaps court her, not bloody seduce her on the Persian rug.

Minutes later the door opened and the butler ushered Annalee in.

"Mr. Westerman! What a surprise!" Her charming smile lit up her face.

She was gorgeous in her frilly pink dress, tight-fitting as fashion required but covered in an exuberance of ruffles and lace. The type of dress a young woman of her age could wear so well, while a woman of Lady Threxton's age would look rather pitiful in an attempt to recapture her youth.

Something the confident and poised Lady Threxton would never seek to do.

Charles flushed. Why in hell was he thinking about *her* at that moment? He had far better things to think about. Like the extraordinarily pretty Annalee.

She reached out her hands to grasp his. Charles flashed a glance at the butler.

"Shall I fetch tea, Miss Brockhurst?"

Annalee seemed startled, as if she had forgotten the butler's presence. "Oh, yes please, Evans." She returned her smile to Charles. "Does Papa know you're here? I'm not certain he's even at home."

Evans shot Charles a look of caution before he closed the door behind him.

"No. I came to see you." He gave her hands a squeeze, then let go.

"That sounds ominous." Annalee strolled over to the sofa and sat, patting the space next to her in invitation.

"It was so lovely to see you last night." Charles took his place at her side.

"It was, wasn't it?" Happiness reflected in her blue eyes. Despite her flirtatious disposition, she still exuded the innocence that came naturally with being so young.

Charles cleared his throat. "I'd like to see you more often."

Annalee's luscious lips parted as she emitted a quiet gasp.

Oh, God. She wasn't as free as he had thought, had hoped. He stood. "Annalee, I apologize if I have insulted you. I just assumed from what you said last night that you were unattached."

She gaped, then smiled. "But, Charles, of course I am free. I'm simply amazed you are even interested."

"Did I not show enough interest in France?"

She laughed softly. "You showed a great deal of interest in a girl who was engaged to be married and willing to let another man give her a peck or two on the cheek. Especially a famous man."

"It was a bit more than a peck." There were a couple of occasions where it was so very satisfying and thorough a necking he practically came in his trousers.

Her cheeks turned a gorgeous shade of rose. "I really should be quite vexed over my behavior," she admitted softly. She gazed up at him with her beautiful eyes, the blue the very color of the spring sky in France. "You and I both knew you would only be at *Le Bocage* for a month or so. And then I would be married. It was a harmless dalliance on both our parts."

Mortification spiked his gut as the pounding of his heart crashed in his ears. "So you never gave it another thought after I had left?"

"Of course I did," she exclaimed. "I thought of you too often." She wrung her hands while the rose of her cheeks deepened a shade. "But, Charles, you can have any woman you want."

"Ah." He nodded. It wasn't quite true, but almost. "And what makes you think I do not want you?"

A knock on the door announced the arrival of the tea. For several moments, Annalee and Charles stared at each other in silence as a maid set the tray down, then quickly left.

Annalee went about pouring the tea. "I guess I had fantasies of you saving me from my fate," she finally said.

"You mean your impending marriage?"

"Yes. I didn't much like Gilbert. He was a bit of a brute."

Charles waited, but Annalee did not elaborate. Apparently the scandal was to remain a secret. She merely handed him a gilded porcelain cup.

"I had no idea." Charles sipped his tea. "I suppose even if I had known, any actions on my part would have been quite scandalous as well. Perhaps it was for the best things happened the way they did."

"Except now I am a year older and still unmarried." She sighed. "There are few options for a woman of gentle breeding to pursue."

She looked so forlorn at that moment. The unknown crushing down on her young shoulders, her heart and mind only aware of one path in life. She did not yet realize there were so many paths. Yet, that was a lesson one learned in middle age, certainly not at twenty-two.

"Annalee, I request the honor of your presence as my guest at the Waterhouse Gala." He blurted the words. He positively blurted without thinking of the consequences. He couldn't take it back. Lady Threxton would see him with Annalee at the affair. "It's an event after the Royal Academy Banquet. For Academy members and their special guests." His hand trembled as he raised his teacup to his lips.

Annalee studied him, her gaze searching his face. "Do you really mean that, Charles?" She was no fool. She understood the implication.

He did mean it. At least he thought he did. Anything to keep his mind off Lady Threxton.

Bollocks. He had to stop thinking about her.

"Yes, darling," he said, squelching his doubts. Francesca had been expecting to be his guest. He'd have to explain everything to her and brace himself for the ensuing onslaught of reprimands.

Annalee pressed her palm to her chest, fingering a bit of frill near her neck. "I should ask Papa for permission before I respond."

He put down his tea and knelt at her side. "I understand. It is a very public proclamation. And if your father wants to be your escort, I will understand."

It was a means of escape, probably their only one. Unless Annalee simply declined the invitation.

But she did not.

Instead she went pale. "Is it a very grand occasion? What shall I wear?"

He cupped her cheek, a grin spreading across his face at her enchanting consternation. "The Prince and Princess of Wales will be there, if only momentarily. I'm sure your seamstress will love the chance to create an elegant gown."

She smiled, the action returning the rose to her cheeks. She was so very pretty.

He leaned in, holding the back of her head steady in the palm of his hand. She flicked her tongue to wet her lips and closed her eyes.

He didn't want to close his for fear of who he might imagine.

Blast it.

He stopped, his lips warm and moist from her panting breaths.

He pulled back and picked up his tea. Annalee gaped at him, confusion clouding her eyes.

"Annalee, darling, no sneaking around this time. We'll do this properly."

She sighed. "Yes, Charles." Her lips stretched into a thin smile as she took up her teacup. "I understand."

Charles slid down the warmed porcelain of his tub, letting out a long exhalation as the water lapped at his chest.

With Annalee accompanying him to the post-Banquet gala, his life would be on track. He was at the height of his career and expected to take a wife. A very beautiful wife who would look good on his arm and was intelligent enough to support him in his career.

Annalee Westerman. Mrs. Westerman. Would there be children, as well?

A chill crept across his flesh despite the heated water. At forty-five he had just assumed he would never be a father. But Annalee was so young and most certainly would want children. All women wanted such things, didn't they?

Well, his prominence as a painter would not be forever. He would have to have a plan for when his career had ebbed. Fatherhood seemed as good a choice as any.

He chuckled to himself. That would mean he and Annalee would have to make love. A prospect he had contemplated far too much while at the Brockhurst estate in France.

Dinners at *Le Bocage* always meant she would wear such attire as to make his trousers tight. Gowns and necklines reflecting the height of Parisian fashion despite their country setting, fashions invented to lure men from their cigars and billiards. The décolletage of her evening gowns revealed alabaster shoulders and the shadow between her breasts. Her upswept hair exposed the delicate flesh of her neck.

And when he and Annalee pursued their dangerous dalliance in the glass greenhouse one night, Charles had made sure he tasted all of that which was presented to him. And she had let him.

His erection nagged him for release under the bath water. He grabbed the shaft and let out a groan.

It had been too long since the last time he had masturbated. He really shouldn't wait so long between friggings.

That night in the greenhouse Annalee's body had flexed and curved under his command, her breathy moans egging him on.

"Charles...please," she had begged.

Please satisfy her.

But he could not. She wasn't his, and anything beyond what they allowed themselves to do would have been noticed by her fiancé. The man would have known if she had been divested of her virginity, or worse, if he'd been deprived of his chance to witness her first orgasm.

For surely she had never known a man's sensual touch until Charles had taken advantage of her.

Charles stroked his cock, his rapid movements jostling the water into little waves. After the Waterhouse Gala, he would have his chance to satisfy her, and take his satisfaction as well. He'd never had a virgin, had never even given such a notion a thought, but suddenly relished the idea of a nubile, innocent, willing young woman beneath him, her body arching and writhing in her struggle to understand the pleasures washing over her flesh.

The unfamiliar need surging in her veins.

He would sweat and grunt as he slammed into her. *My God* she would be so tight. He would render her delirious from the pain of initial invasion and the ensuing pleasure of deepening penetration.

He would wait for her orgasm, wait for her scream of release, wait for her to look up at him in incomprehension, her brow furrowed under her golden-brown hair, her amber eyes beseeching him to give her just one more—

He came under the water, pumping his cock, stretching it until every last drop had been released.

He hit the iron rim of the tub, stinging his hand, uncaring if he sprained a finger.

Damn it. Annalee did not have brown hair and amber eyes. *No.* But he knew damn well who did.

He really needed to stop thinking about Lady Threxton.

CHAPTER FOUR

Rosamund hadn't been to the Vicereine Social Club in quite some time. She hadn't needed to. The men she kept on retainer had been quite satisfactory. They were, each one of them, well-trained, good-looking after a fashion, and asked no questions about her personal life—except perhaps to inquire after her mood and which implement she might favor on that particular afternoon.

But since the night of Uncle Bradley's Salon two weeks ago, Rosamund had discovered a new fascination—or, rather, a new obsession. The handsome dark-haired men who had been coming to her house to service her no longer filled her with anticipation.

She had developed a new taste, one that fed her fantasies at a fevered pitch, leaving her agitated and irritable. She had to find relief. She had sent a note to the club with her muddled thoughts, then visited in person the next day.

The concierge at the Vicereine understood immediately by Rosamund's presence that something was amiss. He fetched Madame Laperne without question.

Valeria Laperne, the proprietress of the Vicereine and as such known affectionately as "Madame," was perhaps ten years older than Rosamund, but her hair had far more gray than one might expect. It gave her a matronly aspect, calming and reassuring to all who sought her services.

Madame met Rosamund in the waiting room. Rosamund tried to explain her need.

Madame nodded at every lament, offering soothing words tinged with a faint French accent. "Lady Threxton, I am at your service." She exited with a slight bow.

Moments later, Madame returned. She entwined her arm through Rosamund's as she led her upstairs to the viewing gallery on the second floor.

"I am sorry the others no longer excite, my lady." It was said with a modicum of concern but utterly without censure.

Rosamund squeezed Madame's hand. "Oh, Valeria, please know Alfred and Martin and Frederick are, each one of them, simply wonderful. They have done no wrong. It is simply my predilection which has suddenly changed."

Madame smiled and nodded. "Of course, my lady. I have witnessed such a phenomenon in clients before."

Rosamund sighed. It was only a little comforting to know she was not alone.

At the top of the stairs, they turned right to continue down a richly paneled corridor, their footsteps muffled by dark green carpet. Madame stopped before a narrow door. She pulled a key threaded with a red ribbon from her dress pocket and slid it through the keyhole. The door opened onto a cozy room. A velvet curtain, the color of Chinese celadon, hung along the far wall before which were two plush armchairs.

Madame tugged on a pale green satin bell-pull. "When one is exposed to a pleasure one never knew one desired, the ensuing need for the desire must not be neglected."

"Yes, of course."

Since Rosamund had discovered her letch almost ten years prior, she had reveled in exploring it. Initially, everything had been new and wonderful. Madame Laperne had provided her with men who had encouraged Rosamund to stretch her boundaries, had taken her to new levels, new ecstasies. Yet, despite the excitement and the release she always achieved, eventually she realized pursuing her letch lacked something. She could never quite figure out what that was.

Until her chance encounter at Uncle Bradley's Salon. Now she knew precisely what was lacking.

Unfortunately, she would have to do with a substitute.

At Madame's bidding she sat in one of the armchairs. A distinguished male servant entered, holding a silver tray laden with refreshment. He offered a sherry in a delicately etched crystal glass. The wine subdued her. She sank deeper into the chair to watch the show.

Madame drew aside the curtain, revealing a large window. The view of the sumptuously decorated private room was slightly obscured by a fog on the other side of the glass. The occupants of the room would only see the glass as a mirror surrounded by a gilded frame. But from her vantage point, Rosamund had a fine view of the proposed selections. Madame had obviously paid great attention to her rambling attempts at description. Rosamund had specified a certain athletic build, with blond hair and blue eyes. The nose must be straight, almost Roman, the cheekbones angular. Not too young. About mid-twenties would do, a little older would be most appreciated. And perhaps six feet or taller, although that was being generous to the source of her desire.

Most important of all, though, expert aptitude in a particular skill was required.

Rosamund downed her sherry. Madame had garnered five glorious specimens, each fitting her physical description precisely. The sight through the window sent a titillating flush to warm her flesh. Five gorgeous men, their shirtless bodies revealing sculpted muscles, lined up along a wooden trestle bench over which a dark-haired young woman was bent. The girl wore only her underthings. Her head was turned away, her face unseen.

The first man plucked a short-handled paddle from a portable rack along one wall and walked around behind the girl.

Rosamund's heart pounded as the man drew his hand over the girl's posterior, tugging on the white fabric of her drawers, smoothing it. He gripped the paddle and raised his arm, then landed an audible smack on her butt.

Rosamund jumped in her seat.

She stared, riveted, as the second man, then the third took their turns with the girl. The fourth man added a bit of a difference when he angled over her and stroked her hair, his blond locks a striking foil to her chocolate brown. The girl's fingers flexed as he whispered in her ear, rubbing the flat side of the paddle on her bottom.

A sensual warmth slid down Rosamund's spine. The fourth man straightened, a bulge apparent at his crotch. He walked around to the short end of the table, a gentle touch of his fingers keeping a continued connection with the girl. He once again placed the flat edge of the paddle on her bottom, seemingly mapping the best spot, calibrating the best angle. He drew back his arm, his biceps flexing, then swooped the paddle down. A dulcet *thwack* resonated in the air.

Rosamund gasped. Heat pooled between her legs. She barely watched the fifth man perform his expected duty. Her gaze followed the fourth man as he took his place in line. He did have the perfect nose and chin…and lips.

"I'll take number four," she said, her voice hoarse as if she had run a race.

"Adam is the perfect choice, my lady," said Madame. "And the one I had expected you to make."

Jeremy stepped back from the oversize canvas to observe his most recent work, a stormy landscape Charles Westerman himself would praise. Over the last few weeks, he had discovered painting theatrical sets was really not all that difficult. Especially under Malachi's direction.

"You see," the stage manager had observed a few nights prior, "it is much like the Impressionists have discovered. The eye only sees so much from a distance, and the eye only needs so much color and detail to interpret the scene."

Jeremy was impressed. "You know of the Impressionists?"

"You forget, my lord viscount," Malachi said with a snicker, "I am from an area of Africa colonized by the French. We are imbued with their culture as if it were our very own. Oftentimes as if it were the only culture of value."

"But surely you have your own art?" Jeremy could not fathom a culture without some form of art. The Africans must create *something* artistic.

"Ah, my people do, of course. We have a great tradition of making the ordinary very beautiful. But our art is not worthy of your Academy."

Jeremy had shook his head at that. Malachi's judgment of color and perception of line were unfailingly correct, his skill in the theatrical arts quite remarkable. He'd probably be a very fine Academician.

It was Malachi who had suggested it was preferable to paint at night, the dancing light of the oil lamps lending more depth to the flat canvas, helping to deceive the eye. It was more like what an audience would see.

But night was not the best time to be in Lambeth. Jeremy was consoled by the fact that the building housed other tenants, artists and craftspeople who gave the area a lively feel. Added to this, the theater was relatively isolated, a bit of an enclave one might escape to if one were seeking a respite from frenzied preparations for the Royal Academy Exhibition.

Rosamund had balked at first, but he'd reminded her he was still painting; it was simply painting that would not be judged as painting. It would be judged as stagecraft. But, if he had to admit, it was rather brilliant stagecraft.

Of course Malachi had helped add that touch of brilliance.

Jeremy put down his palette to adjust the oil lamp on its hanging stand. The stormy sea should have a little boat upon it, Prospero's boat being tossed about before it reached the island years prior to when the play begins.

But what sort of boat? An ancient Roman boat? A Renaissance boat?

A white sail, of course, and a red barge. White and red against blue and green. Jeremy dabbed his brush into the lead white on his palette.

"O, wonder! How many goodly creatures are there here!"

He turned to see Lisette dressed in a pale blue *robe de chambre*—an exquisite hue with her coloring—her arms crossed over her bosom.

"How long have you been watching me?"

"Only a moment, really. I was reviewing lines with Malachi, but he left me for 'metal more attractive'."

Jeremy chuckled. The entire theatrical crew had a penchant for quoting Shakespeare. Any Shakespeare.

Lisette approached. "You were about to change the seascape, weren't you?" She gestured at the upper right corner of the painting.

"I thought a memory of Prospero's boat might add a bit of flavor."

"But will the audience know it to be Prospero's, or will they think it Antonio's?"

Jeremy smiled. "Does it matter?" He stepped forward. "Surely there are boats upon the ocean at any given time?"

In the night-dimmed light, the shadows of the oil lamp flickered and played upon Lisette's face, while the flame glinted in her amethyst eyes. "I suppose."

She did not move as he stepped toward her, wanting desperately to unbutton the ruffled placket to discover what lay beneath. A simple dress? Her underthings?

Absolutely nothing?

The thought spiked arousal in his loins.

He stood before her, desire burbling but tempered by a gentleman's reticence. Gingerly he touched her shoulders. And when she did not flinch, he skimmed his palms down her arms to hold her hands, squeezing briefly. Still she did not pull away.

He grasped her at the waist and drew her more closely to him.

She eased against him as he angled his head and took her in a soft kiss.

Her palms fell flat against his chest. He wore only his shirt, his waistcoat and jacket tossed over a nearby chair. She clutched at the cambric as she pressed her mouth more fully against his.

It was time to discover what lay beneath the robe.

He picked at the tiny buttons, excitement making his fingers fumble as a youth's in the first flush of desire. She adjusted herself under his ministrations, her actions the only permission he needed to continue.

And, as he had hoped, she wore absolutely nothing under the filmy garment.

He broke free from the kiss to gawk. He froze before her, struck dumb by the sight of her womanly curves and by his sudden craving to lick every part of her flesh.

"Lisette," he breathed, his mouth salivating, hovering over a dark areola.

She cupped his utterly hard cock, the heat of her palm delicious through the fine wool of his trousers.

He pulled the nipple into his mouth, twirling his tongue slowly around the taut peak.

Lisette groaned. "Oh, yes, Lord Jeremy," she sighed pressing his head against her breast. "Please."

She uttered the word not as a mere entreaty, but as a hungry beggar seeking that which would slake a need.

He lifted her and carried her to the column of the proscenium arch, setting her back on the boards to press her up against the plaster, once again devouring her with his lips and tongue.

Lisette moaned and wrapped a leg around his thigh.

"Darling," Jeremy breathed against the tender flesh of her neck. "I want you. Do you want this?"

She tugged free the buttons of his trousers and unhooked his braces. "Yes, oh, yes." She slipped his cock from beneath the layers of trousers and drawers, then once again wrapped her leg around his hip as she guided his cock between her thighs.

He thrust up and in, the heat of her ripping a growl from his throat. He stayed embedded for a moment as she pulsed around him, on the verge of climax.

Instinct and desire took control. He pulled back to slam inside, the force driving her up the plaster column. She dangled like a rag doll as he plowed into her almost savagely, motivated by a lust so pure he forgot the woman beneath him. She clung to him, her head buried against his shoulder, emitting clipped yelps as he plunged deeper and deeper.

He reached the point of no return with a groaning rumble, continuing to slam into her desperate for the final peak. He slid his hand between their bodies to yank himself free at the last possible moment, but she closed the gap, crushing his hand against her belly. He came, spurting his seed inside her, the release perfect for one glorious moment before realization hit.

He had not used precautions.

"Lisette," he panted, "darling, I apologize, I could not restrain myself."

She cradled his cheek in her palm. "It's all right, Jeremy."

"But you should wash, douche, you know, as a woman does, to prevent…" He couldn't say the word out loud.

"Don't worry. I'll take care of it in my dressing room."

"Yes, of course."

"And you should go home."

"I'm not leaving you here. Alone at night."

"I'll be fine. What would your wife say?"

Jeremy smiled. Most likely, *did you enjoy it, dear?*

"My wife does not necessarily expect me home every night."

Lisette stared at him with her big beautiful eyes, sucking her lower lip between her teeth. "Then stay with me. I have a very comfortable bed in my dressing room."

A very pleasant prospect indeed.

"Uncle Charles! Uncle Charles!"

Charles got down on one knee as his nieces and nephew tumbled forward into his open arms. He hugged them, holding them steady while they threatened to fell the lot of them into one mound of giggling and guffawing barbarism.

"Charles, you'll spoil them into expressing emotions they're supposed to keep in check."

Francesca's tone held no chastisement, only humor as she smiled upon the tableau.

"All of you, off!" Charles heaved the children away, stumbling as he stood up. He feigned brushing dust off his jacket as he scowled mockingly.

Eight-year-old Gemma tugged on his hand. "Mama says you're taking us to the park."

Charles grinned at Francesca. "Does she now?"

"Will you watch me draw?" squealed Charlotte. "Please, Uncle Charles?"

He grasped her outstretched fingers. "Of course I will, Lottie." At twelve, she was already an excellent artist. Most assuredly, he would mentor her every step of the way. "And while you're setting up your drawing board, Bobby and I will look for bugs for you to sketch."

That brought a smile to young Robert's lips.

The children hushed the moment their nanny entered the room. "Mrs. Burridge, are we ready for our stroll through the park?"

Francesca nodded. "Yes, Matilda." She waved the children out of the door and into the waiting carriage.

Upon arrival at The Regent's Park, Charles drew in the fragrant spring air through his nostrils, exhaling trepidation. As they strolled down the Broad Walk, Francesca leaned against him, her arm looped through his, something she had only started doing since the death of her husband.

Charles would still be there for her, and they would still be as close after he was married. He was sure of that.

"Frannie, will you take walks with me once I am married?"

She stopped and turned to him, her hand on his arm. "Are you serious about this girl?"

"I think so."

Francesca resumed walking. "Charles, Miss Brockhurst was engaged when you met her, was she not?"

"Yes, Frannie."

"Yet that did not prevent her from seeking you out for indiscreet pleasures, even harmless ones, as you have called them."

The implication stung. Of course, she was right. Francesca was always right. "Her fiancé was a brute. I will not be such a man."

"So she will have no cause to stray." Francesca's tone conveyed a hint of cynicism.

Charles sighed. "I suppose this is when I should tell you I've invited her as my guest to the post-Banquet Gala."

Francesca stopped again. "The affair held by John William Waterhouse? Oh, brother, you know how I looked forward to the event."

"I know. It was a difficult decision to make." At least it was a decision he was probably going to regret.

She stared at the close-clipped green grass bordering the gravel path. "Well, I suppose you must be seen with Miss Brockhurst or your engagement will come as quite a shock."

"Perhaps not so much. Her father is hosting a soirée in my honor a week after the Banquet."

"How wonderful." Francesca smiled.

He tugged on her arm to continue their walk. "Everyone will be there, I am told."

She snorted. "Mr. Brockhurst has piles of money, so he can afford to invite everyone."

"I should like it if you would accompany me to Brockhurst's affair, dear sister."

"To appease my wounded pride in not being your guest to Mr. Waterhouse's?"

Charles chuckled. "Precisely."

He led her along the path circling the Griffin Tazza, the sculpture's four winged lions supporting a wide bowl brimming with bright pink and purple posies.

Francesca studied the stone vase. "Charles, do you love her?"

Well that was the problem, wasn't it? "Not yet."

She scowled. "Not yet?"

"Given time, love will grow. Like with you and George."

Francesca cleared her throat. "I never loved George, and George never loved me. There was tremendous admiration and respect. Mine, for his generosity and kindness. His for my ability to manage the house and children. Except for the moments we scheduled to create our three children, we didn't sleep together—"

"Frannie!"

"Charles, as much as you may find it distasteful, that is the reality of a loveless marriage. Is that something you wish to pursue?"

Charles heaved a sigh. "No. But I hardly think that applies in my case. We've already been, well, partially intimate."

"So the flirtation was not so harmless, was it?"

A flush of embarrassment crept up his neck. "No."

"Charles, you don't have to marry. You can stay a bachelor for the rest of your life." She smiled as they approached Matilda grimacing over something in Bobby's outstretched hand. "You have my children to dote upon."

"Which is something I promised to do this afternoon." He gave her arm a gentle squeeze. "Thank you for being my wise younger sister."

She shouldn't have to endure such a reckless, incautious brother.

CHAPTER FIVE

London, May 1880

"Charles, you could, at the very least, pretend to be cheerful," Francesca chided. "You *are* the star of tonight's event."

Charles sat as comfortably as he could in the brougham sent around by Lawrence Brockhurst. It wasn't just the bumps in the road and Francesca's obvious irritation that annoyed, but his own thoughts which hectored him.

It had been a week since the near disaster that was his and Annalee's attendance at the Waterhouse post-Banquet gala.

He sniggered darkly to himself. Of course he was exaggerating. Annalee had been the model of English womanhood. Quiet and complacent, she had comported herself with deference and the utmost care before the Prince and Princess of Wales, members of Parliament, and the president of the Royal Academy of Art. She had dressed exquisitely and had received not just a few compliments on her attire.

No, Annalee had not been a problem at all. Charles had been the problem.

Or, rather, Charles's obsession with Lady Threxton had been the problem.

She had been there, of course; why did he even think for a blasted second she would not have been? She and Jeremy were a picture of the perfect couple: poised, fashionable, cordial, personable—and very gracious, as Charles had been the center of attention at the event. He was used to such fawning by now. But a sudden need for Lady Threxton to bear witness to his success had taken over his senses. He had made sure she was within earshot of conversations and comments of praise. Annalee had tried to keep up with his antics of roaming about far too ardently, and, at one point, had glimpsed sidelong at Lady Threxton, probably wondering why the lady was always following them.

Individually and as a couple, Charles and Annalee had seemed out of place.

Charles sighed. They were either ill-suited for the event or each other. Luckily, no one had seemed to notice so could draw a conclusion of neither.

"The Brockhursts have been very generous to *fête* you."

Francesca's sardonic tone reminded him he was attending a soirée in celebration of British arts and crafts as a guest of Lawrence Brockhurst. Undoubtedly, Brockhurst was using his personal connection with Charles to garner influence, but it did not matter. Charles was using Brockhurst's daughter to create an aura of respectability. Who was the more despicable?

The carriage arrived with a jolt, yanking Charles into the here and now. As he stepped down to the pavement before the arched entry gate, he drew in a long breath and braced himself for the evening ahead.

From the outside the mansion stood out as an elegant, almost classical house set between narrow terrace houses. Brockhurst had wanted to set himself apart from the regular denizens of town life, so had created something of a country manor at the edge of the city.

Charles entered, pausing as a servant took his hat and cape. He looked up to see Annalee rushing toward him, beaming, as if so pleased he was there.

She nodded a greeting to Francesca before intertwining her arm around his. "Mr. Westerman—Charles," she said in *sotto voce*, "I'm so glad you've come. I'm having a beastly time. Everyone is so, well, old and stodgy. There's no one here my age."

Charles reined in his grin. At most events in support of the arts, the guests were usually well above thirty. Unless they were the too-young wives of some barren aristocrat. Or the fresh-faced intended of a barren celebrity artist.

"I understand, darling."

"Lord and Lady Threxton are here. At least I've *met* them."

Charles quashed a sigh. *He* was the more despicable.

Annalee squeezed his arm. "Papa is gossiping in the library. Come."

She dragged him away from an unamused Francesca. They made their way to the library where, the consummate impresario, Brockhurst was holding court, the small crowd laughing at his jokes.

Annalee held them a small distance away. "Let him finish," she said. "He likes the attention."

So astute for one so young. She *would* make a fine wife.

Brockhurst finished and a moment later spotted Charles.

"Westerman!" He threw his hands in the air and approached. "So glad to see you," he said shaking Charles's right hand with both of his.

Annalee still clung to his left arm and smiled at her papa.

"Brockhurst," Charles said. "I'm parched."

Brockhurst guffawed. "Follow me."

They walked to the refreshment room, Brockhurst greeting passersby as if he were an intimate. Most nodded politely at Charles, having knowledge of his reputation yet perhaps surprised to discover what he looked like. Others greeted him with courteous words.

And when they came upon the elegant display of food and drink spread before them, Charles forgot civil manners. Hunger and thirst descended all of a sudden. Annalee was so perceptive in attending to his needs. She handed him a glass of champagne after he had swallowed a delicate sandwich.

"Darling," he said his mouth full of food. "I thank you."

She smiled, a smile tinged with something other than mere deference. A smile tinged with desire.

Charles flushed and turned his head away.

He gulped his champagne. He should be grateful a young, beautiful woman was paying him mind. He should flaunt it. Should flaunt her.

He should learn how to fucking act in society.

Instead he was wondering when in hell he would see Lady Threxton.

He tamped down his lust. Annalee deserved his undivided attention. He turned to face her.

She smiled when he did so, then ever so furtively, slid her tongue over her upper lip.

Charles's cock responded instantly, excitedly. Annalee should not do such things in public. Well, actually she should. She was his only hope of distracting his mind from more wicked thoughts.

For one moment she owned every bit of him.

And then Lady Threxton came into view.

She flickered on the edge of his peripheral vision. He dared not turn his head to focus on her. He dared not turn away from Annalee. She was an innocent in the whole affair. Well, perhaps not wholly an innocent, but not complicit in any way.

"Mr. Westerman, I fear I have embarrassed you." Annalee seemed genuinely sorry.

Embarrassed? "How so?"

"I thought to merely play. And then you looked askance."

She'd noticed. "I apologize, Miss Brockhurst. There are so many people here tonight I feel I must keep apprised of appearances."

"I understand."

She was so sweet. And so out of her element. All around them men and women of experience flitted and conversed. It was nothing like a society dance where there would be young girls of her age with whom to giggle and gossip.

"Annalee," he said quietly, "perhaps we could escape for a moment to the garden."

She gasped as if stunned. "I would like that very much, Charles."

He nimbly led her to a pair of French doors leading out to the terrace. There were a few circles of conversants on the flagstones, but he ignored them and pulled Annalee slowly and unobtrusively down the steps to the garden bathed in lamplight to ward off the darkness of the new moon.

Beyond the lights, at the back of the garden, a tree spread its branches and its shadows. Charles steered Annalee there, maneuvering her around the backside of the trunk.

She relaxed against the bark. "Charles, we should not tarry."

He slowly drew his fingers along the hairline at her temple, down to her cheek and chin. "No, we should not."

He cupped her cheek and leaned in to kiss her.

She mewled in astonishment against his mouth. He persisted with tongue and lips until she relented, opening for him, letting him explore. Her acquiescence inflamed him, inciting him to push his advantage, grasping at her waist, letting his hands scoop upward until he cupped her bosom. She rocked against him, and he followed her innocent lead.

What the hell was he doing? He had been there five minutes and already he was attempting to seduce the daughter of his host.

Charles pulled back, grateful Annalee could not see his flush of abashment in the dark. "I just…I just wanted to make sure you felt a bit more at ease," he said stupidly.

"Thank you, Charles," she said, breathless. "Perhaps we should rejoin the party?"

"Yes. Yes, of course."

They retraced their steps back to the French doors, slipping inside unnoticed.

Annalee clung to him.

"I don't believe it!" she said, quite out of the blue. "It's Amelia. She's arrived with her auntie." She faced him, her cheeks glowing from the excitement of seeing a peer or from his recent debauchery, it was not clear. "We used to be neighbors when I was a girl. May I leave you alone for a spell?"

"Please." He slipped his arm out of hers.

She smiled and hurried off to her friend.

Charles grabbed a glass of champagne from a passing footman, gulped the contents, then exhaled. He'd best dive into the fray. He was, after all, the star of the occasion.

Rosamund knew Charles Westerman would be at the Brockhurst soirée. Why, he was the very purpose of the event—he *had* to be there.

If she were being honest with herself, she would admit she *hoped* he would be there, or, rather, hoped to connect with him, to converse with him, to immerse herself in his presence. Their intercourse at Waterhouse's post-Banquet gala had consisted of meaningless chit-chat. And when she had returned home in the early morning hours after that affair, she had retired with a curious sensation of yearning.

She surveyed the crowd. Brockhurst had insisted on formal attire, so the only way to distinguish those who earned their excessive wealth from those who inherited theirs was the way they expressed amusement. Businessmen guffawed while the aristocracy more or less sneered.

Except for Charles Westerman. He wasn't expressing amusement at all.

He had just swept back into the massive, elaborately decorated drawing room, Miss Annalee Brockhurst on his arm, the very same Miss Brockhurst who had already had him all to herself at Waterhouse's. All of a sudden, Miss Brockhurst darted to the right while Charles slunk off to the left, leaving Rosamund wondering in their wake.

"My brother is being a bore at his own fête, is he not?"

Rosamund turned to the displeased feminine voice at her right.

"Mrs. Burridge. How lovely to see you."

"Likewise, Lady Threxton."

"And such a dazzling ensemble. The vibrant shades of orange reminds me of a sunset in Italy."

A bloom of rose colored Mrs. Burridge's cheeks. "I have been so long in mourning, perhaps I have taken my freedom in costume a bit to excess."

Rosamund laughed softly. "How droll you are. It is a relief when a woman can dress to suit her coloring and mood rather than according to society's dictates."

Mrs. Burridge eyed her. "You've suffered a close loss, as well," she said with comprehension.

"A son and a daughter."

A gray pallor replaced the blush on Mrs. Burridge's cheeks. "Oh my lord, Lady Threxton, I had no idea. Please accept my sympathies."

"Thank you. It was many years ago. At the time, in the depths of my grief, I thought it odd that I should have to be fitted for a new gown."

"And I had been prepared all too well, having married a much older man." Mrs. Burridge sighed. "I do believe widow's weeds were part of my trousseau."

"Oh, dear. Were you married very young? That must have been frightening for a young girl."

A liveried servant with a drinks-laden tray approached and offered champagne. Mrs. Burridge took hers daintily. Rosamund restrained herself from grabbing two glasses.

"I was eighteen," Mrs. Burridge said with a smile, "and a bit of a morbid creature, I must admit. In my adolescence, I had fallen in love with one of my brother's friends, a soldier. He came calling in his uniform one afternoon, and I was instantly in a swoon. I obsessed over him—it's simply embarrassing to reread my journal from the time." She laughed softly, then shook her head. "He was killed in the Crimea. I mourned excessively and refused to ever fall in love again. So my parents arranged marriage to a business partner of my father's."

"Did love eventually find you?" Sipping champagne afforded Rosamund the opportunity to resume observing the drawing room and whether a certain artist would make an appearance once again.

"I suppose I loved my husband after a fashion. Or perhaps it was merely amicable tolerance after a period of acclimation. But my children..." Mrs. Burridge beamed. "I adore my children. I am grateful I had children with George." She glanced at Rosamund and paled. "Oh, my lady, I apologize. That was thoughtlessly cruel."

Her genuine regret was soothing. "The pain still lingers. It always will, I expect. But I try to remember the joy. When given the opportunity, children exhibit such unfettered enthusiasm for life, and I must find strength in those memories." Rosamund stared blankly at the party guests. "After the deaths of Alexander and Isabelle, my husband and I decided we would change our lives radically, pursue passions we previously thought frivolous or, in my case, unsuitable for a woman. Jeremy took up portraiture. My father, it turned out, had been wanting me to work for him. Now I edit his articles, provide a bit of research, and every once in a while actually write the damn things myself."

"My! That is impressive."

"Then my uncle refused to be outdone by his younger brother and hired me on as his librarian." She wouldn't tell Mrs. Burridge about the other part of her agreement with Jeremy: to pursue passions of a more venal nature.

"Your father is Spencer Rutford, is he not? The art critic?"

"Yes, the very same."

"You realize it was your father's review in *Kallitechnis* that set Charles on the path to stardom?"

"I'm certain it was Mr. Westerman's skill with a paint brush that brought him fame. He's a master of the landscape."

Mrs. Burridge laughed. "Yes, of course he is. But he languished in obscurity until that review was published." She thinned her lips and, for a moment, looked askance. "I don't suppose you could make an introduction, Lady Threxton?"

"Between your brother and my father?"

"That was too forward of me, wasn't it?"

The poor dear looked positively distressed. "I'd be happy to make the introductions, Mrs. Burridge. I'm certain both artist and critic would benefit. However, I have a confession." Rosamund drew in a breath. "It is a scandalous secret, really, so you must not tell a soul."

A wrinkle deepened between Mrs. Burridge's wide blue eyes. "I promise I will not tell a soul."

"It was I who wrote that article." Rosamund practically whispered her confession. The truth of it unsettled her now that she had been intimate with the man.

"You?" The wide eyes blinked very slowly. "But surely Charles should know this? I mean I would never tell, but…surely…"

"Perhaps. There is the danger he might be insulted, knowing his career was bolstered by a mere woman."

Mrs. Burridge chortled softly. "Lady Threxton, believe me when I say Charles is nothing like that. He can't afford to be. He has to take patronage where he can. That's why he is so tolerant of Mr. Brockhurst."

Which possibly meant he was merely tolerating Miss Brockhurst hanging on his arm. "I will think about it. It does seem deceitful to not reveal the true author. It would have to be revealed in strictest confidence. The truth could damage my father's reputation."

"Yes, of course. How foolish of me to not consider such a thing." Mrs. Burridge drew in an inhalation. "But enough of that. I should ask you how the Waterhouse affair was. I was so disappointed to have missed it."

"Lively, as always. Have you ever been?"

"Oh, no. I was expected to go as Charles's guest, but, alas, he felt it politic to bring Miss Brockhurst."

"Because of Mr. Brockhurst's patronage?"

"Well, yes. And he thinks he's taken a fancy to the girl." Mrs. Burridge lowered her voice. "How did she act? Did she seem in her element?"

Rosamund shouldn't gossip, really she shouldn't. "Miss Brockhurst seemed somewhat out of her depth. She often had a worried look about her, as if she were trying to keep up with conversation. She's not been exposed to the art world much, has she?'

"I don't believe so. Her father made his money in textile manufacturing, if I recall correctly. His only interest in art is buying it for status and investment. Her mother is French, though, so perhaps there's an art connection there? Charles behaved himself, I hope?"

Rosamund smiled behind her champagne glass. "He did." Unfortunately so.

"Isn't that your husband over there, my lady? That woman he's with is familiar, but I can't quite place her."

"Why, yes, that is indeed Jeremy." He was with, of all people, Lisette LaFleur. The Brockhursts really did have unconventional tastes in their guest list. "The woman is an actress and he is painting sets for her latest production."

"How very fascinating."

"He thought it might prove to be an interesting endeavor."

"Well, my lady, I must take my leave. Charles wants me to mingle. Wants me to meet people."

"Men, I presume?"

Mrs. Burridge laughed. "He's a good brother." She smiled and gave a slight nod before she swirled away in a froth of orange.

Rosamund downed her champagne and deposited it on the tray of a passing manservant. She needed a bit of a respite from the sight of her husband fawning over his latest conquest.

She headed for the terrace and its promise of fresh air.

The price of fame apparently included remaining stoic while tolerating a bloviating man who fancied himself an amateur critic of art.

"Don't you feel, Mr. Westerman, that if an artist had true talent, he would express it with a realistic depiction of a scene, rather than an 'impression' of it?"

"Realistic such as *The Birth of Venus* by Monsieur Bouguereau?" Charles mocked, clinging to the hope that his taunting was not too obvious.

"Exactly! I say, what is really meant by the term 'impressionist'? Does the artist mean to say this is my impression of good art?" The man laughed too heartily at his own joke.

Charles held his tongue. *Good God*, he had to escape.

He excused himself with a forced smile and quickly headed for the French doors again. He needed fresh air, something other than the perfume and sweat-laden humidity of the drawing room.

Out on the terrace, partygoers gathered in small groups and conversed in subdued tones. In a shadowed corner, a young man and young woman chatted, their proximity and furtive handholding suggesting they would rather be doing something other than talking.

Annalee deserved a polite young man such as that, and not a self-centered lecher as old as her father.

Charles sighed and dragged his fingers through his hair. He needed just one moment to get his emotional bearings. One moment alone, in the dark.

He descended the stone steps into the garden and wandered along a path. In the daylight the Brockhursts' garden was quite lovely. At night the colors of the flowers had dulled to shades of gray, manicured bushes to ominous balls of black.

Without directing, his feet brought him back to the tree where he had kissed Annalee. His gut twisted. *God*, that had been idiotic.

He turned and continued in a new direction along the path, toward a small iron-and-glass greenhouse. The entryway was flanked by two glowing lamps casting intersecting circles of dull light across a mini-terrace. A bench near the doorway beckoned.

He would sit and gather his thoughts. He would take as much time as he could without provoking accusations of being unsociable. Really, the garden was not so vast a guest would never find him. But clearly not many had cause to wander so deep into the shadows.

He sat. Awareness of another instantly prickled the back of his neck. He focused in the dimness. A woman sat on a bench across the tiny terrace. Not just any woman. *She* was unmistakable.

"Lady Threxton. How lovely to see you," Charles said softly.

"Mr. Westerman. I'm surprised you've ventured so far from the madding crowd."

He chuckled at her literary reference and relaxed his posture on the stone bench. After his burst of confused passion with Annalee, for some reason Lady Threxton was like a shelter in the storm of emotion.

"And are you here to escape the crowd, as well?"

"My husband has encountered his paramour at this event. I'm giving him a bit of time to indulge."

Paramour? Threxton?

"Are you disturbed by this?" He restrained himself from jumping to her side in support. "About his having a paramour, I mean?"

"Oh, not at all." She smiled easily, displaying a calm self-assuredness only a woman of her age might. "My greatest objection is that I do not find her wholly agreeable. He could do so much better." Her casual air about the matter spoke of something else, something indescribable, almost *lascivious* about her.

And at that moment he remembered he had been *her* paramour. It had lasted mere minutes, but it had happened.

And he still wanted her.

He stood to pace the flagstones. "Was it tit for tat, then? Was that why you pursued me?" His heartbeat quickened. Her positive response would annoy him, of course. He had taken his indulgence, yes, but he still wanted something more, something, apparently, very much like what Threxton was doing.

"I was attracted to you, Mr. Westerman. That was my motivation."

He faced her in the dark, confusion and desire coursing through him, hoping the shadows obscured his real emotions. "And would you be attracted to a man if your husband were faithful?"

She sighed. "If my husband were faithful, that would be his choice." She stood and stretched out her hand.

An invitation. Surely he should refuse. But he could not.

He slipped his hand in hers.

She tugged him into the shadows behind the glasshouse. They stood facing each other in the dark, hand in hand.

His heart pounded in the silence, yet he could not hear hers. Was she so adept at such liaisons? He wanted to kiss her, *God* he wanted to kiss her. Really do so much more, but they were virtually in public. Yet she stood her ground, not moving. Waiting? Or was she simply over him? Had she got what she wanted and was now only humoring him?

He had to know.

He dipped his head toward hers, needing, wanting to kiss her. He scraped her lips as she turned, and landed on her cheek, pressing the soft, warm flesh with his mouth, flicking his tongue to taste her.

She laced her fingers through his as he continued undeterred down her neck, along her pulse point, relishing the burn of her heated flesh on his lips.

"Charles, please, not here." Her quiet voice held a hint of a quiver. "Not now."

He pulled back. "Why? Why not here? Why not now?"

Her breaths puffed hurriedly. "I want something else. Something more."

"I don't understand, Rosamund," he said softly in her ear.

"I barely understand myself."

She pulled away, stripping her hands from his. "I should go. I'm sure Jeremy is wondering where I am."

"He has his paramour," Charles said caustically. "Or did you forget?"

Rosamund chortled. "It would not be politic for the girl to be around him too much at a public event such as this. I'm sure she's moved on by now."

Charles stared at her in the dark. "It is a strange world you inhabit, Lady Threxton."

"Would that you might understand one day, Mr. Westerman." Lady Threxton turned and walked away, leaving Charles to contemplate what the hell had just happened.

Despite Rosamund's every effort of subduing her desire for Charles Westerman, the craving persisted. The enchantment went beyond simple attraction. The *need* for him pulsed through her, growing stronger when he was in proximity.

She walked back to the party, trying not to be obvious in her haste to escape the source of her agitation. She returned inside coolly, as if she had been outside having thoughtful conversation with very interesting people and had not almost let herself be seduced.

As she had expected, Jeremy was alone, or rather, *sans* Lisette. He spotted her and beamed. As she joined him with his circle of friends, he grasped her hand.

"Gentlemen, you all know my wife, do you not?"

And if anyone had been confused over Lord Threxton's feelings after spying him with Lisette, they were assured by the presence of his wife that he was wholly a conventional married man.

"Lady Threxton," greeted Mr. Brockhurst. "I was just telling your husband what a wonderful portraitist he is. So perspicacious of the human condition."

That was a fine assessment of Jeremy's talents. He not only conveyed a realistic depiction of a subject, but was able with seemingly a few strokes of his brush to convey the subject's innermost sentiments.

"I agree, Mr. Brockhurst."

Miss Brockhurst approached. As she surveyed the group of her father's colleagues, her cheeks colored a pleasing shade of pink, highlighting how gorgeous a girl she truly was.

Mr. Brockhurst beamed at her and draped a boastful arm around her shoulders.

"Gentlemen, Lady Threxton, may I present my beautiful daughter, Miss Annalee Brockhurst."

Rosamund smiled politely. "We have already had the pleasure, Mr. Brockhurst."

Low masculine greetings and bows ensued, while Miss Brockhurst curtsied and blushed.

Just then, Mr. Westerman came into view. He spotted Miss Brockhurst and she him. He colored with a glance at Rosamund, then came forward to join their little group, standing between Mr. Brockhurst and his daughter.

"Ah, Westerman," Mr. Brockhurst greeted, with a slap on the artist's back. "You know Lord Threxton, do you not? Have you seen his works in the Summer Exhibition?"

Mr. Westerman cleared his throat. "Threxton is an exquisite portraitist," he said with a nod toward Jeremy. "No one rivals him today."

Mr. Brockhurst guffawed, again slapping Mr. Westerman, this time on the shoulder. A momentary wince sharpened his features.

"I will have only the best, then, upon your estimation, Westerman." Mr. Brockhurst turned to Jeremy. "Sir, will you do me the honor of painting a portrait of my daughter? I would like to hang it at my estate in France." He beamed at the girl. "When she is married and gone from my house, I would love to see her smiling face grace me with its beauty every day."

Rosamund's gut twinged. She flicked a glance at Mr. Westerman. Should Jeremy decide to agree, Miss Brockhurst would be in his studio for several weeks.

And Mr. Westerman might accompany the young lady.

She turned her attention to Jeremy. Her husband did not seem to notice her agitation. He merely grinned, full of professional pride. First accolades from fellow artists, then commissions from rich patrons. Her husband had truly arrived in artistic society.

"I would be honored to create a portrait of your daughter, Brockhurst."

"Then it's settled." Mr. Brockhurst stuck out his hand, and Jeremy shook it. "Now, how does one go about these sorts of things?"

"I can visit you at your house, or you can visit me at my house where I have my studio." Jeremy smiled at Miss Brockhurst. "Should you wish to dress in a costume, I have several of those as well."

"Costumes?" Miss Brockhurst blushed as all eyes focused on her. "Whatever do you mean?" Surreptitiously she tangled her fingers with Mr. Westerman's before folding her hands before her.

"Shepherdess, Greek poetess, ancient queen—anything you fancy," Jeremy said.

"How delightful." The girl smiled at Jeremy, then glanced at her father and Mr. Westerman.

"When are you free, Threxton?" Mr. Brockhurst said excitedly.

"Well, the Summer Exhibition has been hung, so I am more at liberty these days."

"What about tomorrow?" blurted Mr. Brockhurst.

Jeremy's expression remained composed. Rosamund almost laughed at her husband's restraint. He should have, at the very least, appeared stunned at so forward a claim on an acclaimed artist's time.

"Tomorrow would be fine." Jeremy turned to Miss Brockhurst. "How does two in the afternoon sound?"

"Very well, thank you, my lord," Miss Brockhurst said cordially.

"Westerman," Mr. Brockhurst interjected. "Can you accompany her?"

A smidgen of shock flitted across Mr. Westerman's face. "Tomorrow?" He thought for a moment. "I believe so." He smiled at Miss Brockhurst. "I'll fetch you. Be ready by one thirty."

"Yes, Char—Mr. Westerman."

Mr. Westerman shot a glance at Rosamund before returning his attention to Miss Brockhurst.

The cad.

Rosamund smiled.

CHAPTER SIX

Charles appeared promptly at Annalee's house at one thirty in the afternoon on Sunday.

He rang the doorbell, and a chilling sweat prickled his skin. Once they were at Threxton's studio, Annalee would surely know. She'd figure it out. He couldn't possibly maintain the fiction that he wanted Annalee when *she* was in the room.

Except *she* might not even be there. He and Annalee were to see Threxton, not his wife.

Charles calmed a bit as he cooled his heels in the marble-clad foyer, having told the footman he did not want to wait in the parlor.

Annalee descended the stairs, glowing with excitement, wearing the simplest frock he'd ever seen on her.

She twirled before him. "I dressed so I could try on costumes. What fun! I've never worn a costume. It will be like being on the stage."

Charles held out his arm and led her to the waiting carriage. Once inside, he kissed her tenderly on the lips.

She flinched. "Oh, Charles, you mustn't." She pulled back to rest against the tufted leather. "I don't want to appear flustered in my portrait. *Grand-mère* will see it. I need to maintain my composure."

Indeed.

The jostle of the carriage on uneven pavement mirrored his agitated nerves. Charles had never been to the Threxton house. He and Threxton had socialized at their club or at some art-related event. While he considered the viscount among his friends, Charles's sojourns outside London had stalled progress toward more intimate social interaction.

As the carriage curved along Wilton Crescent, the house on Wilton Place came into view. A small neoclassical entry porch fronted the middle bay of the white stucco town home. The clean lines of the five-story building were an aesthetic from one hundred years prior, not the overly exuberant version of the style his modern house sported. The Thrextons were an old aristocratic family, and he, Charles, merely a middle-class man with newly acquired wealth.

He simply could not compete with Jeremy.

What the hell was he thinking? This wasn't a bloody competition. Jeremy had already won by being *her* husband.

As the carriage stopped, Charles's heartbeat picked up its pace until it pounded furiously. He escorted Annalee to the front door, trying desperately to steady his breath—and steady his hopes. What if Lady Threxton was there?

God. What if she wasn't?

"I hope Lady Threxton is at home," said Annalee. "It would be wonderful to have a woman's opinion for my costume."

Charles wanted to melt into the porch. "Of course, darling," he said.

The butler—Mr. Higgins, as Charles learned from a brief exchange with a maid—led them up several flights of stairs to Threxton's studio, a large space on the top floor, a room that was perhaps meant to be the governess's quarters and nursery at one time, but remodeled to be the quintessential artist's atelier. One whole wall had a generous bank of windows, while another corner was partitioned by screens, perhaps a dressing area of sorts.

Threxton stood at his cabinet, organizing supplies. He grinned as they entered the room.

"Miss Brockhurst!" he said, striding forward. "How lovely to see you."

Annalee curtsied. "Lord Threxton."

Threxton turned to Charles. "Westerman," he greeted with a nod.

"Threxton."

Threxton took Annalee's arm and led her to a corner where an easel held an unfinished portrait with a depiction of some rather unspecific Greco-Roman ruins in the background.

"This is but one example of the type of backdrop I can offer you, Miss Brockhurst," Threxton said.

As Threxton and Annalee discussed backdrops and costumes, Charles wandered around the studio. Threxton was a fairly organized artist, his notebooks shelved tidily, his drafting table strewn with drawings and oil sketches of what was obviously a commission—a portrait of a distinguished-looking middle-aged man with bushy whiskers.

There were a few easels set up with works in progress. One in particular caught his eye. A woman. A *nude* woman.

Her. It was unmistakably *her*.

His lungs complained for want of air. He sucked in an inhalation.

The woman stood casually next to a half-height column atop which was balanced a leafy plant, her elbow resting on the edge of the column, her gaze staring out into the distance, contemplative. Her long brown hair hung down her back, curling tendrils embracing her waist.

Her figure—he had to remember to breathe—her figure was divine. Her luscious breasts buoyant above a nipped-in waist and generous hips. Below her belly a glorious thatch of dark hair obscured the prize beneath.

The frank depiction of realistic nudity was shocking, and deliciously arousing.

Charles's heart continued its frantic pumping, rushing blood to his face and cock. If the woman herself came before him, he would not be able to maintain his control.

Annalee's sharp, hearty laugh drew him out of the fantasy laid before him.

"What do you think, Charles—I mean, Mr. Westerman?"

Annalee held a Renaissance-style dress against her and swished the skirts side to side. The ocean blue and celadon green suited her coloring quite well. Threxton, of course, would have instantly determined that from one look at her. He'd probably suggested the costume.

"It was Lord Threxton's idea. Isn't it divine?"

"Indeed. The viscount has exquisite taste."

"Shall I put it on?" Annalee said excitedly. She looked around the vast space and spied the corner with the screens. "There?"

Threxton nodded. "If you like."

"But what about my hair? Should I send for my Veronique?"

"That won't be necessary."

All turned to the woman who'd said the words. Lady Threxton.

Rosamund.

Damn. She was wearing clothes.

Threxton went to his wife and greeted her with a kiss on each cheek.

"Such an important commission, darling husband, and you did not tell Miss Brockhurst she would need her lady's maid? I shall bring in my own Gretchen."

Lady Threxton rang the bell-pull near the door. She showed Annalee to the screened area behind which they disappeared. After a few moments, a plainly dressed youngish woman, presumably Gretchen, appeared. Threxton waved her toward the women.

Threxton went about setting up the sitter's area. He positioned a chair, the requisite potted plant, and a book.

Charles took the opportunity to examine the oil study of Lady Threxton once again.

This time, though, he would have the lady herself with which to compare.

She appeared from behind the screens and strolled toward him, her placid expression assuming a mien of curiosity upon meeting his gaze. She must have read something on his face. She lifted a brow as she studied the back of the sketch, then blushed. She stopped before the easel and stared at him, the blush fading.

Charles had a perfect view of both the lady in the flesh and the flesh of the lady.

A smile tugged at his lips as he surveyed the lifelike drawing and the model simultaneously. A touch of astonishment crinkled her expression. She caught his gaze each time he glanced up from the study. Blood pumped excitedly through him once again, stirring his cock to excitation. He grinned. She flushed, but did not look away, her gaze challenging him to bare his desires as naked as her body.

Had they been alone, he would not have been able to stop himself from seducing her. She most likely would have insisted the seduction be on her terms.

"Finished!" Annalee's chirp of excitement came from behind the dressing screens.

Threxton immediately went to her to lead her into position. He dismissed Gretchen with a wave of his hand.

Annalee beamed. She was stunning in her costume, the picture of a fine Renaissance lady.

Her expression darkened when she saw Charles. She looked between him and Lady Threxton.

Bollocks. He had been too obvious.

Annalee came around, curiosity creasing her brow. She perused the oil sketch, her face turning a deep pink as she realized what she was looking at. She glanced up at Lady Threxton, then back at the painting.

"Why, that's you, isn't it?"

Lady Threxton smiled. "It is."

"Oh, how utterly scandalous!" She glanced at Charles, blushing further, then at Threxton. "Will this go to the Academy?"

Threxton laughed nervously. "Ah, no, my dear. This is a private work. It's what an artist does to study the human form."

Excellent response, my friend.

"Don't you paint portraits?" Annalee was ingenuous.

Threxton cleared his throat. "Yes, yes I do. But in order for me to understand proportion and shape, I need to know how the body carries itself." He pointed to the nude, drawing attention to the lower part of the study. "See how the legs stand and the hip angles?"

Annalee stared wide-eyed. "I suppose."

"With this positioning, I understand what lies beneath a woman's dress—"

Annalee blushed crimson as her hand flew to cover her mouth.

"In the general sense, of course. But if the hips are angled like so," Threxton pointed once again to the nude, "then the dress covering the hips will be thusly positioned."

For a moment, Annalee seemed to be deep in thought. She turned to Charles. "It's like when you draw just one flower. But you never really paint the flowers in such detail. You only paint the entire field."

Charles exhaled relief. "It is very much like that."

"Ah, well, then, we should never tell my father this. If he knew artists did such things as paint portraits of their wives with no clothes on, he would not want me to be here on my own. But I know my poor dear Veronique would be so utterly bored if she had to attend me for hours on end."

Lady Threxton wrapped an arm around Annalee's shoulders. "Darling, don't have a care. If your father inquires, let him know I work as my husband's assistant and am present much of the time in the studio."

Annalee smiled at her. "Thank you, Lady Threxton."

Threxton clapped his hands. "Well, shall we begin?" He gestured toward the chair and other props. "I thought it best you sit, Miss Brockhurst. With a sort of dreamy expression, your book fallen on the floor."

Annalee's face lit up. "Like I'm swooning from reading poetry?"

Charles dared not chuckle aloud.

"Mr. Westerman, you need not stay on my account," Annalee said. Her gaze flitted toward the nude on the easel before returning to catch his eye.

"Yes, Mr. Westerman," Lady Threxton began. "I'll be here to attend to Miss Brockhurst for a little while. I have work of my own, but I'll look in on her from time to time."

"Give me two hours, Westerman," Threxton said, setting up sketching paper on his easel. "We'll just be trying out poses to discover which accentuates Miss Brockhurst's charms the best. You are welcome to stay if you like." He winked as he gave Charles a sidelong glance. "You know, watch the master at work."

Charles chortled, then bowed to Lady Threxton. "Thank you, my lady, for your offer to chaperon Miss Brockhurst, but I think I shall stay. I'll take the opportunity to study Lord Threxton's techniques, review some of his sketches against the works in progress."

Threxton cleared his throat. His wife colored briefly.

"Very well," she said. "I'll send for tea."

"I would like that very much," Charles said.

As Lady Threxton went to the bell-pull, he was certain she had a little swish to her step that had not been present earlier.

"Will I be able to drink tea?" Annalee inquired.

"Absolutely, Miss Brockhurst. We will pause many times today so you may rest," Threxton said as he rummaged through a box of charcoal sticks.

The tea ordered, Lady Threxton sauntered over to a chair, a subtle wiggle to her backside.

Charles moved to the shelves of notebooks and pulled one out. His new vantage point afforded him a view of Lady Threxton. He turned the pages, hoping desperately to find more salacious sketches amidst the mundane anatomical studies. Even if he found nothing, gazing at the viscountess herself would be a lovely way to spend an afternoon.

The light cast by the flame of a solitary oil lamp danced along the stripes of the wallpaper in the playroom. The sizzle of the burning wick was the only sound in the otherwise eerily quiet space.

Rosamund shifted on the divan. Waiting was positively vexatious, putting her in a mood. Surely the clock in the hall had chimed six o'clock a quarter hour ago? She smoothed her *robe de chambre* into place around her legs, her hands trembling. Mr. Westerman's presence earlier that day had greatly disquieted her, inciting an agitation that could only be confronted in one way. Her usual way.

She leaned back and stared at the ceiling, her gaze lazily drifting to the polished brass grille running along the top of one wall. No one would be watching her in the shadows behind the elaborate arabesques piercing the metal. Good. She needed to face her desires unshared that afternoon.

Adam, with his resemblance to a young Charles, was the perfect choice to perform the service. And now he was taunting her with just how perfect he was by making her wait for her satisfaction. Every muscle in her body tensed and gripped with anticipation. She blew out an exhalation and concentrated on sinking into the cushions. The best way to endure torment was to remain relaxed.

The click of the door latch shot a thrill through her nerves. Adam entered, the sight of him—tall, athletic, blond—almost sending Rosamund into a swoon. He was dressed as a hunter returned from the chase, buff breeches tucked inside glossy knee-high boots. He wore no jacket or waistcoat; his black braces drooped at his sides. The buttons of his shirt placket were undone, revealing a hint of chest hair. His sleeves were rolled up over muscled forearms.

A curled horsewhip hung from a belt slung across his hips. Rosamund's breath hitched.

He strode across the hardwood floor, the rap of heavy steps harsh in the quiet space. He raised a censuring brow as his steel-blue gaze raked across her casual and supine form. She stiffened, the action betraying the wetness already beginning to pool between her legs.

He sauntered around the divan, all the while fingering the braided leather of the whip. "You will take better care next time in anticipating my arrival, my lady."

In one movement the whip was off his belt and unfurled in the air. The crack echoed a shiver down her spine.

Rosamund sat up straight on the edge of the divan, planting her feet flat on the floor, folding her hands primly in her lap. She bowed her head in obeisance.

He knelt before her and lifted her chin with two large fingers. His blue eyes bore into her, probing the darkest recesses of her soul. "Well done, my lady."

He stood and circled her again, slowly, each click of his heels on the wooden boards reverberating in her core.

"Tell me, Lady Threxton, are you distressed by recent sins?"

His voice sang in a deep bass, not quite matching the man inhabiting her reality, but perfectly matching the man of her fantasies.

"Yes, sir." Her tongue hissed weakly against her dry palate.

"Would you like to absolve your mind of this distress?"

She swallowed and stopped a smile. He would allow her to wallow in her sins, but not the ensuing agitation. "Yes."

He stopped, his presence weighty behind her, his breaths measured and heavy. He was waiting.

"Yes, sir."

He continued his pacing. "And will you submit to my demands on the road to absolution?"

She closed her eyes and drew in a breath. The scent of him, raw and masculine, filled her nostrils. "Yes, sir."

He came around to stand before her. "Look at me."

She opened her eyes and looked up, her gaze traversing his sleek form to the waves of his dark blond hair. He tossed the whip onto the divan, its dull thump at her side unsettling. She flinched.

He smirked and flashed a teasing glint. "I thought you better disposed to correction."

She wanted to tell him she was, to beg and plead with him that he must know she was. Instead, she remained silent.

He chuckled, a rumbling sound that reverberated deliciously in her sex.

"Take off your dressing gown."

With jittery fingers, she pulled the buttons free, then slipped the garment from her shoulders. He yanked the robe out from under her and tossed it to the floor.

A chill spread across her, piquing her nipples under her corset. He untied the string at the neckline of her chemise and loosened the garment until it hung off her shoulders.

"Are you wearing drawers?"

Surely he could see the answer to that question.

She lowered her eyes. "No, sir."

"Good."

Once again he lifted her chin. He patted her cheek softly then stood back and stripped off his shirt.

Rosamund gasped.

She stared at his well-honed torso, so close she could reach out and touch had she dared. Firm muscles angled and planed, with a dusting of dark blond hair growing thicker where the trail disappeared down his breeches. He was a magnificent manifestation of her fantasies.

He knelt before her, pushed up the hem of her chemise, the cambric smooth against her thighs, then grabbed her knees and opened her legs. The sound of her, damp and sticky, filled the space between them.

His narrowed gaze penetrated. "You wanton little whore."

"Yes, sir."

He raised his hand as if to strike her. She cowered.

He lifted her off the divan, tossed her over his shoulder, then took her vacated space. He maneuvered her until she lay across him, her belly on his thighs. His erection pressed into her side, hot and potent.

"If I wish to strike you, my lady, you will allow me the privilege." He slid his hand down her thigh, then gathered the fabric of her chemise at her knee.

"Yes, sir."

He pulled the cambric up, cool air swirling over her naked buttocks until the heat of his hovering hand imbued her. He tickled the flesh of one cheek, drawing gentle circles with a thick finger, avoiding delving into the cleft.

"Such beauty should be enjoyed by all men," he sighed. "I am a lucky man to behold this sight so closely."

He pressed his palm against the undercurve of her cheek, briefly curling his fingers around her hip. He rubbed slowly, delicately, in a circular motion, each pass a tiny bit faster as if polishing her to a shine.

Suddenly he drew his hand away.

"I am also a lucky man to mar this sight."

He struck, jarring her against his erection. The burn at the point of impact slowly suffused her skin to meld with the wetness at her sex.

He rubbed the spot he had just swatted. "Is it possible I have just made you more beautiful?"

The cool emptiness of the absence of his hand lasted for only a minute, but an excruciating minute. She wriggled slightly in invitation.

He grabbed her hair and pulled. "Did I give you permission to enjoy this, my lady?"

The position constricted her neck. "No, sir," she said hoarsely.

He let go. His swat was cruel, stupefying. She gasped and went limp against him.

"That is more like it, my lady."

Again he rubbed the tender flesh, his fingers flicking tantalizingly close to her sex. He pushed her leg, opening her to blow on her labia. Instinctively she contracted.

He growled in delight.

"So delicious. A man would pay to fuck your quim."

She contracted again.

He struck her, his palm slapping against her heated sex, sending reverberations up her channel. She clenched the vibrations within, blinking back tears of release, choking on an orgiastic cry.

He leaned over her, his breath hot on her cheek. "Have you had enough, my lady?"

"No, sir."

He spanked again, this time his fingers touching her cunt.

"That is not the correct answer."

Tears wet her lashes. "Whatever pleases you, sir."

He picked her up off his lap and set her down to kneel before him. He smoothed back her hair and studied her face, wiping a tear from her cheek.

"So beautiful."

He kissed her, openmouthed, plunging his tongue into her depths. She wanted to collapse, but he held her steady at her shoulders, his strength flowing through her. He tasted glorious, as a man should—as the man of her fantasies should. She wanted to pleasure him, to suck his cock until he came in her mouth. She would do anything, anything for him at that moment.

He broke free from the kiss, still holding her steady, staring deeply into her eyes, a tear at the corner of his own, a quiet acknowledgment that their performance was over.

She expelled a hard breath then broke down in tears.

He pulled her up to sit on the couch, wrapping an arm around her.

"Shh, shh, my lady."

She covered her face in her hands. "I just wanted… I just wanted…" She heaved inhalations between sobs.

"I know," he said gently. "We all just want. And those that can help alleviate wants are here to serve."

Such truth from one so unlikely. She looked up at him, offering a smile. "Thank you, Adam."

He grinned and wiped a tear from her cheek. "My pleasure, my lady."

Jeremy watched the morning sun shine weakly through the worn but cheery curtains in Lisette's bedroom. Beside him, Lisette still slept. He wrapped his arm around her, and she nuzzled drowsily against him.

He enjoyed moments like this. They were both riding high with their successes, yet ordinary moments were reminders of the simple joys of life.

Jeremy was quite satisfied by his inclusion in the Summer Exhibition. While 1880 was "a great year for landscapes"—both in the sense that the canvases were well executed and that there were a great many of them on display—as far as portraiture, one reviewer noted, the 1880 exhibition "unquestionably excels all previous exhibitions."

Jeremy had beamed as he archived the reviews in his notebooks. He himself had not been singled out as exemplary, but neither had he been singled out as bringing down the quality. He was simply one of the "unquestionably" excellent portraitists.

On the other hand, as far as Lisette's career was concerned, *The Tempest* was not a hit, but it had been well received—by critics of the lesser newspapers. Reviews never made the *Times* or the *Evening Standard,* but then the theater was not officially part of the West End companies. Lisette—and Malachi—seemed to take it all in stride.

They were all of twenty-three, each of them, so really had no stakes in the game yet. They were just happy to be on the stage.

And Lisette was happy to be in Jeremy's arms. Or so it seemed, as she had been spending a lot of time with him in bed—sleeping, and probably too often. But she was working hard. He could either sleep with Rosamund, whose temper had been brooding of late, or he could sleep with a young woman who did not fend off his sensual advances. She just never did any of the advancing herself.

He had attended the previous night's show. He had seen a preview and opening night, of course, as his own artwork was so much of the production, but had decided to see one of the less well-attended shows in the middle of the run. As always, Lisette and her cast were very good, and Jeremy's scenery was still spectacular. The audience responded with gasps, applause, and laughter at all the right moments.

It had been an uneventful performance, with no adoring fans to keep at bay. So Jeremy had accompanied Lisette home to Camberwell and spent the night.

There had been no sex, just naked, sleepy cuddling on Lisette's part and frustration coupled with half masturbation on Jeremy's part. But a new day had dawned and, as far as he knew, Lisette had nowhere else to be but in his arms.

She stirred against him, the softness of her breasts pushing into the side of his chest. He had been rock hard ten minutes ago and was rock hard once more. He stroked down her waist to her hip.

Her eyes fluttered open. "Good morning." Her voice was wonderfully gravelly.

"Good morning, darling." He rolled to be half on top of her.

She nudged him away. "I have to piddle."

She extracted herself from the bed and went to the chamber pot, squatting and showing off her magnificent derriere before pissing the night's contents from her body. She staggered a little as she walked back to the bed, her abundant breasts swaying tantalizingly. She climbed back under the covers and gave him a twisted smile.

She touched the tip of her finger to his nose. "You want to fuck, don't you?"

He most certainly did. "Only if you do, love."

She giggled. "And what if I don't?"

He'd been incautious too often, not pulling out. She had reason to be worried. "I'll understand."

"You'll just go fuck your wife, right?"

The remark stung. He'd rather leave Rosamund out of their conversations. "I'd satisfy myself."

"Does she mind much?"

Rosamund hated when he masturbated without her— "What do you mean?"

"That you have sex with me. Marriage vows and all that."

"Ah. Lady Threxton and I have mutually agreed upon a loose definition of fidelity." He grabbed her around the waist and rolled on top. "Which means you and I are allowed our pleasures."

She giggled again and spread her legs.

He smoothed his hand over her belly to tangle through the hair of her motte before reaching his prize. She was wet and ready for him. He found the little nubbin of her clitoris and rubbed. Her eyes closed as her expression melted into oblivious desire.

"Darling," he said. "Do you ever touch yourself?"

She looked at him with a furrowed brow. "I do, sometimes. Not since I've been with you." She nuzzled against his arm. "I haven't really needed to much," she said with a smile.

"I'd like to watch you."

The smile vanished. "Watch me?" It was as if she had never considered such a thing. A bit odd for a professional performer.

"Yes," he said. "I'll watch you pleasure yourself while I pleasure myself."

She eyed him with a twisted smile. "But, darling," she said as she stroked his cheek above his beard. "Why would we bother when you can be inside me?"

Why, indeed. "Because it's enjoyable." He raised a brow. "And fun." And one way to avoid pregnancy.

She twirled her fingers through his chest hair. "I like what we usually do." She clasped both hands around his waist. "I think that's fun."

Inwardly, Jeremy sighed. Not all of his lovers had been this unadventurous. "All right, love. Whatever my lovely little Lisette wants."

She giggled and grabbed his cock. He almost came in her hand.

She placed him at her entrance, moaning encouragement as he entered her. He growled relief as he pressed forward. She was so wonderfully responsive, enveloping him with her warmth and sighing her pleasure.

Yet something changed in her violet eyes. A sort of sadness tinged them. Or maybe it was his own mood. He needed the physical release—he was at the point of desperation. Just her presence excited him, and he could not go on for very long without spending.

Too quickly he reached the point of no return, but he held on, as a gentleman ought. Finally, Lisette climaxed around him, sending him over the edge. He pulled out and aimed his cock at her belly between them.

Lisette yelped, then rolled to her side, pushing his arm at the elbow. He collapsed and toppled over, still holding on to his cock as he jetted his emission on himself and the sheets.

He lay there, panting, not really quite sure what had just happened.

Lisette gave him a little swat. "I thought you were going to spend all over me."

That had been the idea. "Of course not, darling. I would never do such a thing." Jeremy sighed.

Their initial attraction had been so deep, so intense, and yet as lovers they were so mismatched. It was his utter compatibility with Rosamund that made him cherish his wife so much. He had yet to find any such connection with a secondary lover.

Lisette sat up on the edge of the bed. Their lovers' afterglow had clearly ended.

"I'm famished," she announced. "Let's see what the landlady has in her larder." She stood and wrapped herself in her shabby *robe de chambre*. "You can take me for a proper meal later."

CHAPTER SEVEN

Charles knew he should not accompany Annalee to the Threxton house for her portrait. Really, she should bring her lady's maid as a companion and chaperon. But Annalee encouraged him. She respected his good opinion as an artist.

"And," she had said one night after dinner at the Brockhurst house. "I want your opinion as a beau."

Charles had almost spit out his port at that. Was that what he was? Her beau?

Of course he was, but he acted more like a cad. He spent every waking moment thinking about Lady Threxton.

Over the last month, he had found himself in Threxton's studio, hoping for just a glimpse of Lady Threxton as he watched Annalee's portrait take shape and bore witness to Annalee's questions regarding Threxton's aesthetic decisions.

"What's that in the background?" she had asked, pointing to a stone structure atop a mountain.

"A castle." Threxton had sounded rather pleased with himself.

"A castle? Why?"

"You've been reading poetry and dreaming of knights and such."

"Like *Idylls of the King*?"

"Something romantic like that."

"Aren't I dressed as a lady of the Italian Renaissance?"

To which Threxton had just laughed. "Oh, my dear. Perhaps I should have painted you plainly, and not as a romantic heroine."

Annalee had blushed at that. She was terribly pretty when she blushed, the pink in her cheeks augmenting her coloring to her advantage. Her beauty had interested Charles upon first meeting, and her naive inquisitiveness had made him pursue her dangerously.

During the times he and Annalee had returned to the studio, Lady Threxton had rarely been present. Once, she had stopped by to say her good mornings very briefly, and another day had been in the studio when they had arrived. Both times, she was the picture of cool confidence, of calm collectedness, a woman not easily rattled.

Yet, both times, she had quickly scurried away. As if she were avoiding Charles.

Busy, she had said. Work for her uncle and her father, she had said. He wanted to ask her what it was precisely she did, wanted her to take him deeper into her confidence, wanted to laugh with her, wanted the thrill of flirting with her.

Alas, he merely mumbled "good day" when he saw her, then sat in a chair watching Threxton. Occasionally, he would peruse the viscount's sketches and drawings, hoping for another exciting study, but he never saw any more nudes of Lady Threxton. Disappointment reminded him he was taking time away from his own work.

His obsession with Rosamund was wreaking havoc on his career.

The final day of Annalee's portrait sitting was very much the same as the other days.

"Well, Miss Brockhurst, I have all I need from you at the moment," Threxton announced. "Now comes the finessing of the work. We'll arrange an unveiling when it's ready."

"Ooh! I like that idea," Annalee said with genuine glee.

Charles took her home, listening to her continued effusion in the carriage.

"I've never had such a thing as a portrait of myself. And now I am to have an unveiling. Oh, how marvelous."

She clung to his hand a little too long as she descended to the pavement. "Will you kiss my hand in farewell, Mr. Westerman?"

He bent over her bare hand and pressed his lips to her palm.

She blushed and drew her hand away, only then noticing she wore no gloves. "My gloves!"

Charles searched the seat of the carriage. Annalee searched her reticule.

"Oh bother, I must have left them in Lord Threxton's studio." She batted her lashes at him. "Oh, Charles, be a dear, will you, and fetch them for me? I think I left them behind the dressing screen."

He shouldn't, he really shouldn't. She should send a note, send her maid, send anyone else.

"Yes, Annalee. I'll go right now."

She smiled. "Thank you"—she looked askance, side to side—"darling." She touched his lips with a featherlight kiss. "I'll tell Papa you'll be staying for dinner."

"All right."

She skipped away up the steps to the Brockhurst residence.

Charles directed the driver to return to the Threxton house, then sank back against the leather squabs, unsure whether it was anticipation or dread that roiled his gut.

Rosamund paced the foyer, her steps light against the marble tiles. She'd sent a note to Madame Laperne, saying she needed Adam's services desperately. Was he, perchance, available that afternoon?

The messenger boy should have been back by now.

The doorbell rang. She froze in place as Higgins dealt with the caller.

"A message, my lady." Higgins handed her a missive on a silver salver.

She opened it with trembling hands. Tears threatened but propriety demanded she keep them at bay.

Her heart sank. He couldn't come. He apologized profusely. It would have to wait until tomorrow. He would love to see her then.

Damn. She drew in a breath. Perhaps Jeremy could help her, just this once.

"My lady?"

The butler stood before her once again.

"Yes?"

"Mr. Westerman is here. He says Miss Brockhurst left her gloves."

Rosamund almost collapsed from incredulity. "Mr. Westerman?"

"Yes, my lady."

She looked past Higgins's shoulder to see Mr. Westerman standing near the door, turning his hat in his hands.

"Mr. Westerman," she greeted as she came toward him. "How lovely to see you."

He paled. "Lady Threxton. The pleasure is mine." He gripped his hat at the brim. "I am here to collect Miss Brockhurst's gloves. She left them in the studio. I can wait while a servant retrieves them."

Here was opportunity presenting itself. "Why don't I take you upstairs myself and we'll search for them together?"

He glanced at the floor before meeting her gaze. "I would not want to disturb Lord Threxton while he works."

"Jeremy is taking tea in his study." *Thank God.*

He hesitated for a moment, a thoughtful expression molding his face until it softened into something close to mischievous. "If it is not too much of a bother. Miss Brockhurst told me where to look."

"No bother at all, Mr. Westerman. Follow me."

Rosamund mounted the stairs, and Mr. Westerman followed a few steps behind in silence. His weighty presence sent a tingling thrill up her spine, hardening her nipples against her corset. She was hopeless to prevent the exaggerated sway in her hips his presence provoked.

Once at the studio, she opened the door and invited him in with a wave of her hand. He strode to the center of the room and sighed.

"Such a lovely atelier." He gazed around. "I am not so lucky with mine. It's small. The light is not as good as I'd like."

"Oh? I'm sure it is much finer than what you describe." Rosamund closed the door behind her and stood by his side. "I would love to see it one day."

He turned to face her. "And I would love for you to grace it with your presence."

She flushed, the heat of her reaction tickling her sex. "I'd like to do more than merely grace it."

He raised his brows. "Oh? Such as?"

"I'd make sure you were making the most of your attributes."

He chuckled. "I'm sure you would," he said with a suggestive air.

Was it an invitation?

He looked around. "She said she left them behind the dressing screen."

She? "Of course. Miss Brockhurst's gloves." Rosamund pointed to the corner of the room. "Just there."

"Am I allowed? There might be unmentionables."

She laughed. "I'll fetch them." She looked back at him. "I don't suppose you have a dressing corner in your studio?"

She ducked behind the screen. The gloves were on the slipper chair.

"Perhaps I should."

She turned at his voice. He was right behind her.

He looked around. "It's very cozy."

She stepped forward. He didn't move away.

Another invitation? At least not a refusal.

Her heart beat faster as she reached up and glided two fingers across his cheek. The skin was rough and warm and flushed pink a moment after contact.

He licked his lips. His luscious lips. Just a taste, that's all she wanted, all she needed. Just a taste.

She stood on tiptoe and brushed her lips against his.

He grabbed her around the waist and pressed his mouth to hers, urging his tongue inside. Rosamund devoured what he gave her, tasting him thoroughly.

Satisfaction turned to fresh need. She needed him to…to… But he wouldn't understand, would he?

And he had his own idea of what she needed.

He crushed her against the wall, trapping her there with his hip as he nibbled on her earlobe, then laid kisses down her neck. She melted under his touch, dazed, fading into a dream she had every night of him.

Until he began to pull up her skirts.

She livened. He wanted her, to be inside her.

She unhooked his braces at the front, unbuttoned the fly of his trousers, the fly of his drawers, freeing his cock, already thick with arousal. She wrapped her hand around the shaft, squeezing a droplet of excitement from the tip. She smoothed the wetness over the glans.

He sucked an oath through his teeth.

He grabbed her buttocks, strong fingers pressing into her cheeks, inciting frenzied lust. He angled into position, lifting her, sliding a hand along her thigh to urge it upward. His cock prodded her entrance only a moment before he slid inside in one swift movement, his erotic groan reverberating in his chest under her palms.

He pulled back, then slammed into her, over and again, saying nothing, a man possessed, determined to slake his lust. She wrapped her arms around his neck to gain purchase as he jostled her mercilessly along the wall.

Sweat sheened his temples, his grunts filled her ears. This was not lovemaking; this was not passionate bliss; this was a vulgar act of ridding himself of some base urge, an urge she provoked. An urge she thoroughly understood.

"Don't pull out," she whispered.

He thrust forcefully one last time and came with a clipped howl, shuddering, sputtering as he emptied himself inside her.

His face twisted in something akin to agony. He pushed away, shoving his still-erect cock inside his trousers, fumbling as he righted his clothes. He grabbed Miss Brockhurst's gloves and stormed out.

Rosamund crumpled to the floor and let the tears flow.

* * * * *

Charles rushed down the stairs to the Thrextons' foyer, clinging to his emotions with every bit of control he could muster, barely saying a word to the butler as he dashed out the front door.

Once in the carriage, he slammed his hand against the leather seat.

He had to get out of London. He had to get very far away from Lady Threxton and her temptations. But where?

Scotland. He'd go back to Scotland.

No, he'd had enough of the Scottish countryside for a while. Somewhere else.

He'd go to bloody America just to get her out of his mind.

He drew in a long inhalation. He had the world at his beck and call, really. He could choose to go anywhere.

He'd think about it later. Right now he had to go home and dress for dinner. An evening with the Brockhurst family and their set would have to suffice as distraction for now.

Thank God he wouldn't be alone tonight.

"Well, Westerman." Brockhurst slapped him on the back as he sucked on a cigar. "How's the life of an artist?"

Charles sidestepped a puff of smoke aimed in his direction. Brockhurst had clearly had a bit too much port that evening. But he'd allow the man his indulgences. He'd been good for his career. Very good.

A mustachioed man approached, an industrialist. Charles was fairly certain his name was Boulton. "Westerman." He nodded. "You've had good reviews this summer, haven't you?"

Charles smiled behind his port glass. An industrialist interested in art. A potential patron. "Thank you. I suppose I have."

"Ah! You should not be bashful of such accolades, my good man," said Gooch, who very definitely did something involving wool. "It's all well deserved."

It was. He'd worked long and hard, had developed his skill, had honed his talent. A man deserved accolades after all that.

"Well," began Brockhurst, "your celebrity may just keep you here in London, but I would love to tempt you away to France again."

France? Of course. France. "The Île-de-France?" He wouldn't have to bother with America after all.

"Yes. We're planning to return to *Le Bocage* in August for a few months. I'll take that portrait of Annalee. Threxton says it will be finished by then." Brockhurst blew out more gray smoke. "I'd like to commission a new set of murals from you."

Charles raised an eyebrow. "Oh?"

"The Fields of Elysium. In the south parlor." Brockhurst placed the stub of his cigar in a dish. "You remember the room? It's Chantal's favorite."

"Of course." It was one of the rooms in which Annalee had flirted with him. "Your wife has reason to enjoy the room. It has good light and a lovely prospect."

Brockhurst placed a hand on his shoulder. "Which will be made that much more lovely with a Westerman landscape." He gave Charles a friendly pat. "Think about it. There's plenty of time for packing and arranging passage."

The idea was very attractive. And would be very lucrative, if the last commission was anything to judge by.

And Annalee would be there to distract him from thoughts of Lady Threxton.

"Come," Brockhurst said to the men. "Let us join the ladies in the drawing room."

Charles caught Annalee's attention the moment he entered the room. She immediately went to his side.

"Mr. Westerman." She smiled provocatively.

Charles had been separated from Annalee during dinner. She had been seated between two of her father's colleagues on the other side of the table from him. Charles had been seated between two lovely women. They had been a bit starstruck, and each wanted to buy paintings from him. He had no doubt that they would. Their jewelry proclaimed they were positively dripping with money.

He offered his arm, then strolled with her to a quiet corner. "Miss Brockhurst, why did you not tell me you were returning to France?"

"I'm sorry. It was not for me to say. It was a sudden change of heart on Mama's part. She misses her *Maman. Grand-mère* is ill."

"Please forgive me. I did not know. My condolences."

Annalee looked past his shoulder. "Did Papa tell you?"

"Yes."

"What else did he say to you?"

She knew. One corner of his mouth lifted in a knowing smile. "He asked if I would paint another set of murals."

She batted her lashes. "And will you?"

He chuckled at her enthusiasm. "I have not given him my answer yet. But, rest assured it will be 'Yes'."

She let out a little squeak, then quickly covered her mouth with her hand. "I won't tell Papa. I'll let you tell him." She gazed at him, her blue eyes twinkling. "Oh, Charles, I am so glad. It will be like last year, only so much better."

He could only hope.

CHAPTER EIGHT

London, August 1880

Jeremy stared at the letter unfolded on his desk, the flamboyant handwriting slowly blurring as thoughts bombarded his brain. Lisette was gone. She'd left for Paris with Malachi. They'd packed up the theater but expected to return to London the following spring. She thanked "Lord Jeremy" for everything he had done for her.

That a lover thanked him was disquieting. Of course, she must have meant his help with the scenery. She didn't specify. His first instinct was that she was thanking him for the sex.

He sighed and stared out the window. Lisette leaving was for the best. Her youthful body had been a pleasant diversion, but it was time for Jeremy to take his career more seriously, join a few clubs, hold a few salons. Rosamund would love to play hostess at such affairs.

Except she had been morose of late, due to Westerman's repair to the French countryside. How oddly coincidental: husband and wife who had permitted each other their personal freedoms suddenly had only each other.

And they themselves were departing soon for Langley Heights, their estate in Norfolk. The countryside would offer distractions for a spell—the Hammonds' annual hunting party would be the best of them, and the occasional visitor from London would surely provide some entertainment. But mostly it would be just Rosamund and Jeremy, their solitude compounded by Rosamund's dashed hope that Charles Westerman might have been lured by the prospect of painting serene autumn vistas.

It was Rosamund's despondency that had inspired Jeremy to give her a memory to occupy her mind whenever she felt the oppression of a broken heart.

Jeremy had sent a private note to Madame Laperne, purchasing Adam's time and services for Rosamund's exclusive use while they remained in London for the month of August. Adam had agreed readily. He liked Rosamund. He especially liked that being spanked roused her immensely and wasn't simply a fashionable aristocratic exercise. For that reason, Adam had said, he always looked forward to their next encounter.

Adam had arrived about an hour ago. Before he had gone upstairs to Rosamund's playroom, he had suggested—with polite enthusiasm—Jeremy might want to participate that afternoon and not simply act the voyeur. Jeremy had said he'd think about it.

And then the letter had arrived…

What better way to rid Lisette from his system than to goad his wife toward climax?

Jeremy chortled as he refolded Lisette's missive. His time in the theater had enabled him to comprehend how much he was not an actor. He was really an audience member, perhaps, at most, a backstage hand. And this lack of skill in the performing arts made him ill-suited to fully participate in an elaborate chastisement scenario. Luckily, Rosamund accepted his hands-off handling of her letch, and Adam was fabulously skilled in the art of acting a rôle.

But every once in a while, for his wife's sake, Jeremy could deign to play a part.

He left his study, taking the stairs two at a time to arrive at the corridor that led to the playroom. He crept quietly until he reached the door, then knelt and pressed his ear against the keyhole to listen.

Rosamund's muffled moans were steady, as if she were being pleasured continually and not being swatted at intervals. Jeremy cracked the door open and peeked inside.

A paddle had been tossed carelessly onto the floor. The four-poster bed had been pushed askew into the center of the room. Atop the bed Rosamund was on her knees bestride Adam's face. She was gagged, her wrists tied to the front bedposts by an elaborate series of twists and knots. She wore only her stockings. Adam was thoroughly nude and quite the magnificent example of British masculinity. He held her firmly at her thighs as he tormented her with his tongue, his toes flexing and curling at the end of the mattress, his prick proudly erect and angled toward Rosamund's arse, still pink from having been paddled.

A thrilling chill ripped down Jeremy's spine. The sight of his wife in bondage stirred his cock until it ached within his drawers. Rosamund's lovers had never been so creative. Although he'd never known her to require so much creativity.

Jeremy was definitely not going to let the moment pass without his involvement. He stripped down to his shirt, then knotted the hem around his waist, exposing his stiff and bobbing prick.

Adam noticed him and gave a wink.

He approached the pair. Adam continued his oral ministrations without a respite, as if Jeremy's climbing onto the bed to join them was customary.

As the mattress dipped under Jeremy's weight, Rosamund turned her head with a muffled "Oh!" her eyes wide in fear or surprise. Possibly a little of both.

Jeremy straddled Adam's torso and slid up behind his wife, wrapping his arms around her waist, his erection prodding the cleft of her buttocks.

"Darling, I see you're enjoying yourself," he murmured in her ear. "Would you like to enjoy yourself even more?"

Adam chuckled into her quim.

Jeremy took his cock in hand and aimed it at his wife's cunt. Adam's wet breath on his glans excited him, shooting a tingle of lust to curl within his stones. Adam adjusted his position as he sucked on

Rosamund's clit, allowing Jeremy room to push forward and sheathe himself inside her soaking cunt.

Rosamund cried out, her ecstasy muted against the gag but apparent from the force of her grip around his shaft.

Jeremy fucked her slowly, cupping and massaging her breasts before pinching her nipples, eliciting pulsating squeezes in return. Below, Adam worked his sensual magic with his tongue. Rosamund swayed against the ropes, weakening under the onslaught of orgiastic delights, melting into Jeremy's embrace.

Adam's devilish tongue flicked against the top side of Jeremy's prick, perhaps purposefully, perhaps unintentionally, it did not matter. He was fucking his wife in a new and glorious way, a way his previous lover would never have allowed.

And Rosamund's yielding form meant she was giving in to the new experience readily, a carnal adventure so wildly different from her experiences with Charles—from what she had told him. Certainly the two had done nothing like this.

This was a sensual memory to suppress any lingering regrets regarding other lovers.

Rosamund would remember being bared and vulnerable before two men as each took pleasure from her, giving it back tenfold. She would remember Jeremy's cock, the hardest it had ever been, filling her, she clenching tightly with his every thrust. She would remember Jeremy pulling her hair with such vigor she was forced to tilt her head backward. She would remember his tender touch before cruelly twisting a nipple. She would remember her own husband calling her a whore because Adam's mouth was otherwise occupied. She would remember Jeremy slamming inside her mercilessly until he came with such intensity the bed shook.

She would remember crying in gratitude as Adam untied her and cooed soothing words.

She would remember her husband's joyous grin flashed in her direction before he left the room.

Jeremy sighed as he leaned against the closed door to the playroom. Rosamund was a treasure of a wife. He barely deserved her. But he would do anything for her.

Anything.

* * * * *

Le Bocage, Île-de-France, August 1880

France in late summer was every shade of gold and blue a painter could imagine. The landscape outside the Brockhurst estate was glorious to study and sketch, and over the last fortnight, Charles had availed himself of every chance to do so.

He sighed as he gazed out the ancient panes of the windows of the south parlor. He could truly settle down in such a place. And Annalee presented him with such an opportunity. Well, at least with the possibility of an opportunity.

Flirting and mashing were pleasurable to be sure, but he had to consider the long term. Annalee would be a pleasant enough wife the first year or so, especially in bed. It did not matter that he did not love her at that moment. Surely love would grow over the years. But a wife had to be so much more than a companion, a lover so captivating he would think of no other. She had to be a manager of the home, a partner in his business. Could Annalee be all those things? Perhaps with a bit of discipline and guidance. She was only twenty-two. She had many years ahead of her to settle into the role. But he was already forty-five and at the top of his career. He needed the role of Mrs. Westerman filled as soon as possible.

He would have a few months to think about the prospect. In the meantime, Annalee was busy with French lessons, exploring the gardens, and spending long hours with her mother, grandmother, and other extended family. She would learn a great deal from contact with generations of female relatives, their traditions, their advice. She might be ready for the role of wife if he waited to propose to her in several months' time.

And while he contemplated such a move, he had his work to occupy his days. The south parlor had been emptied of all furnishings and was for Charles alone. His working situation had never before been so gratifying. The room was situated on the southwest corner of the ancient mansion, with wrap-around windows affording a spectacular view of the wild fields of the estate. Brockhurst had said they might develop the wildness into agriculture, but for now the expanse was the gloriously untamed Champs-Élysées, the Elysian

Fields, the final resting place for the souls of heroes and virtuous men. An ironic vista for someone as dishonorable as Charles had been of late.

Instead of Rococo tableaux between the windows—which Brockhurst had suggested—Charles had decided the mural would integrate the views beyond the glass. He had positioned his sketching easel at the best vantage point from which to take in the view as he laid out the scenes for the interstices and headers. Brockhurst had hired a local boy to assist him, which reminded Charles of Lady Threxton's comment about whether or not he employed assistants. Yet the boy was employed for menial tasks like fetching tools and the tea tray and keeping the protective cloth covering the parquet floor. He held no prurient interest despite Lady Threxton's suggestive remarks about what a helpmate could do. The boy was a sweet fellow, singing folk songs and reading poetry while waiting for instructions in Charles's mediocre French. Charles would eventually teach him to be a proper artist's assistant, but for now, during the design phase of the commission, the boy was simply there.

Sometimes, though, Charles wished it were Annalee at his side assisting him. Like Lady Threxton was assistant to her artist husband.

And sometimes, as his brush caressed the wall, Charles imagined Lady Threxton as his assistant.

And so much more.

CHAPTER NINE

Norfolk, October 1880

Jeremy surveyed the guests in the billiards room at Hammond Hall, the estate of Viscount and Lady Hammond, his country house neighbors in Norfolk. The event was, ostensibly, a hunting party, yet each cigar-smoking, brandy-swilling chap was an unlikely man to climb on top of a horse. Well, except perhaps Lord Hammond's son, Harland, whose tailored suit hugged his broad shoulders flawlessly as he strode across the carpet, then turned with a casual flair to announce he was about to head off to the drawing room for a bit of cards and whisky.

Hunting was a the most frivolous excuse for a party.

There was one thing not frivolous about such affairs, though, and that was the opportunity to flirt with women who would still be at the house the next morning. If the flirtation continued over breakfast, then the pursuit of the prey could be continued on horseback into the far reaches of the estate.

Sex out in the woods was delicious.

And there was one woman in particular Jeremy had been fantasizing taking into the woods since the first day of the party.

Her name was Maude, and she was the daughter of Bennet Bowles, a Radical politician who was abysmal at winning a seat in Parliament but a master of the political pulpit. Miss Bowles was something of a Radical herself, as she insisted on insinuating herself into the domain of men, including Lord Hammond's billiards room. She had enticed a couple of girlfriends to join her, one of whom was bent over the felt, a cue in her hand and a man at her backside instructing her on the best position in which to shoot. Occasionally, in her attempt to adjust herself, the girl wriggled her arse right into the crotch of the man helping her, which only inspired the man to bend against her more fully. It was as if one were a voyeur to a sex act with clothes on.

Quite invigorating.

Miss Bowles sidled up to Jeremy. "I don't know if it is more fun to play billiards than to watch billiards." She smiled. "What is your opinion on the matter, Lord Threxton?"

Jeremy chuckled. "I enjoy both, Miss Bowles. It does depend on the company, I suppose." He wrapped his lips around his cigar for a long suck. "Do you play?" He blew smoke in the direction of the billiards table.

"Would it be scandalous to say I do?"

"Oh, terribly so. And do you play the game well, Miss Bowles?"

"Very well, Lord Threxton. Quite masterfully, if I do say so myself."

She was indeed a master of the game at hand.

"And when will I have the opportunity to see you play?"

"Tonight, Lord Threxton, if you are up for it."

He was. "I think I need to hone my technique, Miss Bowles. Will you offer me some instruction in the library? There is a grand table there upon which we may practice."

She smiled. "I would enjoy that very much, my lord."

"Maude!" A brunette rushed to Miss Bowles's side, flushed and flustered. "I just heard a juicy bit of gossip." The girlfriend suddenly noticed Jeremy's presence. "I'm dreadfully sorry, my lord, where are my manners?"

Dare he be shocking? "Quite possibly on the carpet outside the billiards room door."

Miss Bowles laughed out loud. Her friend blushed and muffled her giggle behind her hand.

"I was just about to seek out the library," he said. "I'll leave you ladies to your conversation."

He bowed and flicked a glance at Miss Bowles as he licked his cigar. She smiled knowingly. He turned to leave.

"Maudie, remember that horrid little actress we met at the Summer Exhibition?" the brunette said quietly.

He took a couple of steps, a safe distance to listen.

Miss Bowles groaned. "The one who said she was sleeping with a famous painter and somehow that made her know absolutely everything about art?"

Jeremy pretended to look for something in his pocket.

The brunette giggled. "That's the one. Liesl or something—"

"Lisette," Miss Bowles said. "Lisette LaFleur."

He froze, then quickly recovered. No need to draw attention to himself. He took a long puff on his cigar.

"Yes! That's the one."

"Well," Miss Bowles murmured, "what about her?"

"She's pregnant."

The room and its occupants spun until the scene blurred into a morass of colors and sounds where the display on the billiards table devolved into something quite obscene and the enunciation of all the words containing *p*s and *g*s and ending in *t*s were hyperexaggerated.

"Lord Threxton? Are you quite all right?"

Miss Bowles's concern-laden voice yanked him out of his funk.

He smiled at her. "Miss Bowles," he began quietly, "I'm exceedingly sorry, but it appears I've had a bit too much to drink. I'll have to postpone our rendezvous. I think it best I crawl off to bed."

Miss Bowles smiled. "It would be best if you were at the peak of your game when we had our match, my lord. I wish you good night."

He bowed before his escape. He needed to sleep on the news, needed to convince himself that the child could be anyone's, except if Lisette was visibly pregnant now, then it would have been perhaps five months ago—

Bollocks.

Le Bocage, Île-de-France, October 1880

Charles sat cross-legged on the floor in the middle of the south parlor of the Brockhurst mansion. He extinguished his oil lamp. It was midnight, and the house was asleep—the perfect time to see what his mural looked like in the glow of the moonlight.

He always scrutinized his paintings at night and, if he could, in proximity to the original vista. He wanted to know if the landscape looked like mere paint on canvas, flat and unchanging. Or if it succumbed to the vagaries of night and day, as nature did. The mural in the south parlor seemed to integrate well with the view just beyond, except for the curlicues of the Rococo molding surrounding the windows.

"Charles?"

He looked up at Annalee's voice. She stood in the doorway dressed in her robe, her hair undone. The quintessence of sultry innocence.

He patted the space to his right. "Come sit on the floor, if you like, and look."

She closed the door, then took her place at his side, her legs tucked under her, leaning a little against him.

"What are you doing?" she asked softly.

"I'm looking." He smiled at her. "What do you see?"

She followed his gaze to the mural and seemed to genuinely study it. She laughed softly. "It looks like it's outside, like there's a window there"—she pointed to the painted wall—"or, rather, that the window continues endlessly."

Anxiety fled in a rush of relief. "That is what I hoped you would see."

"You're very good." She rested her head on his shoulder, the faint scent of lavender flaring his nostrils. "You know that, I suppose. All those prizes and commissions."

Her closeness stirred him, rousing his lust. "Thank you." He had been thinking of her of late, of what they had done last year and how it might continue. How it might progress.

She reached for him, and he slid his hand in hers, smoothing his thumb over the soft skin. Annalee's sigh fanned warmth across the pulse point of his neck. He turned to find her lips near his, her breath puffing in rhythm to his increasing heartbeat.

He leaned in and kissed her.

She tasted of desire and promises. He clung to her as he explored her depths. She let him lead her to the floor, unfolding her legs until she was beneath the weight of him. He rolled the bulge of his rock-hard cock against her belly.

She sighed. "Charles," she whispered. "Darling."

She wanted him. She wanted him but could not possibly understand what that meant, what pleasures he could give her.

What pleasures he was going to give her at that very moment.

He lifted her robe, her nightgown, exposing her to the cool night air, and bent over her nakedness. He kissed the hair of her motte, then slid his tongue through her innocent slit. She bucked up with a quiet gasp, pressing her sex into his mouth. Her moans filled his senses as he licked her tender flesh, holding back the enthusiasm that coursed through him, pushing his erection into the floor as if that would pacify his lust. He had so wanted to give her pleasure, and now she was his.

He took a breath, then sucked her clit into his mouth.

She grabbed his hair, pulling at the roots, drawing him into her, as her hips and back undulated. He followed the wave of her movements, determined to give her the ecstasy she never knew existed.

She bucked up with a choked cry, holding herself aloft as she shuddered.

Had he just been witness to her first orgasm? The thought astounded and humbled him.

He extended himself over her. She placed her hands on his cheeks and kissed him.

"Charles, darling, please, I'm ready."

Ready? *Good God.* Was he? His cock ached to be inside her.

"Annalee, my sweet, if we do this, we cannot go back."

Her eager gaze bore into him. "I understand, Charles." She reached down and slipped free one button of his trousers.

He sat back on his heels and tore off his waistcoat, his braces, unbuttoned his trousers and drawers, and grabbed his cock. Annalee stared, wide-eyed, first at his face, then at his erection. She touched him gingerly, then wrapped her warm hand around his shaft.

"Charles." Her eyes pleaded.

God, he could spend just from her touch. "Darling, I don't want to hurt you."

"I'll be fine. Please," she begged. "I want you."

He stretched over her as she opened her legs. He hovered at her entrance, reticence holding him for a moment before he pushed inside just an inch. She fluttered around him, the thrill excruciating. He plowed farther. She was slick from his earlier pleasuring, easing his slide into her depths.

She groaned, a sensual sound without a tinge of pain, without a hint of shock. A sound instead suffused with knowing satiety. A sound which should have encouraged him.

It did not.

He stopped, and she rocked her hips in an invitation to continue.

Only a woman who had experienced sexual rapture would do such a thing.

Damn.

Annalee was not a virgin. No. And she was practiced in the art of lovemaking.

He pressed forward, undaunted. Or, rather, his cock was undaunted. His brain was perceiving her in a new light.

Well, if she was no virgin, then she should at least have a few surprises during this their first time. He slammed into her with a harshness borne of jealousy and betrayal. She gulped air, possibly unused to such sexual coarseness. He hoped at least.

He did not hold back. He knew better than to stay inside. It would be prudent to pull out. But he did not want to. He needed to show her he owned her, that she would be his, despite any other who had previously delighted in her charms.

He came with a rumbling snarl, pumping his seed deep inside her.

When it was over, he crushed her, panting, wishing his body's release would extend to his mind and his heart.

"Annalee, we'll announce our engagement tomorrow."

"Yes, Charles."

He liked her; she would be a good companion. But it would take a long time before love would grow.

A very long time.

Jeremy dished out a generous helping of eggs at Lord Hammond's lavish breakfast buffet. A floral fragrance roused him to the woman suddenly at his side.

"Lord Threxton, I hope you slept well last night," Miss Bowles said in a tone far too coquettish for morning. "I slept quite soundly and undisturbed."

Jeremy smiled. It was a very good sign Miss Bowles's flirtation was continuing over breakfast.

"Thank you, Miss Bowles. I did indeed sleep very well," he lied.

"It's a marvelous day for a hunt. Will you be joining us today?"

"I think not. I'd like to take a walk over the hill." He angled over her. "Truth be told, I'm not much of a hunter. I'm here for the company."

Her lips stretched with an upward curl. "There's a lovely meadow over that hill. It's perfect for a bit of solitude and poetry."

Her seductive smile shot straight to his crotch. She was suggesting a future liaison, although granting him the opportunity to take the lead. That he was married was not a secret—and clearly not a problem. He just needed to be careful.

So he avoided Miss Bowles most of the day—she was hunting for a good part of it—until the after-dinner port and cigars were once again brought out and the evening's entertainments had begun.

By midnight, Jeremy ended up in a corner of the library, listening to a reading of ribald limericks from *The Pearl*, thoroughly enjoying himself.

His nostrils flared at the seductive lilac scent before he saw her.

"Miss Bowles." He nodded.

"Lord Threxton, I thought such frivolities beneath your intellect."

He chuckled softly. "Oh, no. Most definitely on par with my intellect."

Her shoulder brushed his upper arm, jostling his port glass. Tawny liquor ran over his fingers as his cock livened in his trousers.

A most ingenious contrivance.

"I apologize, my lord." She ran her fingers down his jacket, her gaze traveling even lower. "Shall I fetch your handkerchief?"

"In my inside breast pocket. Over my heart."

She smiled as she reached in. Did she feel the rapid thump of desire?

She unfurled the handkerchief and took his glass from his hand, wiping the stem and base. She handed him the linen as she swallowed the remaining liquor.

"It appears as if you need a refill," she said. "Shall we repair to the study? I hear that is where all the good spirits are kept."

Her eyes were dark with lust. He doubted very much they would be going to the study.

In the hallway, she urged him into the shadows of a wood-paneled corner. Her mouth was on his before he could offer a protest. She was soft and warm and so very willing.

"My lord, I recall I have a decanter of port in my room. Would you care to join me for a nightcap in more private circumstances?"

"I would very much like that."

Five minutes later, Jeremy was in Miss Bowles's bedroom, kissing her senseless as she stripped him of his jacket and waistcoat and slid off his braces.

He reached for the buttons at the back of her dress. She let him unfasten them, then urged his hands away.

"Let me reveal myself to you while you sit and watch, my lord."

The girl was not without experience of a man's desires, that was sure.

She divested herself of her gloves, dress, and hair ornament quickly with no fanfare. The petticoats came next. She stood before him in combination and corset, stockings and shoes.

"I fear you are overdressed, Lord Threxton. For every garment I remove from now on, I expect you to do the same."

Besides shoes, she wore four articles from what he could tell. He wore five.

She removed her corset. He removed his shirt.

Her expression remained impassive as she slipped off her shoes and he removed his. She ungartered a stocking, then the other. He did the same with his socks.

Slowly, she unbuttoned her combination underwear. He unbuttoned his trousers, revealing his drawers underneath. An eyebrow ticked upward, the only sign she comprehended her impending defeat.

She slid the undergarment down the curves of her glorious, youthful body. He pulled off his trousers. She stepped out of the combination and smiled as her gaze raked across his erection under his drawers.

She stood before him utterly nude, except for earrings and a diamond necklace that set off her buoyant breasts quite elegantly. She was simply gorgeous.

"Lord Threxton, it appears you have won."

Indeed, he had, in so many ways. She came forward and held out her hand in invitation. He clasped her and followed as she led him to the bed.

She sat on the edge of the mattress and wrapped her legs around his hips, pulling him to stand between her soft, milky thighs. One by one she unfastened the buttons of his drawers. His erection sprang free from the open placket. She bit her lower lip as she wrapped her hand around his cock.

He sucked air between his teeth as she slid her hand up and down, drawing the foreskin over the head. Too soon she let go. She scooted to the middle of the bed and peeled back the sheet. He jumped on the bed to join her.

Under the covers they continued the embrace they had started against the paneling in the hallway.

He feasted on her mouth, her neck, her luscious breasts, as he fingered her sticky and moist cunt. He wanted her and she was ready for him.

He maneuvered on top and opened her thighs for his invasion. His hardness sought her silken folds. He pushed inside and found heaven.

She moaned as she rocked her hips, trying to match his rhythm, then giggled when she could not keep tempo. She was no virgin, but neither was she experienced. Would she understand when he pulled out?

Pulling out… He'd have to. He couldn't risk another mistake.

Mistake? A *child* for God's sake.

His prick softened.

He fought against nature to regain his hardness. But sexual congress had become impossible, he shoving his flaccid cock against her warm, wet quim.

"Ouch!"

He was trying too hard.

"It's all right. I've heard this happens sometimes."

What could she possibly know of such things? She was all of twenty-five. Most likely every single one of her lovers had been potent virile stallions.

At the very least he could give her pleasure.

He slid to her side and bent over her breast, skimming his hand down her belly to her motte. He touched her clitoris, eliciting a jumpy flinch. Did she even know what an orgasm was? Had she only sought to satisfy the male?

He stroked and teased, pressed and provoked. Miss Bowles writhed on the bed, gasping and gulping, her eyes wide as if startled by the pleasure she was experiencing. She lifted her hips, her mouth agape, emitting guttural and clipped yelps from her throat. She pushed her hips into his finger, rolling and rocking as if being fucked, until she growled a wail of ecstasy. She dropped her hips to the mattress and stared at the ceiling as she panted.

"My God, Threxton. That was marvelous."

Marvelous indeed. And all he wanted to give her. Morning might be equally disastrous as far as his prick was concerned.

He got up and began to dress.

"Don't you want to stay the night?" Her tone was pleading, as if she had just discovered being fingered could be more pleasurable than being fucked.

"I shouldn't. For appearances' sake."

She understood. She had her own fragment of a reputation to keep intact.

Jeremy stumbled down the hall to his and Rosamund's bedroom.

She was sleeping, her sprawled position on the bed indicating she slept very soundly. His wife had no demons to fend off, no guilt of betrayal.

He climbed into bed beside her. Rosamund stirred with a quiet grumble.

"Jer? I thought you had a conquest tonight."

"I did," he said enfolding her in his arms, her back to him. "But I couldn't follow through."

"What's wrong, darling?"

Of course his wife would know that lack of performance meant something was weighing heavy on his mind.

"Someone was talking about children earlier." He kissed the crown of her head. "It put me in a mood. I couldn't help thinking of Alex and Isa."

Rosamund turned around to face him, then pushed him to arm's length. She studied him in the dark. "Darling, we have to accept they are at peace now."

Would that he could feel the same. He brushed a loose strand of hair behind her ear. "I know. And I had thought I had truly accepted it until—"

He couldn't tell her. He couldn't tell her about his betrayal. Not in bed.

"Sometimes I remember them and I am greatly affected," he said. "I cannot explain it."

Rosamund rolled over to spoon against him. "Hold me." She pressed her buttocks into his hips. "We still have each other."

Jeremy wrapped his arms around his wife. She was the best wife a man could hope for. She deserved so much better than what he could give her. What he had given her.

He was the worst villain in the world.

Charles announced his and Annalee's engagement the next day to Annalee's father.

"I can't say I'm surprised. I've noticed a deepening friendship between the two of you," said the slightly stunned but proud Brockhurst.

So it was official. Charles Westerman and Annalee Brockhurst were engaged to be married. The wedding would be the following year in June.

And once that became public knowledge, it was as if all propriety went out the window. Or perhaps it was because they were in France.

Annalee came to his bed at night. She admitted she did have to sneak around a bit, make sure the floorboards didn't squeak and such. But she made no effort to leave before the light of dawn. More than once, Hubert, the valet supplied to Charles, discovered the two in bed in the morning.

Of course, Hubert cared not a fig and went about his regular expected tasks.

During the day, Charles painted, Annalee studied French literature and acted as companion to her grandmother. Sometimes Annalee was given a respite. Those days she read newspapers and magazines out loud to Charles as he worked.

"The queen is enjoying her stay at Balmoral."

Charles snorted a laugh. "Of course she is. Scotland is beautiful."

Annalee smiled briefly before returning to the newspaper. "Hmm. There's some sort of crisis involving the Ottomans and a seaport called"—she hesitated—"Dulcigno." She remained quiet as she read. "Oh my, there may be a war. Did you know that?"

"I did not."

"I hope Mr. Gladstone can stop such a dreadful thing."

Annalee had become a bit more interested in politics since having met so many politicians at the Waterhouse post-Banquet gala. She seemed determined to keep abreast of society gossip and world events. It was a pleasant presage to what the future would hold for their lives as a married couple.

By mid-October, the mural was finished. At the private unveiling to the family, Brockhurst effused praise.

"Marvelous, Westerman. Simply marvelous." He draped an arm around his wife's shoulders. "Don't you agree, Chantal?"

"*Oui*. Yes, it is very splendid, *Monsieur* Westerman."

Brockhurst grinned ear to ear. "We'll have a fête, a ball to show it off."

The event became a celebration of autumn as well as a celebration of the new artwork. The mansion was exquisitely decorated, the guests even more so. Charles had never had to speak so much French in his entire life. He was certain he got most of it right.

As the evening wore on, eventually he became less important than the champagne and waltzing. He exited through the south parlor and escaped to the fields beyond the glass doors.

The moon lighted his way, and the shadows kept him obscured. He found a patch far enough from the house to not be bothered and lay down to look at the stars.

The glittering dark was a landscape he had yet to explore. It was a brilliant idea. He chuckled at his stupid joke, then began to reconsider.

A woman's laugh distracted him.

It sounded like Annalee.

"*O...vous me flattez trop.*"

You flatter me. It *was* Annalee.

A deep baritone laugh indicated she was not alone.

"*Mon chérie*," the man cooed.

As the pair traveled farther away amongst the grasses and moonlight, their words became indistinct.

Annalee and a man? What man? She had no male relations, really. Two cousins who were mere boys, some uncles who, last he saw, were engrossed in cards. Who besides Charles—her fiancé—would be an appropriate man for Annalee to go running off into the fields with in the middle of the night?

Well, he was going to find out.

Charles stood, remaining quiet for a moment, listening for Annalee and her friend.

A squeal indicated her direction.

He walked slowly, not wanting to disturb them. What if she had a legitimate excuse? A priest, a solicitor, a doctor, someone who might need to meet with her in private for her grandmother's sake?

A chill crept up the back of his neck heightened by October's cool air. What if she were with the man who had deflowered her?

He stepped lightly, always listening. Finally, they were right in front of him, his view slightly obscured by tall grasses. But only slightly. He had enough of a view to know the man was definitely not a priest.

The couple lay on the ground on a blanket, Annalee's stocking-clad legs wrapped around the bare buttocks of the man stretched on top of her, moving his hips—

Fucking her.

His peasant attire, shaggy dark hair, and robust bulky form gave him away as Anton, the Brockhurst gardener.

Charles watched, frozen in place, disbelief mingling with betrayal icing his veins. Anton grunted, sputtering expletives in French, Annalee moaning encouragements. The act was not new to either of them. They had each done it before. And with each other.

Anton picked up his pace. Then, with one final thrust, he growled and held himself still on straightened arms.

The bastard didn't even bother to pull out. The damn gardener came inside his Annalee, *his* fiancée.

Charles wouldn't cause a scene. It was so unlike him to do so. But this was unlike anything he had to deal with.

"You bloody fucking whore."

Annalee scrambled out from under her lover. "Charles?"

"He didn't even bother to pull out."

"Darling! Please! I had to."

Had to? He would not even grace that with a request for an explanation.

He stormed off, ignoring her protests, not wanting to wait for her to right her underwear and party dress. What had been the scandal involving the other beau? She had implied the man had been at fault in the affair. But what if it had been Annalee herself who had been the scandalous one? She had been no virgin when Charles fucked her. How many years ago had she lost her innocence?

He wouldn't be able to sleep now. No. Instead he would pack and plan. He would go to Paris. He would drink absinthe with the Impressionists and the modernists. Visit the Louvre and ruminate over his place in history. Discuss betrayal with poets and possibilities with philosophers.

He would forget he ever met a woman named Annalee Brockhurst.

And maybe start fantasizing once again about a woman named Rosamund Chambers.

CHAPTER TEN

London, January 1881

Jeremy distractedly swirled his crystal snifter of brandy as the dull light of winter passed through the windows of his art studio. He stared at the unfinished portrait before him. The subject was the wife of a minor politician, a young woman who flirted every time she visited the art studio. She had decided to dress as a Roman poetess and had chosen a diaphanous stola, a garment that barely concealed the dark areolae atop her bouncy breasts, and with the cold of winter, revealed her puckered nipples. She flaunted her figure, even asking Jeremy to help secure the golden girdle under her bosom.

He should have fucked her by now. She clearly wanted him to fuck her. But he hadn't. He had barely flirted, except to let her know her pose was "perfectly provocative" and to continue holding it. He had lost all taste for such games.

He shifted his gaze to his brandy, to the golden liquor clinging to the crystal as it dribbled down the sides of the bowl. He gulped the contents of the snifter, the alcohol burning a path down his throat.

The clock struck noon. He grimaced in defeat.

Rosamund had recently chastised him about his newly acquired habit of drinking too often and too much.

The incident had been during their annual Twelfth Night party, when he had to play host. "Put that down," she had said as he raised his glass to his lips when no one was toasting.

He had looked at her in bafflement. She had returned a stern gaze.

"Jeremy, you just finished a glass. I do not know what has been troubling you of late, but it needs to end. You cannot continue drinking to the point of sleep or embarrassment every night."

So, instead, he started to spread the drinking out to all hours of the day. Rosamund's pursed lips and chilly glares during evening meals showed she was no fool.

She never asked why, though. But one day he would have to tell her.

He would have to tell her about the illegitimate child, the result of a passing fancy with a woman he could never love.

He doubted he could ever love the damned bastard either. It would never be a substitute for the two children he still adored with all his heart.

Jeremy stared at the empty glass, then placed it on his painter's table next to the palette muddied with ill-considered attempts at color blending. He dared to look up at the portrait with dabs and blobs done with shaking hands.

He had to get the hell out of there. Had to get away from the house that taunted him with its absence of children's laughter. And his failure as an artist.

He had to stop drinking alone. He needed some company.

He'd go to his club.

The club room of the London Museion was never very quiet. Of course, a man *could* read his newspaper, but the atmosphere favored socializing and camaraderie. Painters and sculptors discussed new and modern artistic techniques, or passed along work to those who needed it. Oddly, professional jealousy was rarely a concern. It was far more beneficial to support each other in the long run.

The Museion was where Jeremy had first met Charles Westerman, at the time only a hardworking painter and not yet the famed artist. So he should not have been so surprised to see the very man upon his arrival.

"Westerman! I thought you in France."

Westerman rose from the leather club chair to shake his hand. "I was. Paris, actually. Wonderful city. So much art."

"Ah, the perfect venue for newly wedded bliss." Jeremy motioned toward the liquor cabinet. "And how is your bride?" he asked as they strolled across the room.

"Headed into spinsterhood on her father's country estate, I hope." There was a bitter edge to his voice.

Jeremy started. "I take it there was no marriage."

"I am once again a free man."

Jeremy poured two glasses of cognac, and handed one to his friend.

"To Rosamund, then." Jeremy raised his glass.

Westerman flushed briefly before he took a sip.

Jeremy downed his drink and poured another glass.

"Threxton?" Westerman eyed him with astonishment. "Is something wrong between you and your wife?"

Jeremy took Westerman's arm and led him to the bank of windows. He sat in the window seat, inviting Westerman to sit across from him on the cushions.

Jeremy leaned against the polished wood paneling lining the cozy space and stared out the window at London. "I am the most vile of villains."

"How so?" Westerman intoned with incredulity. "What could you possibly have done?"

"I got a woman with child."

Westerman sucked air through his teeth. "Ah. Is she blackmailing you?"

"I've not heard a word from her since last summer." Jeremy gazed at the golden liquor in his etched glass.

"Then how do you know?"

"Rumor. Gossip."

"Bollocks." Westerman swore under his breath. "Then she must be worth gossiping about. Who is she? Perhaps I can help."

"Lisette LaFleur," Jeremy said as quietly as he could.

"The actress?" Westerman hissed.

"The very same."

Westerman emitted a scoffing grunt. "Why, that's impossible!"

"I'm afraid it is quite possible."

"No." Westerman grabbed his shoulder and caught his eye. "Listen to me very carefully, my lord. I was just in Paris, living among artists. I knew all the Bohemian expatriates. Every single one of them. I saw Lisette and her baby. Trust me, the child is not yours."

"How on earth can you possibly know?"

"Because the child is mulatto."

All blood drained from Jeremy's head. He stared at Westerman through dizzy eyes. "Mulatto?"

"Yes. Which means it's not your child, do you understand? Absolutely not your child." Westerman laid a hand on Jeremy's knee. "And despite it being Paris and excessively Bohemian, everyone is talking about it. Really, it is quite the scandal."

Of course. "Malachi."

"Pardon?"

"Malachi. Lisette's stage manager. She left London with him. I should have known they were lovers."

"I presume the gentleman in question is black?"

"African. From Senegal." Relief spread over Jeremy like honey dripping from a spoon, slowly but assuredly. He leaned his head against the paneling and puffed out an exhalation laden with all the pain of the last four months.

Westerman gulped his liquor.

Jeremy looked at his friend. New lines had formed on his face since last he'd seen him. He was troubled as well. "I've been too mired in my own hell to notice yours. Tell me about Miss Brockhurst."

"The gardener," he muttered.

"And what did the gardener do, exactly?"

"Annalee."

"Ah."

Westerman puffed out an equally long exhalation. "I simply left. I sent a note to her father saying I had evidence of her inconstant heart, that I could not undertake a marriage based on lies and deceit." He swallowed another gulp of cognac. "Threxton, I have something very horrible to tell you."

"Christ, she's not pregnant too?"

Westerman flashed a look of shock, then shook his head. "No. Nothing like that. However, I have been keeping my own deceitful lie." He looked Jeremy in the eye. "About your wife."

"My wife?" Jeremy contained a smile. "What about my wife?"

Charles grew hot under his collar. Threxton, however, seemed cool and collected.

Charles swallowed more cognac in an effort to fortify himself.

"She and I…I…" He'd have to say it. Simply had to say it. "We had an affair." Charles drew in a deep breath. "I took advantage of her in the library at Lord Creslow's exhibition. I swear I had no idea who she was, which is despicable in and of itself. But had I known it was your wife, I would have never done such a thing. *I* am the most vile villain to have betrayed a friend."

Threxton chuckled quietly. "I know about Creswell's library. And about the incident in my studio—"

Charles chilled.

Threxton offered a wry smile. "She told me."

Charles's mouth dropped open. He searched Threxton's expression for a hint of *something*—anger, hatred, humor. But his friend sat next to him with just a hint of a smile.

"She told you?"

"Ah. I see there is something you do not know about Rosamund and myself."

That the husband did not seem to give a damn was beyond comprehension. "You don't need to be magnanimous, Threxton, because of your own indiscretion."

"Believe me, I am not being magnanimous. I've seen the two of you together. The mutual desire is palpable." Threxton patted him on the back. "And, it seems, you're a free man now, Charles."

Threxton's reaction was simply incredible. "But Rosamund is not a free woman."

"No, she is not." Jeremy grinned briefly. "Because she is tormented by thoughts of you."

"My lord, this is not amusing."

Threxton placed a hand on Charles's shoulder. "I apologize. I'm being purposely vague."

The viscount pressed farther into the box seat, toward the window. A nod indicated Charles should move deeper into the recess as well. Threxton took a swallow of cognac.

"Charles—I may call you by your Christian name, may I not?"

Was he about to reveal something so intimate? "Please. I have no objections."

Threxton smiled. "Well, Charles, I must ask you to abandon all preconceived notions of love, of marriage, and of erotic fulfillment."

So they were traveling down that path. "All right."

"You and I have only known each other for a couple of years. You know that I'm married, that I am an artist, and I have the title 'Viscount'. Beyond that, you do not know much else."

"You're a bloody brilliant portraitist. I know that, as well."

Threxton smiled as a blush colored his cheeks above his beard. "Thank you. But about my personal life, you know almost nothing, except what I just revealed about Lisette."

"Granted. Go on."

"I've been married to Rosamund for almost twenty years. It seems such a long time, and yet, as our life together changed suddenly a few years ago, it seems only as long as that." Threxton drew in a breath. "After we had been married a few years, Rosamund gave birth to our son, Alexander."

Charles tried his best to not convey his shock at the revelation.

"He was a beautiful boy. Gentle and studious, and yet so rambunctious when he was at play. He had Rosie's eyes, I remember. When Alexander was eight, we gave him a little sister. Isabelle. She, too, was beautiful. Like her mother. We were the happiest of families for two years."

Threxton's lashes dampened. "I received an invitation to paint a series of portraits for an industrialist in York. Rosamund convinced me to take the commission, not for the money, of course, but the prestige and notoriety. At the time painting was merely a frivolous endeavor. I never contemplated pursuing it seriously. But word of mouth brought me to the attention of this patron. I was expected to stay in York for several weeks. I was there for only a fortnight when disaster struck."

A pang spiked Charles's gut. *The children.* In the two years he'd known Threxton, the viscount had never mentioned children until now. Something terrible had happened.

"Alexander became ill. Rosamund wrote it was an illness typical of boys. But a few days later a new letter begged me to come home. I left as soon as I could, which was not soon enough. I arrived at my house in London and was turned away at the front door by a nurse. I could not even see my own wife."

The viscount stared out the window at the bleak London winter. "Alexander was seriously ill. Scarlet fever, they said. Rosamund and I corresponded hourly by messenger. Alex was receiving the best treatment, she assured me.

"And then the dreaded letter came, the one not from my wife, but from a nurse. Rosamund herself was too ill to write. Isabelle was also bedridden." He thinned his lips. "I was beside myself, I had to see my family. The worst that could happen was they would die. What the hell would I have to live for then? I resolved to die with them.

"I went home and pushed my way through, up the stairs to the bedrooms. It was worse than I imagined. Alex was at death's door."

Threxton sucked in a shuddering breath. "I held my son to my breast. He died in my arms. I had no one with whom to grieve. Rosamund was feverish and bedridden.

"I went to her. She cradled little Isa in her arms. My God, it is a horror to see a child barely out of infancy struggling to live." A tear slithered down Threxton's cheek. "Isa died later that night in her mother's arms after Rosamund had fallen asleep."

Threxton cleared his throat. "I was lost. Was she next? My wife? Whose company I had thrived on for over a decade, who was the center of my existence?

"I lay down next to her, not wanting to live if she died, willing the fever to take me next. The fever broke the next day. She would live. My Rosie would live." The viscount smoothed the hair around his mouth.

"When she was well enough to sit up in bed the news was given to her. Not only had we lost our two children, we would never have children again. She was left barren."

Threxton reached into his inside breast pocket and pulled out two cigars. "Each of us remained in our own separate hell for many months thereafter. I finished the commission, and Rosamund set her mind to regaining her health and strength." He offered a cigar to Charles and waved to Godwin, the club manservant, for a light.

Godwin obliged readily, maneuvering a pair of standing ashtrays next to the window seat before he bowed and sauntered off.

Threxton sucked on his cigar. "When I returned from my commission, Rosie sat me down for a conversation most married couples do not have."

Smoke escaped his nostrils as he exhaled. "She had almost died, and because of that she wanted to live. And to live she wanted to experience pleasure and pain and all life had to give her. Including experiencing other men."

A cold sweat crept up Charles's spine.

Threxton chortled darkly. "It is natural for a man to want more than one woman, but woman is built to want only one man. Yet, death changes the lives of those left behind. And meeting Death face to face only to have him turn you back changes everything."

Threxton sucked in a draught of smoke. "What is life but hopes and wishes and dreams and desires? An individual will seek out those dreams and desires and sometimes discover they cannot be met by one person. That person can best support the other by letting them go. As long as they return."

The viscount stared at the glowing ash at the end of his cigar. "We decided upon an arrangement. We would each of us choose our own paths, including the paths of our desires. We had a few rules: I would father no children, and we would remain committed to each other. We would neither separate nor divorce. Most of all, we would have no regrets, no what-ifs." Threxton took another draw, expelling the smoke slowly. "On her path, Rosamund developed a sensual confidence she never had before."

Charles had been seduced by that sensual confidence.

Threxton met his gaze, quirking his right eyebrow. "She wants you, Charles. I know you've already had each other. But it wasn't enough. She *craves* you. And—" He leaned in. "I want you two to be together."

Despite Jeremy's efforts, Charles would not meet his gaze. Instead he stiffened against the wood paneling on the opposite side of the window seat, ignoring both his drink and his smoke.

"This is preposterous, Threxton."

Jeremy nodded. "It sounds odd, does it not? Man and wife willingly and knowingly sharing the beds of others. As a man, I'm allowed that freedom, expected to avail myself of such opportunities with little or no consequences." He sighed. "Social consequences anyway. Society just expects it of our class. We have our mistresses, propriety be damned. But women like Rosamund, virtuous to a fault yet lusty by nature, they are not allowed to follow their own desires. If they do, society shuns them, gossips about them, chews them up, and spits them out. They have to disappear for a while, let it all die down before they make a comeback. There is no freedom in that." Jeremy swirled his cognac, staring at the rivulets as they trickled down the crystal. "But what if a husband and a wife agreed upon a mutual arrangement?" He once again sought and finally found Charles's gaze. "Surely this must go on more than we think? As long as there is mutual support, there is no need for the woman to hide." He took a draw on his cigar.

"Unbelievable," Charles breathed. "Is this some sort of trick? A game, perhaps? A contest to see who can acquire the most lovers?"

"Oh, I hadn't thought that would be your reaction." Jeremy guffawed as he set his snifter on the window frame. "I would have won such a contest long ago." He blew out gray smoke deliberately before balancing his cigar on the ashtray. "No, it is not a game, and, if it were, after the scare with Miss LaFleur I am no longer playing. I need to take a step back. But that does not mean I cannot meddle in Rosamund's affairs when I see her intended needs some motivation."

"Her intended?" Charles's eyes widened. "Meaning me?"

Jeremy leaned in, his hands flat on the cushion between them. "Yes, Charles, you."

Charles heaved a sigh. "I'm stunned, dumbfounded." He shook his head. "My God, this is…this is…" His brow crinkled. "What the devil should I do? Send a note to have her join me at a house of ill repute?"

Jeremy chuckled. "Well, there is only one she would meet you at anyway, and I'll leave that up to her to inform you about it or not. You might want to start by inviting her to an event—a poetry reading or an art exhibit. Then go for a coffee afterward. Send her flowers the next morning." Jeremy grinned. "You know how to court a woman, don't you?"

"Court a…*court* her?"

"I would say you could just continue fucking her as you have been, but I think Rosamund wants something more than that from you."

"To what end? She's already married."

"You've never had an affair, I take it?"

Charles gaped. "I've never been married, Threxton."

Jeremy laid a hand on his shoulder. "And my wife has never had an infatuation like she has with you. She's head over heels."

"Damn and blast," Charles muttered. "I'll admit I'm quite fond of her myself. Too fond."

Jeremy laughed and slapped Charles on the back. "Good." He sat back against the paneling and resumed sucking on his cigar. "Now, there is a matter of some delicacy that I would like to discuss."

Charles shook his head. "Besides fucking your wife?"

"Ah, yes, it is how she would like you to fuck her."

"*What*?" Charles blanched. The crinkle on his brow deepened.

"Come by the house tonight. Nine o'clock. No need for evening dress. Wear something comfortable. A smoking jacket if you have one."

"A smoking jacket?" Charles shook his head. "Of all things." He sighed. "All right. I'll wear a blasted smoking jacket. What can I expect?"

"I have another story to tell you. And it comes with a…sort of demonstration."

CHAPTER ELEVEN

What in hell compelled Charles to arrive at nine o'clock sharp at the Threxton residence, he did not know. No, that was wrong. Rosamund compelled him, or thoughts of her. Fantasies, more like it. That she was in love with him was a dream beyond his wildest dreams. But that man and wife would willingly seek out others was an unbelievable notion. There had to be a catch.

He inhaled his trepidation, letting it out slowly to calm his nerves before he rang the doorbell. Threxton himself answered the door and ushered Charles into the foyer.

"I've given the staff the night off."

Which possibly meant Jeremy did not want the staff to witness the events of the evening.

Good God, what had he got himself into?

Jeremy took Charles's overcoat and hat and draped them casually on a gilded side chair set against the marble dado.

"Ah, good. You've worn your smoking jacket. And such a fine one it is."

"Thank you, my lord," Charles said with a grin. "It's Turkish." It was indeed fine, of silk velvet with a touch of shearling around the collar. His very favorite article of clothing.

They mounted the central staircase to the second floor, then walked down the hall. Along the way Jeremy pointed to *objets d'art*, briefly noting their origin or aesthetic value. As if that were the very purpose of Charles's visit.

They came upon another, less grand staircase and took it to another, nondescript hallway. Perhaps the servants' wing. They stopped before an ordinary door painted a brownish green.

Jeremy took a key out of his jacket pocket and unlocked the door. He gestured a polite invitation for Charles to enter.

The room was small but decorated like a grand pasha's palace. Curtains lined one wall above a banquette padded with richly brocaded cushions. Tasseled pillows of velvet and embroidery were scattered about. A deeply hued Oriental rug graced the floor. In the center was an ornately carved table, upon which were a decanter and two glasses, plus an intricately carved cigar box and two etched brass ash pans.

Jeremy motioned to a spot along the curtained wall. "Please, my friend. Make yourself comfortable."

Charles sat and stretched his legs. Jeremy poured two unequal glasses of liquor and offered the one with more to Charles.

"Since your news this afternoon, I have returned to my usual levels of drink."

Jeremy pulled two cigars from the box and offered one to Charles.

For a moment they sat and smoked in silence, the haze adding a mysterious allure to the exotic room.

Jeremy broke the peace. "Earlier today I alluded to my wife's newfound sensual confidence after our agreement to explore our individual desires. Rosamund's path led her to unusual lascivious pursuits."

"Good God, man, is this really appropriate?"

He chuckled. "Don't worry, Charles. I will not inquire about your own predilections in the bedroom. But you should know of Rosamund's if you are to pursue something further."

The idea of a woman's husband divulging the details of her sex life should have been disgusting. Instead it was highly intriguing. If anyone would know how to pleasure a woman, it would be her husband.

Jeremy sucked on his cigar as if in thought, blowing the smoke out slowly. "Rosamund visited clubs of a certain nature, exploring her prurient needs with freedom and abandon. In these venues, she discovered a particular letch she did not know she had."

Charles set his cigar on the ashtray and grabbed his cognac. "A letch, you say?" He took a deep swallow of liquor.

Jeremy leaned forward and drew back the curtains along the wall of the banquette, revealing a metal grille intricately cut with arabesques. "Yes, a letch. A sexual practice that is considered, by and large, unusual. I participate in this letch willingly because Rosamund is my dear wife, but not wholeheartedly as it is not my own. It is time to show you." Jeremy reached behind and tugged a servant's bell-pull. "Look below, beyond the grille."

Charles looked through the arabesques carved in the metal, his vantage like a balcony overlooking a small, sparsely furnished room. Various implements resembling curious sporting equipment—a table tennis paddle, a cricket bat—hung along one wall. Against the far wall was four-poster bed—nothing particularly ornate or overly large, but having a suggestive presence.

The door to the room opened, and Rosamund walked in.

Charles's breath quickened at the sight. She was wearing only undergarments, her hair hanging in waves down her back. She glanced back at the door.

The door opened again, and a man stepped through. A tall man, young, lean, blond—

Charles flushed. The resemblance was uncanny. The young man was the very image of himself at about age twenty-five.

"His name is Adam," Jeremy said quietly.

Rosamund flung her arms around Adam's neck. He took her in a deep kiss.

Charles's cock livened at the sight. He should feel jealousy. He did not. Witnessing the scene was like watching a dream. A dream involving himself and Rosamund.

Adam led her to the bed. He brushed her hair off her shoulders, caressed down her arms—gestures imbued with feeling and sentiment, as if he cherished her.

Because Rosamund should be cherished.

Adam gently urged her to bend over the mattress. She did so. He took her left hand and stroked it, then kissed it.

And then he tied it to one of the bedposts.

The sight sent a chill along his spine. Rosamund did not protest; she did not flinch. She wanted to be tied. She allowed Adam the same liberty with her right hand.

Charles squirmed, attempting to alleviate his rock-hard erection. Rosamund was in the very same position as the night of the Creslow exhibition when he'd taken her in the library. Was Adam about to do the same? His heart hammered in anticipation.

Adam pulled up her chemise, tucking a bit of the hem under her corset. He reached around and untied her drawers. The garment slid down her legs to lie limply at her feet.

Charles swallowed the saliva pooling in his mouth at the sight of her beautiful buttocks, the flesh milky white and perfectly rounded.

Adam smoothed his hand over the gorgeous mounds. Charles gaped at every stroke, wanting desperately to be that young man at that moment. To be in possession of Rosamund's charms.

He would bend down on one knee and kiss her, lick her, taste the plump pale skin as he pulled his cock free and stroked in anticipation of entering her. He would finger her sex, surely finding her wet with desire, hearing her voice plead with him to fuck her—

Smack!

Charles flinched at the sound of skin against skin waking him from his fantasy. Adam was not kissing his lady's rump, nor was he fucking her. He had just done the most extraordinary thing.

Adam had spanked Rosamund. Hard.

Rosamund had not cried out. Instead she had thrust out her now rosy bum—in invitation?

Adam caressed where he had hit her. He bent over and murmured into her ear. She nodded.

The young man went to the wall and pulled down the table tennis paddle. He twirled it in his fingers, then tossed it from hand to hand, weighing it, finally settling on his right hand.

Rosamund's butt cheeks clenched.

Good God, he wasn't about to—

Whack!

The sound of wood hitting flesh was jarring, disconcerting, grievous, and yet, somehow amidst the jumble of emotions, arousing.

Rosamund held still as a dark pink circle formed on her right buttock. Adam pressed his hand against the spot and rubbed tiny circles.

"Yes."

Rosamund's breathy affirmation was barely audible.

Adam played with the paddle once again, pacing behind Rosamund as he did so. Was he going to—

Slap!

Charles's cock ached inside his trousers. Were he alone, he would be frigging himself at the erotic sight.

Adam soothed his captive's bottom, this time his fingers straying to the cleft, then farther to the apex of her thighs, delving in.

She would be wet, Charles was sure of it. She would be wondrously wet.

God, his cock needed release. Preferably inside the wicked Rosamund.

But Adam stepped back, raising his paddle once again. It was unimaginable. How could she possibly stand any more?

Thwack!

It was between the cheeks, too near her cunt. She must be in horrible pain. He would save her.

Rosamund wriggled her bottom as her moan drifted through the brass grille. Adam approached her again, stroking her naked arse.

Charles could stand it no longer. He stood, ignoring the wanton bulge in his trousers. He paced along the banquette.

"How long does this performance last?" he asked in a low growl.

Jeremy sniggered. "It's no performance. It's what my wife desires." His gaze briefly flitted to Charles's crotch.

Charles flushed and turned away. In the room below, Rosamund was being pleasured by the blond and handsome Adam, his fingers between her legs and his lips near her ear, whispering as she huffed and moaned.

Charles plopped back down on the banquette and closed his eyes, letting the erotic sounds imbue him. He gripped the seat cushion as Rosamund's wails of pleasure filled the conjoined spaces.

Then silence.

It was finished. He glanced through the grille. Rosamund and Adam exchanged intimate pleasantries, then exited through the same door they had entered.

Charles let out the breath strangling him for want of release. What in heaven's name had he just witnessed? And why was he so aroused?

He glared at Jeremy. "Do you mean to watch me fuck your wife?"

Jeremy recoiled with a wince. "Good God, no. Adam is paid for such displays." He eyed Charles. "I would only watch you if you demanded it. If that were *your* letch."

Charles looked away. It was all too much to take in.

"Charles, trust me. She wants you. And I want you to have her." Jeremy leaned forward and laid a hand on his knee. "And she wants you in the way you just witnessed."

The world had just turned upside down.

One look at Jeremy revealed the viscount was absolutely serious.

Panic gripped Charles's gut. He had to get out of there, away from the madness of his friends.

Away from the madness of his own desires.

Charles stumbled down the several flights of stairs, grabbed his coat from the foyer, and ran outside, slowing to a walk when he reached the pavement. He continued in a direction he thought might be toward home.

The rumble of a cab jostled him to his senses, and he hailed the driver. He needed to be hidden away from the world, not exposed on the street for all to see.

Besides, it was too bloody far to walk.

* * * * *

"Charles left in a hurry, Rosie darling. I think you shocked him."

Rosamund stopped brushing her hair and placed the silver-backed brush on her dressing table. She looked through the mirror to the view behind her. Jeremy sprawled casually on the bedroom divan, his untied robe revealing the dark mat of hair on his chest and abdomen trailing to the shadow at his groin. His well-groomed beard only hinted at the surfeit of masculinity covering his body. The attributes of a mature man were so much more riveting than those of youth. Adam was a wonderful partner, but in twenty years' time, he would be so much more attractive.

Like Charles Westerman.

"You mean *you* shocked him, darling."

Jeremy chuckled. "When you see him next, be gentle."

"Will I ever see him again? After what you did?"

Jeremy hadn't told her Charles had been invited to witness her chastisement. The spectacle was meant for Jeremy's eyes only. She had been mortified to discover Charles had watched the display, had railed at Jeremy through blinding tears. Jeremy had settled her on the divan and told her—on bended knee no less—about his initial reticence at inviting Charles without her permission; but his strong belief that Charles would find the scene enticing had driven him to reveal this secret of their marriage. Jeremy had acted in her best interest, he assured her, to garner the fulfillment she needed.

He knew precisely what that fulfillment was. She needed Charles Westerman to participate in her letch. Willingly. She had often wondered how that might happen, had resigned herself to accept it might not. Yet now the plot had been set in motion.

Jeremy was absolutely the best husband.

"It may take him some time to comprehend fully what it is you need." Jeremy rose and went to the dressing table, not bothering to tie his robe. "Perhaps he'll do some experimenting of his own." He gave a gentle squeeze of her shoulders and kissed the top of her head. "I remember when you first asked me to spank you. I was horrified. It was unconscionable to hit a woman." He took the hairbrush from her, running a finger around the edge of the silver. "Now I understand." He held out his hand. "Come."

She followed him to their bed. Along the way, he picked up one of her stockings from beneath the slipper chair.

"On the bed," he growled. "On your hands and knees."

His forceful command shot through her like a bolt of lightning in an electric storm. She did as directed, excitement roiling within.

Jeremy wrapped the stocking around her eyes. "Think of him." He tied it tightly, the knot pressing into the back of her head.

He tossed up her robe and nightgown, bunching the fabric around her waist, then rubbed her bare bottom.

"Exquisite, Lady Threxton."

It was the very voice of Charles Westerman. His low rumbling timbre, his middle-class accent.

"Such a glorious bottom. So pale. Like a marble bum on a statue in a museum. Shall I put you on display?"

She flushed at the notion. She loved being watched. It was shameful.

"Ah, my lady. A blush colors your cheeks at the suggestion." He leaned into her, his breath hot on her neck. "I should like to see such a blush on your bottom."

The shudder of pre-climax ripped through her.

He snickered and smoothed his hand over her bottom once again. "You want that, don't you?"

The shock of the cool silver against her bottom tingled between her legs.

"Only wicked girls need such punishment. Have you been wicked? Do you harbor lustful thoughts?"

The swoosh of the hairbrush in the air thrilled her. She gasped in anticipation and braced herself.

Nothing.

He snorted. He cupped her bottom with a warm hand. "You were expecting something?" He took his hand away. "Something like this?"

The force of the impact impelled her forward. She yelped as she fell onto the pillows.

The sting radiated from the sore spot on her bottom through her sex, down her thighs. By feel, she righted herself back onto her hands and knees, spreading her legs just a little bit wider.

"Such a lovely shade of pink. Like a maiden's cheeks. Except only one is colored so. What about the other?"

She closed her eyes under the silk stocking and braced herself.

The blow bit, then burned deliciously. She moaned her approval as her sex clenched.

The brush fell to the carpet with a thud. The mattress sagged as he climbed on. He grabbed her by the hips, rubbing his thumbs on her still burning cheeks.

"Beautiful," he breathed.

His cock prodded between her legs. She angled her hips.

"Fuck me. Fuck me, Charles."

"So wanton." He positioned himself at her entrance. "So wet."

He slammed inside, relief washing over her as she gripped his cock within. Like his swats, he was merciless, driving into her at a frenzied pace, grunting like a rutting animal, digging his nails into her sides.

He pushed her forward, farther onto the bed and wrapped an arm around her waist, taking control, using her for his own satisfaction.

His dominance wrenched orgasm after orgasm from her body until she was utterly spent, limp in his arm.

He followed a moment later, holding his hips against hers as he spewed his seed deep inside.

He pulled free and fell to the mattress, grabbing her, enveloping her in his arms, untying the stocking and tossing it aside.

"Darling," he said as he kissed her face, her hair, his beard tickling her flushed cheeks. "Oh my darling Rosamund. Give it time. Give *him* time."

Tears welled in her eyes. "Oh, Jer." Would it ever be this good with another man? She so wanted it to be.

He held her face in his hands. "Darling, I only want what is best for you. He will be so good for you. Trust me."

She smiled. "Haven't I always?"

* * * * *

Charles stumbled into his entryway, emotional exhaustion threatening to buckle his knees.

Tyler's firm grip on his arm kept him upright. "Mr. Westerman, may I be of service?"

"No." Charles shook his head. "I'll be fine, Tyler."

He needed to be alone. Alone with his thoughts of Rosamund.

And her glorious backside.

The valet scowled fleetingly before slinking away.

Once in the refuge of his bedroom, Charles leaned against the closed door and stared at the bed. Had it always been that large? Big enough for two? The white sheets practically glowed, as if an empty canvas upon which a man and a woman could explore the limits of their sensual desires—

He balled his fists and hit the air. Desiring the wife of a colleague was reprehensible, disgraceful. Then to have that colleague egg him on… It was obscene. Terrifically wicked.

And yet, deep down inside it was wondrously exciting.

A surge of energy revived him.

Could he have her? Could there exist the possibility of a world where Rosamund and he could lie in each other's arms undisturbed? Where furtive encounters were just one of the many ways they would enjoy being together?

Where she would submit to his desires willingly?

In Creslow's library he had found the sight of her exposed backside unduly erotic. Of course, like any man, he found the shape of women's bodies—cinched waists flaring out at the hips—alluring. Yet the fashions of the day emphasized the bottom, with a touch of padding, perhaps a bow, or frills and flounces gathered and draped at the backside. Twenty years ago, women's skirts had been excessively wide, bell-shaped. Back then he had never been aroused by what a woman wore. But upon self-examination, he had to admit he much admired the bustle. Sadly that exuberant fashion accessory had been subdued somewhat in recent years. He yearned to see a bustle on Rosamund, the mound obscuring but utterly accentuating that which lay beneath: Two fleshy pale orbs in need of chastisement.

Good God. He'd never had such thoughts before. Why was he suddenly having them now?

He doused the light, locked the door, and drew the curtains. He tore off his clothes in the dark, unable to look at his body already aroused by corrupt thoughts. Blood rushed from his brain to his overeager cock, dizzying him. He climbed into bed, under the covers, stretching the blankets over his head to block out the world, curling into a fetal position, willing sleep to descend, to take him away from his bizarre reality.

But the images in his brain would not stop. The memory of her naked buttocks hectored him. The pressure in his cock, the heaviness in his balls became unbearable. He'd frig himself surreptitiously under the sheets. No one would know, no one need know. Then it would all be over. Tomorrow he would forget Rosamund, forget what Jeremy had said.

He grabbed his cock. He pumped furiously, uncontrollably, trying desperately to concentrate on the movement of his fist and not on the images flashing in his brain of Rosamund being spanked and controlled by a twin of his younger self. Trying futilely to concentrate on his own guttural growls and not relive her sensual moan of release.

He came on the sheets, pumping what seemed like endless quantities of semen from his spent body.

With a shuddering exhalation, he rolled onto his back, the bed covers hiding his shame-filled countenance and his sinful desires.

He couldn't face Rosamund, just couldn't. Jeremy neither. They knew him too well, understood his desires when he barely understood them himself. He'd avoid the club, avoid any place artists gathered. He'd have Francesca handle the business of his commissions, his excuse being his work was quite in demand and he needed time in his studio.

Eventually time would cool his ardor toward Lady Threxton and cool his peculiar need for a particular part of her anatomy.

CHAPTER TWELVE

London, April 1881

Another year, another Royal Academy Exhibition, although this year was slightly different. Charles was showing two watercolors—a medium he'd never exhibited in before—as well as six oil paintings, all of which had already been sold. That he was still doing well professionally was heartening. Emotionally? Well, that was a different matter altogether.

He still burned for Rosamund.

He had thrown himself into his work the last few months. The requirements of the Academy were that works not be previously exhibited. For a much sought-after artist like himself, that meant new paintings. And there was nothing like mixing the perfect green or gold, laying down the sinuous lines of a vista, polishing and refining a scene until it matched his vision entirely to take his mind off the frustrations of his heart.

Once again, he was among the guests of honor at the Royal Academy Private View, held the night before the Banquet. It was not a tedious evening, especially when Francesca was at his side. Besides, he rather enjoyed dressing to the nines and shaking hands with colleagues and politicians, joking with the Prince of Wales, hearing his name spoken in hushed tones as he walked past awed aristocracy.

Charles was busy being overly in awe himself as he exchanged pleasantries with the Princess of Wales, when suddenly in the corner of his eye he noticed a vision of loveliness dressed in peach and pale purple.

Their interchange over, the princess graciously gave a nod to the next babbling artist and Charles moved to seek out his potential muse.

He found her in one of the larger galleries. He hid behind guests deep in conversation as he studied her.

She stood before one of his grand landscapes, the huge canvas extending over quite a bit of wall space. The scene was based on his sketches from Scotland, a field with the varying purples of heather in bloom amidst the grays of mottled rocks. The woman in peach stood off to the left side, her back to him, her body turned at an oblique angle as if she were gazing off into the distance beyond that which was on the canvas. The way she was positioned, the muted coloring of her dress, the delicate brown of her hair, made it seem she was in the very painting itself and not standing on the gallery floor.

Such a vision. He should introduce himself.

She shifted her weight, the fabric gathered at the back of her dress shifting with her. Would the lady's glorious backside be flushed pink under the profusion of skirts and petticoats? Did she bend over for her lover and let him raise the color of her cheeks with loving swats from his generous hand?

Good God, what the devil was he thinking? He shook his head to get the image out of his brain, and adjusted his jacket to hide his burgeoning erection.

So many months later and still such wickedness festered. And excited.

Since that night at the Thrextons', he had been plagued by thoughts of Rosamund. Every time he heard her spoken of in company, saw or heard someone like her, the image of her buttocks red from his swats came into view.

Except, he always had to remind himself, it was not he who had spanked her.

He had spent countless hours considering what Jeremy had proposed. To be so intimate with her he would share in her letch, be so devoted to her he would do what she demanded of him, and if that demand was that he control her pleasure, then so be it.

It would be a new way of being with a lover. Perhaps he should just be willing to try.

His consideration of the woman perusing his painting suffered a moment's distraction. Lord Somerford shook his hand to tell him how much he loved his work. He thanked the man for his kind words, then resumed observing his muse.

She paced before the canvas a few steps, then leaned in as if to study a brush stroke. She continued on to the far end of the canvas and turned, giving him a fine view of her profile.

His flesh prickled. *Rosamund.*

Of course. Only she could elicit such a wanton response in him.

She did not yet see him. He did not want her to see him. He stepped aside, behind two politicians discussing the uplifting nature of the glories of empire depicted in paint.

"Charles!"

He turned to see Jeremy coming toward him with a grin.

"Lord Threxton."

They shook hands, Jeremy with much enthusiasm.

Jeremy beamed, genuinely it seemed. "So good to see you. It's been too long."

"I've been busy," Charles stammered. "For the Exhibition. I suppose as have you?"

"Yes. I'm delighted to be showing my first allegorical work. *The Tempestuous Daughter*, based on sketches I had of Miss Brockhurst. I'm sure you don't mind."

Charles chuckled. "Not at all." The politicians shielding him from Rosamund moved. He shifted nervously.

"Is everything quite all right?"

Charles glanced at Rosamund. Jeremy followed his gaze.

"Ah."

Charles narrowed his eyes at him. "I've not seen you in months and that's all you can say?"

Jeremy sobered with a sigh. "Rosamund is well. There is no other change in her circumstances." Jeremy leaned closer. "She still burns for you."

She burning for *him*? Every pore on his body was gasping for air.

"Shall I call her over?"

His gut clenched.

"She would love to see you, Charles."

They were in public. It was best their reunion after several months was arranged and mediated rather than an unexpected surprise. "Yes. All right."

A moment later Rosamund was before him. His view of the room blurred around the edges, his lungs constricted for want of air. His body seemed to float as if in a dream.

"Mr. Westerman," she said gaily. "So nice to see you."

The confidence in her voice was belied by her glove-stretching grip on her husband's arm and the pale cast to her face.

"As always, Lady Threxton, the pleasure is all mine."

She blushed and briefly glanced away. Had he been the object of her fantasies? He held out hope.

She smiled. "I've been enjoying your painting, Mr. Westerman. Truly stunning."

And I've been enjoying your backside. "Thank you, Lady Threxton. Your estimation of my work is invaluable to me."

"Scotland, is it not?"

He grunted in reply. "It is lovely countryside. A thousand landscapes could not do it justice."

It was ridiculous. They were talking around each other. They weren't even flirting, which Rosamund was so very good at even in public.

"Lady Threxton, as I value your opinion on art, I was wondering if you would accompany me on a walk-through of the Exhibition on a day when I am not so occupied with politicians and royalty."

Rosamund paled again. Jeremy hid a smile behind his beard.

Charles would not be daunted. "Next week? Pick your day. I know the first few days of the Exhibition can be quite a crush."

Her expression softened. "I would love to, Mr. Westerman. I think Thursday afternoon."

"Very well. Midafternoon, perhaps? We'll have tea afterward. I'll pick you up in a cab around two o'clock."

It was exhilarating just saying all those words. He didn't give a fig if she eventually said no.

"I will be waiting for you at two o'clock on Thursday, Mr. Westerman."

The hall clock chimed a quarter to two.

Rosamund grasped the edge of her dressing table as she stared at herself in the mirror. Was that a blemish on her cheek? A new gray hair at her temple?

She shuddered. She was acting like a debutante on the night of her first ball, hoping desperately that a man—any man—would take notice of her.

But Charles Westerman was not just any man. He sparked sensual thrills deep inside. He invigorated her, and made her feel like an intelligent, attractive woman.

And in her fantasies he was the man who fulfilled her particular carnal needs. The ones Jeremy only indulged because he was an obliging husband.

She stood and let Gretchen adjust her dress, position her hat just so, then help her slip into her coat. She clutched the soft leather gloves and the chain handle of her embroidered handbag.

The clock struck two. The doorbell rang.

Rosamund smiled. Charles Westerman's cab was amazingly punctual, or he had been sitting outside her door waiting for the hour to strike.

She sucked in a breath and let it out slowly. She'd make him wait just one minute more.

* * * * *

Lady Threxton had all sorts of opinions about all sorts of art hanging at the Royal Academy Exhibition. It was quite refreshing to spend time with a woman who was not afraid to speak her mind, to challenge him, to offer points of view he had never considered. There were a few times when Charles laughed out loud, to the embarrassment and annoyance of all present.

Afterward at the café, Lady Threxton had been more subdued, perhaps shy. There was no easy object of conversation like there had been when standing before artworks.

"When did you begin painting, Mr. Westerman?" she asked as she stirred her tea.

"My parents gave me a box of paints for my tenth birthday. I think they didn't see me again for days. Eventually, I ran out of paints."

Rosamund laughed, an invigorating sound. "Somehow I cannot imagine you being ten years old, Mr. Westerman," she said, her eyes twinkling.

"That's because you insist on calling me Mr. Westerman, my lady." He smiled.

"Oh, were you Charlie then? Or Chas? Or perhaps Chuck?"

Charles laughed. "I was Charlie in grammar school, my lady."

"Oh, please. Rosamund."

Charles nodded. "As you wish, Rosamund." Her name rolled off his tongue facilely, his having said it so frequently in his fantasies.

"And what has been your finest accomplishment as a painter?"

"The Brockhurst commission last year, I suppose." Charles snorted in mild disgust. "Despite what eventually happened."

"I saw Mr. Brockhurst a few months ago in London," she said softly. "He did mention the mural was stunning. Tell me about it, Charles." Rosamund looked him straight in the eye as she said his name.

He sighed. "It was a project for a garden room with large windows. The commission was to paint the interior walls with a landscape. I chose to recreate the same scene one sees as one looks out the windows. Of course I had to choose one particular time of the year to depict in paint. The view changes with the seasons." He stopped. "I hope I am not boring you, Rosamund?"

"Not at all. You have such a lively manner of speaking."

He had been gesturing. Sometimes he got carried away. He chuckled as she sipped her tea.

She looked in his eyes, a sadness in her own. "I heard about what happened with Miss Brockhurst. I'm so sorry."

He really hadn't thought about Annalee for quite some time. "Thank you. It was difficult at first, but I feel quite recovered now."

Rosamund toyed with her teaspoon, not looking at him.

"You may have been partly to blame for her leaving me."

She blanched. "I beg your pardon?"

"When I saw your portrait. The sketch in Jeremy's studio."

"My portrait… Oh." Her cheeks returned to their rosy glow, although perhaps a shade deeper than usual.

"Annalee must have felt a measure of jealousy as I stared at the work too long."

"Well, I suppose a man might naturally do such a thing with a nude picture of his friend's wife," she said quietly.

"And then you were right there in front of me." He raked his gaze over her. "It was difficult to not imagine the living model as such."

She looked away, exposing the elegant line of her neck that met the curve of her shoulder. Her dress was modest, but of a gorgeous brown that flattered her hair and eyes, the whorl of the moiré pattern giving the effect of a swirl as one stirred a cup of hot cocoa.

"That dress is quite fine. The colors become you."

"Thank you, Mr. Westerman," she said in almost a whisper.

He eyed her. "Have you forgotten my name already?"

She shook her head. "I apologize, Charles. One becomes used to formalities." She glanced at his cup; her own was quite empty. "Shall we take a walk? It is a lovely spring day, don't you think?"

It was a lovely spring day indeed, made even lovelier by Rosamund's arm wrapped around his, her palm in repose, but her fingers tense. Outside there seemed to be more distractions, more things to talk about. They wandered until they were alone on a path. Charles's heart thrummed impatiently.

"Did you know the Italian Garden was only put in twenty years ago?" she said. "I find that fascinating. It seems as if the garden has been here forever."

Her closeness was driving him mad. Her fingers relaxing and tensing on his forearm—like the pulse of her cunt around his cock—drove him madder still. "No, I did not know that."

She broke free and spun around. "I love London in the spring."

She placed her hand on his left shoulder and grasped his right hand as if to dance a waltz. She bit her lower lip and gazed at him under half-lidded eyes.

They danced a moment, not very well, as Charles was a terrible dancer. Rosamund laughed, a spontaneous, genuine laugh. She stepped back, releasing him.

The thick trunk of a tree was at her back. Her smile seemed to beckon.

Charles glanced around. They were, for the most part, alone. He stepped forward, grabbed her at the waist, holding her steady after her slight flinch. He pressed her against the tree and took her in a passionate kiss, soft but demanding. She tensed, flattening her palms against his chest for only a moment, before relenting in his arms. She parted her lips under his. Arousal flared within.

He slid his hands up to cup her breasts, then skated them along her waist and over her hips. He grasped her backside and ground his crotch into her skirt, growling his appreciation.

He broke free from the kiss and stared at her still in his arms.

She stared back, confusion and desire darkening her gaze, her breath releasing in excited puffs.

"Charles, let me go," she said quietly.

"No." He was cruel, but she did not flee.

Her eyes flicked side to side, her brow contorted in worry. "Not here. We're in public."

"You forget we fucked in public once."

That seemed to fluster her. Her eyes narrowed. "Our encounter was behind a closed door," she hissed.

"Then is all you need a closed door?"

"We cannot flaunt our affair in public."

"Ah." So that was it. Propriety still reigned even in an arrangement that was anything but proper. Well, then, he would let her go, but find a more appropriate place to continue his suit.

She searched his face. "You're plotting something, aren't you?"

"Perhaps." He offered her a half smile as he drew the tip of his tongue over his upper lip.

She gaped as she stared at his mouth, her eyes tracking the path of his tongue.

He pulled away and took her arm in his and led her to Uxbridge Road. He searched right and left for a hansom cab, and hailed a hackney coach—a much better choice as it was larger, with blinds to shield one from prying eyes. He helped Rosamund inside, then gave the driver her address.

The plodding carriage would give them plenty of time to discuss their future.

He climbed inside, taking the seat opposite Rosamund, then knocked on the roof to urge the cabbie onward. Rosamund sat tucked away in the far corner of the carriage, her hands folded in her lap, her face turned to look out of the window.

He leaned over and pulled the blinds shut on both sides of the carriage, leaving her with a view of nothing but himself.

Still she looked away, not at his face, deciding upon the view of the floor next to the door.

"It is I, really, who should be unnerved," he said.

That made her look at him. "Unnerved?"

"I've had affairs, but none with a married woman. How does one act? Especially around the husband? And especially when he is still a colleague and a friend?" He met her gaze. "Do you have advice on the matter?"

She sighed. "Truth be told, no. My lovers have been agents at the club I frequent, never friends."

"So I am your first."

Her lips thinned into a weak smile. "I suppose."

As the carriage bumped along the road, he clumsily sat beside her. He clasped her hand. "Then we are both new to the game, my lady." He cupped her chin and turned her to face him. "Rosamund, ever since I found you, my thoughts have been filled with you, reliving every moment shared with you, conjuring up new fantasies of you."

Her lips parted. She smoothed her tongue across her lower lip as her gaze dipped to his mouth.

"I will confess I am afraid for my heart," he continued softly. "I am uncertain what I want. Almost a year ago I thought I wanted a young wife and the opportunity for children. Now I do not know if I want any of that at all."

A quiet whimper escaped her throat.

"I do know that at this moment in my life I want you. I want to make love to you, wake up with you, laugh with you, share quiet moments with you simply sitting and enjoying your company."

A tear fell down her left cheek.

"Yet you cannot wholly be mine. Will sharing a lover satisfy my needs as a man? And, in order to enjoy those things with you, I know I have to do something I'm not sure about, something I've never done before, something I simply do not know how to do." He wiped her tear away with his thumb, then tenderly pressed his lips to her damp cheek. "I was witness to something shocking. More shocking still, you want me to do this to you. I cannot hurt you, nor any woman."

"It does not hurt me, Charles, it invigorates me."

"How can you say that, Rosamund? What I saw was so…so…violent."

"I chose to be spanked. I want to be spanked. And it was more vigorous than violent. My chastiser was not harming me. He's been trained in the erotic arts very well."

"Darling, you'll have to teach me what it is you want." He leaned in and touched his lips to hers, soft, delicate, wet. Sensation exploded at the point of contact, shooting outward through his limbs to the tip of his cock. She clutched at him, wrapping her arms around his neck as he slid his around her waist.

He kissed her neck, the delicate pulse point fluttering under his tongue. He smoothed his hand over her breast tightly bound under her bodice, then continued down to her waist. He gathered up her skirts and explored under the silk and lace to find her knee, then glided his hand up her cotton-covered thigh to the slit in her drawers. She gasped as he sought her motte.

"Is this private enough for you?" he asked.

She tucked her hips to give him more access. "Yes, darling. It's perfect."

Dampness clung to the curls of her sex. He poked a finger between her labia teasingly, then pulled it through the slick folds, searching for her clitoris.

Her gasp signaled his discovery. He flicked his nail back and forth over the plump, hard nub, smiling as sensuality softened her expression. A pinch elicited another gasp, breathy and yearning. She would let him do anything to her.

And the idea of doing whatever he wanted was absolutely thrilling.

He wanted to give her pleasure, wanted to take his own until he reached that magnificent culmination into ecstasy. But what he was doing to her now, guiding her, holding sway over her desires, suddenly became a need, an urgency he never knew he had. The thrill of controlling her descent into carnality, of watching her climb to her peak but being the gatekeeper to all she felt, was utterly arousing. The wonderment of it chilled him at the very moment Rosamund yelped in climax.

He thrust two fingers inside her, reveling in the clenching force of renewed orgasm. His cock complained as it pressed against his trousers. But his cock could wait. His mind was in control and his mind found orgiastic joy in directing Rosamund's pleasure, in making her feel the moments of lust he wanted her to feel—her cunt, her clit, any part of her that could experience bodily pleasure.

She held his gaze, her eyes glazed over, lost in a rapturous oblivion. He did this to her. He made her feel this way. He could make her feel this whenever he wanted.

She writhed under his ministrations, then bucked with a sharp cry. She lay in a heap in the corner of the seat, panting, staring at him in adulation.

"Darling, Rosamund, I'll be your lover, but you have to show me what you want. Can you do this?"

She nodded, her face flushed and glowing. "Yes, Charles, I will do anything you ask."

CHAPTER THIRTEEN

Upon arrival at the address for the Vicereine Social Club, Charles stared briefly in astonishment. From what Rosamund had told him about the unusual establishment, he had expected something quite different than the building before him, perhaps something more tawdry and sinister. But no. The building was quite ordinary, like any other commercial building in London.

On the ground floor was a milliner's—an actual milliner's, not a false front, a shop from which Charles knew Francesca ordered some of her hats. A stairwell to the right of the shop led to a dance studio on the first floor—which reminded Charles he needed to learn how to dance if he were ever to escort Rosamund to ballrooms.

But through a rather unremarkable door to the left of the milliner's was a stairwell that led to the second floor and above, where Madame Laperne's was located.

Charles had never been in such a place. He knew of men who had, or boasted that they had. And once he was on the inside, it was everything and nothing like the stories he had heard.

The reception salon was indeed luxurious, as rumor of such places proclaimed. But it was far more opulent and lavish than a man without an aesthetic sense might describe. Plush velvets in rich jewel tones and glossy dark wood paneling gave the room a luxurious feel. The lighting was subdued, cast mostly on the floor so a patron might see where he—or she—was going but not so much the faces of others also seeking sensual pleasures.

Because Rosamund had arranged his adventure, Charles was to meet first with Madame Laperne herself. Madame offered him a comfortable chair in her office, then took a seat behind her mahogany desk. A smattering of fine lines indicated she was a little older than he. Her dark hair had faded to a silver gray and glowed like a nimbus around her kind face. She was dignified, not flamboyant, in her dress and demeanor. Her manners pointed to finishing school on the continent.

"Lady Threxton speaks highly of you, Mr. Westerman." The French lilt to her voice was calming.

"Thank you, Madame Laperne." He nodded politely. "Lady Threxton said I should not be afraid of you."

Madame Laperne laughed, glee and a touch of incredulity brightening her face. "Oh, my dear sir," she said wiping a tear from her right eye, "there is no fear in my establishment. Unless, of course, you desire it." She winked.

"I hardly know what I desire, Madame. And I hardly understand my reaction to watching Lady Threxton experience hers."

There. He'd said it. He was not one for mincing words, and Madame was clearly not one for tolerating a man who danced around a subject. And he was a bad dancer.

She smiled a warm, almost motherly smile. "Lady Threxton enjoys chastisement. She explained you had a chance to witness this."

"I did. Unwittingly."

"And for that I apologize, Mr. Westerman. A man should never have to witness an act he is possibly uncomfortable with."

"Thank you, Madame. The experience provoked unexpected sensations."

"Did you feel arousal while watching her?"

Madame's mystique instilled honesty in him. "I did."

"Do you understand why you felt arousal?"

"Hardly. I would never strike a woman and would never consider such an act arousing in the slightest."

"Ah." Madame folded her hands. "But you understood Lady Threxton was experiencing pleasure and arousal, did you not?"

"I did." Charles let an exhalation slowly escape through clenched teeth. "Still, the display was disconcerting."

"Of course it was, Mr. Westerman." Madame steepled her fingers. "Oftentimes when we are attracted to a person, when we watch that person experiencing pleasure, no matter what it is, we experience pleasure ourselves."

Charles thinned his lips.

"Ah. Let me explain with other means. What food do you dislike, Mr. Westerman?"

"Food?" For some reason bread pudding came to mind, although he'd only had it once. "Bread pudding?"

Madame nodded. "Let us say you were with Lady Threxton at a café. She has ordered bread pudding. You dislike the stuff, yet there she is eating it and enjoying it. Sitting across from her at the table, do you smile at her experience of pleasure, or do you rail against the disgusting qualities of bread pudding?"

It was his turn to laugh genuinely. "I suppose I would watch her with some measure of disgust but a greater measure of enjoyment."

Madame smiled. "It is thus with Lady Threxton's enjoyment of chastisement."

"But how can *that* possibly give one pleasure? I understand different tastes in food. But having a man strike you?" He shook his head, aghast.

"Are your pleasures so simple, Mr. Westerman? A woman to suck your cock? To bend over while you fuck her from behind? To gamahuche while she is tied to your bedposts?"

Charles shifted in his seat, discomfited at his arousal at mere words.

"Would you say these pleasures are ordinary, Mr. Westerman?"

He considered the question a moment. "Not ordinary, perhaps. I don't expect my village vicar to indulge in such. But not extraordinary either."

She smiled wryly. "Ah, the upstanding vicar. Of course he does not gamahuche his wife."

Charles flushed.

She tilted her head and narrowed her eyes. "Shall I shock you, Mr. Westerman?"

He snorted. "I believe you already have, Madame."

"Oh, I am sure I have not." She leaned forward on her desk. "There is a man who attends my club, rather infrequently I admit. An older man in his late sixties. You might know him from Parliament or perhaps the society pages. But once ensconced in the privacy of our club he assumes a persona. He calls himself Lord Swaddlemore."

Odd. Charles maintained his composure.

"Lord Swaddlemore attends club functions with a hired nanny, yet he himself has no children."

Charles cleared his throat. "I imagine this is perceived as eccentric by the denizens of the club."

Madame chuckled. "Not at all. In fact, quite the opposite. You see he needs the services of a nanny as he is dressed as an infant with a swaddled bottom."

"Good God," Charles blurted.

"Oh yes, Mr. Westerman. And the man is thoroughly nude on top. He cuts quite a figure as he boxes twice a week. The nanny wears a walking costume."

Preposterous. "What, may I ask, does the nanny do?"

Madame smiled an enigmatic smile. "She chastises him when he soils himself."

"Good God." Charles looked askance in disbelief.

"So perhaps, Mr. Westerman, you can see how Lady Threxton's letch is positively tame."

Positively tame was not a description he would use. And yet... "Yes, I do see how one might consider it as such when compared to others."

"Now, Mr. Westerman, before I teach you how to engage Lady Threxton in her predilection, I must make one more point."

He was all ears.

"Lord Swaddlemore may be strange, yet his desires hurt no one. The nanny is paid quite handsomely, I might add. And she is not really a nanny at all, so there are no children going without her expert services."

"That is a relief."

"Don't mock, Mr. Westerman. It only reveals you are hiding some deeper emotion."

He looked away.

"The lesson is that everyone has their unusual proclivities. As long as no one is being harmed, we must be tolerant. Now the real challenge is to discover what your letch is."

He met her gaze.

She smiled enigmatically. "And how this can be used to Lady Threxton's great advantage."

"And my own?"

She chortled. "And your own, Mr. Westerman, yes. Let us return to the example of Lord Swaddlemore. As I intimated, he is a very powerful man, yet he plays the role of a child. And not a strong-willed recalcitrant boy. No. He plays the role of a very dependent, needy infant."

"The exact opposite of who he really is."

"Precisely. Many people have letches that are unlike their true selves."

"Ah." He understood her implication. His gut twisted. Who the hell was he? "You seek to discover my sensual desires by understanding who I really am?"

"Yes."

"Therein lies a problem. I'm not certain who I am anymore."

"You are a famous artist, Mr. Westerman. Even I have heard of you." Madame Laperne pointed to the wall behind him.

He turned around. Hung in a balanced arrangement were nine small landscapes in various mediums, oil, wash, lithography. He recognized a small oil sketch of the French countryside as his. Seeing his work hung against the rich wallpaper instilled a sense of pride.

He nodded to her. "Thank you, Madame, for your patronage."

"It is a lovely work. It reminds me of the landscape of my childhood." Her eyes took on a faraway cast for only a moment. "As I was saying, Mr. Westerman, you are famous, quite talented in what it is you do, and approach your work with the mindset of a professional, not a dabbler."

Which was, perhaps, an affront at Jeremy. "So what is the opposite of who I am?"

"Ah, I had wondered that when I discussed your situation with Lady Threxton. I inquired further about you and your career with others who know of you."

Charles started.

"No, don't worry, Mr. Westerman, your affiliation with me and Lady Threxton is quite safely hidden. You see I do sometimes purchase works of art. I merely inquired casually at Moulton Gallery about your career. To see if it was worth my money to invest further in your works."

Charles calmed a bit.

"The *galeriste* mentioned that you are not from a wealthy background, so did not grow up with the opportunities afforded the upper classes. That your talent, which in his estimation was unmatched in what he called 'fieldscapes', was due to your tenacious study and practice. He had never known an artist to work so hard as you do, who was as disciplined as you. In short, he did not know an artist who was as in control of his career as you."

Madame Laperne raised an eyebrow at him. "However, I suspect you do not really feel as in control of your career as the art dealer says you are. I suspect your facade of control is a masquerade for something else."

Heat prickled under his collar.

"Why do you work so hard, Mr. Westerman?"

He gripped the arm of the chair. He knew. He truly knew. He had never voiced it before.

"I…I am afraid of it slipping away. I work in order to maintain a level of financial security, enough to sustain myself and whoever may come to depend upon me." Francesca. Her children. His father. "As long as I have paintings to sell, I am still viable. I will still have an income."

"Lack of money in your past has made you fear such a fate again."

"Yes."

"And yet you must be quite successful, Mr. Westerman. I mean, financial success."

"I suppose I am."

"But you feel at any moment it could all slip away."

"Yes."

"You feel a lack of control in your life."

He stared at her. "Control?" There was no control in his life. Yes he was disciplined and his output was prodigious. But financial security? At any moment it could all disappear.

Good Christ. He wanted to be in control.

In control of Rosamund.

And yet, it was Rosamund who controlled him, who commanded his passions. "Am I in a battle for control over my own passions?"

"I beg your pardon, Mr. Westerman?"

He shook his head. "I don't understand. Why do I want to dominate her? Rosamund is a capable and dynamic woman and I greatly admire that about her."

"She is yet another aspect of your life over which you do not have much control. Your love life."

Too true. The disaster with Annalee proved that. And his affair with the very married Rosamund.

"Now, Mr. Westerman, we have discussed a great many deep ideas. I suggest you go away and think about all I have spoken. Come back if you want to learn how to please Lady Threxton."

* * * * *

"Charles, your tea will get cold if you continue to ignore it while pacing my carpet."

Charles stopped midstep and stared blankly at Francesca. "What? Yes. Sorry." He sat and picked up the blue-and-white willow pattern cup and gulped down the now cold tea.

Francesca placed a hand on his knee. "My dear, dear brother. Whatever has come over you?"

Concern furrowed her brow. She knew something. She must know. She knew him too well to not know.

"It's a woman, isn't it?"

She read him like an open book.

"Frannie, you said you never really loved George, right?"

"I did say that. It is, unfortunately, true."

"Well, while you were married to this man you did not love, did you ever think to have, or perhaps you did have, my God, I have no idea what went on…" He stopped, slightly mortified.

"Charles," she said sternly, "out with it."

He met her gaze, her expression now tinged with annoyance. "All right. Just…please don't be angry, Frannie." He drew in a bolstering breath. "Did you have an affair when you were married?"

She flushed and shrank back against the forest-green velvet settee. "No," she said quietly. "No. I never considered such a thing. And then there were the children. I could never do such a thing knowing my children were without their mother. It would be selfish."

"But what if George had suggested it?"

"Suggested it?" she squawked.

"I mean, advocated it, encouraged it, said he wouldn't mind. Something like that."

"I cannot imagine such a thing, Charles." She had a pained look on her face.

He really shouldn't open old heartaches, but he had to know if his virtuous sister had her boundaries. "What if Archie hadn't died? What if he had only been wounded in the Crimea, but Father had insisted you marry George? And then George had let you…be with Archie?"

Francesca squeezed her eyes shut. When she opened them, her lashes were wet. "Why are you asking this?" Her voice was hoarse.

"Because I need to know before I tell you what has been preoccupying me of late."

She sniffled. "All right. I would have wanted to be with Archie. And if George had encouraged such a relationship, I would have pursued it." She shook her head. "But it's more complicated than that. We had children, and what if Archie had wanted to be married with children?"

"Yes, it can be complicated. Or it can be fairly simple. Like with me and Rosamund."

"Rosamund? You mean Lady Threxton?" Francesca gasped. "Oh my word. You're in love with Lady Threxton." Her hand flew to her mouth. "Charles, that could be very complicated. Viscount Threxton is a colleague of yours. I thought you were friends?"

"Threxton has given us his blessing. Actually much more than that. He's encouraging us."

"Have they grown apart? They seem to put on quite a facade of a happily married couple."

"It's no charade. She and Jeremy are truly in love. It's not like he ignores her and she needs to find solace in the arms of another man. It's not like that at all."

A crease formed between Francesca's brows. "Then what is it like, Charles?"

"It's an unusual arrangement, like no other I have ever known. They…they have what can only be described as a free marriage, each of them open and available to relationships with others."

"Oh my word." Francesca nibbled on her lower lip. "Married women have affairs all the time, I suppose. Especially in the upper classes. Charles, is she telling you that you are more to her than just her lover?"

"I'm not just taking her to bed." Charles pressed his palm to his forehead. He hadn't actually taken her to bed now, had he? "What we have is unusual. It's a discovery, of her, of myself even." He looked at Francesca. "I'm not sure I want to say any more to my sister."

She smiled. "All right. Then what is it you *are* telling your sister and why?"

He chuckled. "Frannie, we've always been close. More so since George died. I need to tell you I think I'm in love with Rosamund. I need you to understand. I need you accept this. I need your blessing."

She sat straight against the cushioned back. "I don't want you to get hurt, Charles." Her eyes bored into him, soulful and deep. "I don't want you running away again."

He kissed her forehead. "No, no, I won't. I'll come to you first."

She laughed softly and picked up her teacup, staring into its depths for a moment. "We only kissed, you know."

He had no idea what she was talking about. "Pardon?"

"Archie and I. Nothing else beyond kissing, despite me pressing him for more."

Charles smiled. "I know. He told me." He smoothed a strand of hair behind her ear. "He was going to ask you to marry him when he returned from the war. But he didn't want to leave behind a ruined, possibly pregnant, innocent girl. He feared he might not return."

Francesca broke down in sobs. "Oh, Charles. It still hurts."

He took her trembling teacup and placed it on the side table.

She reached for him. "What might have been. What should have been."

"Shh, shh." Charles cradled her in his arms. *No regrets.* Isn't that what Jeremy had said? No regrets.

He and Rosamund would have no regrets.

The afternoon was too beautiful to spend inside, but Charles had made an appointment with Madame Laperne. He was duly greeted and ushered upstairs to the third floor where the "guest salons" were located. The concierge opened the door, suggested he hang up his jacket, then advised he get to know his surroundings while he waited for Madame.

The private room was cozy and lushly decorated. A large mirror framed by an elaborate Rococo gilded frame hung on one wall papered in deep crimson. Dark red velvet draperies hung in thick folds on the other walls, probably to muffle any sounds that might happen within. That there might be sounds needing to be muffled was made evident by the selection of implements of chastisement available on a portable rack near one wall. Among the choices were a small round wooden paddle, a longer paddle shaped like a cricket player's bat, plus various leather floggers and whips.

In the center of the room was a hip-height wooden trestle bench, the top of which had been rubbed smooth and shiny, particularly along one edge. Charles ran his hand along the dark wood, the indentation eerily resembling an executioner's block. Yet those who bent over this bench desired the judgment they received.

The door opened, and Madame entered with a young woman— her height, her coloring, her shape the very image of Rosamund but at least twenty years younger. Inwardly, Charles chuckled. The man Rosamund had hired had resembled himself. It was peculiar that Madame Laperne was not only able to satisfy a particular letch, but supply a particular model to satisfy that letch.

"Ah, good afternoon, Mr. Norton." Madame Laperne greeted him with the prearranged sham name.

"Good afternoon, Madame." He nodded in greeting.

"May I introduce one of my girls." Madame gestured at the lovely young woman who smiled and bobbed a curtsy. "Lydia will be helping us with the demonstration. She is most expert in the art of spanking and paddling."

"A pleasure," he said. It certainly was a pleasure to see what Rosamund might have been like at twenty-five.

Except Rosamund never would have worn the almost ridiculous short skirt puffed up by too many petticoats and the dangerously low-cut tight-fitted bodice. The ensemble looked rather enchanting on Lydia, though.

Madame ushered Lydia over to the trestle. Lydia knew exactly what she needed to do. She bent over the wooden top and settled her feet hip-distance apart. The flounce of her skirts poofed up. Madame did the honors of smoothing the skirts up and against her back, exposing the girl's lacy drawers.

"Mr. Norton, please take up the small round paddle." Madame pointed to the rack. "It is the preferred implement for today's demonstration."

Meaning it was what Rosamund preferred.

He picked it up and weighed the heft. The handle was heavier than the flat, rounded end. One side of the paddle was smoother and shinier than the other, the handle grooved ever so slightly to favor that side when held in the right hand.

"Mr. Norton, step over here."

He did so where indicated, to the left behind Lydia.

Madame fiddled with the string at Lydia's drawers, loosening the garment and pulling it down. Before his eyes were two gloriously pale and full demi-globes. His cock stirred unwittingly.

"I wish to point out some aspects of anatomy, Mr. Norton." Madame smoothed her hand over Lydia's buttocks.

His damn cock stirred even more.

"Under the flesh there are bones here, here, and here." Madame indicated the upper portions of the buttocks near the spine and at the tail bone. "I would assume you know that, but I wish to emphasize that striking the bone too harshly could cause damage."

Charles knew the basics of anatomy as taught in art school. There, skeletons were displayed as illustration on how to give a body structure.

"I want you to touch Lydia, to feel these areas, to get to know where bones are and are not. You should do this with all your subjects."

So the pretense of his presence there was as a man in training, not a client with a letch.

He touched Lydia's glorious backside, pressing to discover the bones within the pillowy softness. His cock was fully erect under his trousers. Madame, of course, would know. Without shame, he adjusted himself for comfort's sake.

Madame smiled. "Now let me see how you naturally hold the paddle."

He held his hand out. She inspected his grip.

"Very good. You naturally use your right hand. Do you play tennis, Mr. Norton?"

"Alas, I do not."

"There are two ways to strike. One forward with your arm held out to your side. Another way, which delivers a slightly different touch, is to hold it across your waist."

Madame demonstrated by directing his hand and the paddle in the two methods.

"Now I want you to strike Lydia on the fleshiest part of her arse."

Charles pulled back to strike.

"You know where that area is, Mr. Norton?"

Charles touched Lydia again, just to make sure. He pulled back again and swatted her, not hard, but enough to give a hearty slapping sound.

Lydia flinched with the impact and let out a little "ooh."

A pale pink circle formed on the pale flesh. Charles's cock stirred again.

"Very good, Mr. Norton. Lydia, how was that? Too hard or too soft?"

"I like it a little harder, if you please."

Madame stilled Charles's hand. "It is always proper to understand the level of discipline your subject can bear. Increase the force of your strikes in increments." She let go of him.

Charles pulled back and struck harder. A pink circle appeared to the right of the one he had just made.

"Good, Mr. Norton. Lydia?"

"Yes, that was nice."

"Another?" asked Madame.

"Yes, another."

Charles's cock was further stiffened at the breathy request.

Madame smiled at him. "It is always good to understand your subject's limits, as well." She nodded. "You may proceed."

He stared at the blotches and aimed between them. He hit with the same amount of force as before.

Lydia jumped. "Oh, my, Mr. Norton. That was exquisite."

Madame patted Lydia's thigh. "Lydia, dear, shall we give some attention to the other side?"

"Oh, yes, please." She seemed rather excited.

"Now, Mr. Norton, you can either switch hands, or you can stand farther to the side. Or you can use the other swatting method. From your arm bent across yourself at the waist."

"May I try soft hits to test the various methods?"

"By all means, Mr. Norton."

Charles flicked his wrist this way and that, flipping the paddle in his hand to better understand the implement. He lightly patted Lydia's butt and thighs, engrossed by the rebounding flesh.

Lydia giggled and squirmed at his gentle swats.

She was enjoying his playfulness, it seemed. Did she also enjoy the harder swats? The act was doing nothing for him except enlivening his cock, and that, as far as he could tell, was because a beautiful pair of buttocks was on display before his eyes, the flesh rosy and alive.

Charles boldly circled around the table to Lydia's head. He lifted her chin with the paddle. Her pupils filled her brown eyes, her cheeks were as flushed as her bottom. "Lydia, do you like to be spanked?"

"Yes, sir."

"Why?"

She blinked in bemused astonishment. "It feels good, sir."

He released the paddle. "Can you elaborate on why it feels good?"

She settled her head on a cheek and gazed up at him. "It makes me feel warm inside. And there's an excitement to not knowing when I'll be hit."

He turned to Madame Laperne. "Is it thus for all participants of this lustful endeavor?"

She pursed her lips. "No. It is the nature of the participant that drives their lust for the sport. Lydia is a playful girl, so she senses it as play. Another might believe themselves deserving of punishment. The human condition is so varied, Mr. Norton."

Words were never truer. "Yes it is, Madame."

Charles returned to his place at Lydia's backside. He stood a measure away from her and came down hard on the virginal cheek.

Lydia moaned and spread her legs open an inch more. The scent of her sex wafted through the air, filling his senses. It wasn't mere playfulness she experienced. The act of chastisement had aroused her. It was the second time Charles had witnessed arousal achieved in such a way and it still surprised him. And excited him.

"Are you going to fuck me, now?"

Charles flushed at the question. He was hard as a rock, but not desirous of Lydia's services. He flashed a horrified glance at Madame Laperne. Madame smiled calmly.

"No, no, Lydia, dear. Mr. Norton is loyal to his lady friend. He merely wanted to learn a new skill."

"All right." Lydia twisted her head in Madame's direction. "Are we finished, then?"

"I…" Charles looked to Madame for instruction.

"Yes, Lydia. We are finished. Thank you for your time."

Lydia righted herself to standing, shaking out her short skirts. She curtsied with a smile and a blush at Charles, then left.

"Thank you, Madame," he said. "Is there anything else?"

She grunted a laugh. "I think it is time you go home and think upon what you've learned, Mr. Westerman."

"Right." He was hoping she'd say that. He couldn't wait to leave. His cock was screaming for a frig.

CHAPTER FOURTEEN

Rosamund smiled as she took in the sight of swirling couples on the ballroom floor at Lord and Lady Somerford's, the pastel blurs of women's dresses swooshing around the rigid, dark figures of men. A ball was a festive respite from the teas and lectures and gallery shows that made up her usual fare during the Season. She could let down her guard and soften her intellectual veneer as music pulsated within, inviting her feet to take a turn on the parquetry through the haze of gas lamps and the odor of perfume.

A thick masculine hand slipped around her waist.

"You look delicious, my love," Jeremy murmured against her ear, his lips tickling her. "I should like to show you off on the dance floor."

"Yes, please, darling husband."

Jeremy whisked her into the whirling madness. He was a fine dancer, commanding her every move with confidence, easily negotiating their path amidst the crush. A smugness twisted his lips. He always said they made a handsome couple, and that night they turned more than just a few heads.

Several exhilarating minutes later, they were back mingling with the wallflowers and gossips.

"Lord and Lady Threxton, you make a striking pair on the dance floor," said Margaret Longacre, who was both wallflower and gossip.

"I thank you indeed, Miss Longacre," Jeremy said, dripping with charm, which he really shouldn't do around her.

"If I may bend your ear a moment, my lord."

And bend his ear is precisely what Margaret did, with a monologue concerning the dearth of female representation in the Royal Academy Summer Exhibition of 1881. What Jeremy could do about such a matter was anyone's guess.

While Jeremy endured his fate, Rosamund perused the crowd, hoping, foolishly probably, for a glimpse of Charles. While the Earl of Somerford was a noted art collector, the event was a ball, and Charles most definitely did not dance.

A flush swept across her skin when she saw the very man standing with his sister. He stood out, not just because of his stature and good looks, but because of his blond hair and Francesca's striking salmon and lavender gown. Charles seemed distracted as he surveyed his surroundings.

Rosamund surreptitiously nudged Jeremy. He glanced up.

"Miss Longacre," he said with excruciating politeness. "I will do my best to alert the Academy to your concerns. And now I must beg your leave as I see Mr. Charles Westerman, and we agreed to smoke cigars with the other gentlemen tonight."

Jeremy grabbed Rosamund's elbow as Margaret curtsied. Rosamund eyed her husband as he led them forward. "Darling, did you know Charles was going to be here tonight?"

"Not a clue. But it was our only escape. Come. I should be seen being friendly to your lover."

The moment Charles espied them, his dull expression brightened. He said something to Francesca, who smiled and looked up at a handsome mustachioed man to her left.

"Westerman," Jeremy greeted. "Mrs. Burridge." He nodded to Francesca and her friend.

"Threxton, Lady Threxton," Charles greeted back. "May I present Roderick Harbough, a family friend."

As pleasantries were exchanged all around, it was quite obvious from Francesca's blush what kind of family friend Mr. Harbough probably was.

"Once again, Mrs. Burridge, you are wearing such lively colors. The salmon pink brings out a freshness in you."

Francesca's blush deepened. "Thank you, Lady Threxton."

Rosamund hid her own smile behind her fan. How absolutely marvelous for Francesca to have found a beau.

Jeremy placed a hand on Charles's shoulder. "How about we gentlemen enjoy a smoke in the lounge while the ladies have a chat. What say you, Harbough?"

Mr. Harbough agreed, then glanced back at Francesca as Jeremy and Charles led him away.

"Francesca, wherever did you meet the dashing Mr. Harbough?"

"Moulton Gallery. He happened to be viewing a collection of seascapes in watercolor while Charles and I were delivering a canvas."

"And you were such a distraction from the watercolors that he made an introduction?"

"Something like that." Francesca positively beamed. "It's so wonderful to have a man's attention again."

Rosamund linked her arm through Francesca's. "I rather agree."

"Speaking of which…" Francesca nodded at the French doors leading to the terrace. "I think we should wander a little away from the other guests."

"Yes, of course." Rosamund's curiosity was thoroughly piqued.

They walked across the flagstones and down the steps toward the rose garden, gossiping and giggling as any pair of girlfriends might. Just as Jeremy had said it was a good idea for him to be seen with Charles, it was equally a good idea for Rosamund to spend private time with Francesca. The rumormongers would dismiss any closeness between Charles and Rosamund as being quite ordinary.

The din of the party was subdued amidst the roses, the colors of the flowers muted by the grays of night, their fragrance clinging to the cooling air.

Francesca released her hold. "Rosamund, Charles told me about the two of you."

Rosamund tried to hide her initial shock. "Oh, I see." How much he had said would quickly become apparent.

"But, please, do not think him indiscreet. He would never confess such a thing without a reason."

"Oh?" A reason?

Francesca glanced around. "Rosamund, Charles confessed you two were intimates but that you were still very much attached to Lord Threxton."

"I am, indeed."

"Yes, that's what he said. I don't pretend to understand it, but I do know my brother's heart to be fragile and he has already suffered enough threats to break it. I just…I just…" Francesca faced her. "Charles is in love with you."

The blood drained from her head, momentarily dizzying her. "Oh, I see."

"I know it is really not my business, but Charles is my dear brother. I don't know how you feel about him or what you hoped your affair would bring. I just ask you to not hurt him. Don't toy with his heart, Rosamund. Charles is a good man."

Rosamund took Francesca's hands in hers. "Oh, my dear, I would never do such a thing. What did he tell you about us?"

"Only that you have some special arrangement with your husband. That you and Charles are embarking upon an unusual affair."

"Unusual?" An interesting choice of words. "Did he specify further?"

"No." Francesca scrunched up her brow. "It's not corrupt or illegal, is it?" she asked in a hushed murmur. "I mean besides you being another man's wife."

Rosamund gave Francesca's hands a squeeze before she let go. "I assure you that there is nothing you need to worry about." Except now Rosamund feared for her own emotional state.

"I apologize." Francesca shook her head. "I am the one being indiscreet. He's a grown man. He can look after himself."

Rosamund inhaled deeply. "You are a good sister to concern yourself for his sake." She looped her arm around Francesca's. "And now we should return to find your Mr. Harbough. I'm certain he would love a dance with you."

Francesca chuckled. "Perhaps I should have a care for my own heart rather than for my brother's."

As they strolled back to the house, Rosamund's brain was frantic with thoughts. She had tried to smother the emotions plaguing her, but she could no longer continue. Her feelings for Charles were not mere obsession. She was in love with him. The thought rushed relief through her body. What was more, she felt nothing less for her husband. She loved Jeremy with the same level of intensity she had before she began her affair. She simply loved Charles differently. Was it possible for one woman to love two men at the same time? And for Charles, was it morally wrong to fall in love with another man's wife when that woman loved him back, and, more importantly, the husband had full knowledge and acceptance of the affair? Or, was it more acceptable to have a consensual affair, but not to lose one's heart?

She had to find Charles, to talk to him, to tell him how she felt.

They found the men in the drawing room, Jeremy gesticulating as he talked while Mr. Harbough laughed. Charles stood apart with Lord Somerford, nodding intently, his expression impassive. Briefly, he glanced her way before resuming his attention to the earl.

"I'll go see what my Roderick finds so amusing," Francesca said. She left Rosamund with a smile.

Rosamund watched Charles, unable to move from her spot on the drawing room carpet. She wanted to join him, but she had no reason to. She would be interrupting. She would have had no such qualms if it were Jeremy—

Charles flicked his finger in a beckoning gesture.

Rosamund stilled. Had that been meant for her?

Charles turned his head ever so slightly in her direction and lifted an eyebrow.

It must have been meant for her.

She sauntered over to him, greeting guests along the way, holding herself back against the desire to skip to his side. When she was two steps away, he acknowledged her with a nod and a smile.

"Lady Threxton, how lovely to see you."

"Mr. Westerman, the pleasure is mine."

"I presume as you are his guest, you are at least an acquaintance of the Earl of Somerford?"

"Oh my dear sir," Somerford exclaimed, "Lady Threxton has shocked me more than once with her opinions about art."

"But you have never not heeded my advice, my lord, when building your collection."

"So very true, my dear. Now tell me your opinion of Mr. Westerman's skills."

Charles blanched. Rosamund tried not to smile too broadly at the inadvertent double entendre.

"In my estimation, my lord, Mr. Westerman is the finest landscape painter in the British Isles."

Charles blushed.

The earl chortled. "Mr. Westerman, I'll have my man set up an appointment with your agent." He nodded. "And with that, I bid good evening to you both. I'm certain Lady Somerford would like her waltz now." The earl ambled in the direction of the ballroom.

"Thank you, darling," Charles muttered.

"I meant every word." Rosamund flicked her fan in front of her mouth to hide her grin at her very wicked thoughts. "Now shall I shock you by taking you to the Earl of Somerford's private collection of erotic art?" She lifted a brow.

Charles gaped. "By all means, my lady."

Charles followed Rosamund upstairs and quickly discovered that a linen closet on the second floor of Lord Somerford's grand manse was not simply a linen closet.

No, indeed it was not. The space between the shelves piled with sheets and draperies served as a passage to a room slightly bigger than the linen closet but not by much. A room paneled in gleaming chocolaty brown wood upon which hung image after image of prurient art.

"Rowlandson, Fuseli, other British artists," Rosamund said as she slid her finger along a row of framed prints. "Below are all Italian in the Classical vein."

Astonishing. And arousing. "Lady Threxton, how on earth did you know about this room?"

"I'm Somerford's curator."

He chuckled. Of course she was.

"And these"—she pointed to another row of brilliantly colored prints—"are from India, these from Japan." She gestured broadly. "This whole wall is French—"

Images of fellatio abounded. "I see."

She laughed softly. "Sadly, most of the artists are unknown." She grabbed the collar of his jacket and pulled herself against him, her breath fanning hot on his lips. "Unlike the artist I'm about to seduce."

"And what if that artist wants to seduce you first?"

She drew back and circled behind the trestle table in the middle of the space. She placed her hands flat on the polished surface. "Maybe I'll let him."

"I know how you dislike public sex." He raised a brow. "Unless it's your husband who's watching."

She pouted, a ridiculous expression that faded into something more like wantonness. He could stare at her for hours while she had that expression. Especially if it were reflected in a mirror while he was fucking her from behind.

Good God. Where on earth did that thought come from?

He held her gaze. "But we're not really in public, are we?"

She went to the door and locked it. "No, we are not. We are quite alone here."

"Like Lord Creslow's librarian's office."

She colored. "How was your visit to Madame Laperne's?"

He snorted. Of course Rosamund probably knew more than she let on about the matter. "It was very interesting. I was instructed in the art of the paddle with a young girl named Lydia. Do you know her?"

"I don't know many of the girls. Madame only sends men to me. You saw my Adam."

He raised a brow. "I saw how your Adam looks a little like me."

She blushed and perused the wall of French prints.

"Lydia looks a little like you," he said. "A younger you."

Rosamund laughed softly. "How thoughtful of Madame Laperne."

"It was really. It helped put me in the proper mood for the activity."

She gazed at him, something helpless in her expression. "And is the activity something you wish to pursue?" Her soft voice was edged with a gravelly quaver.

"I would very much like to excite you in that way, Rosamund, if that is what you wish."

The helplessness melted into relief. "It is what I wish."

He wrapped his arms around her waist and took her in a passionate kiss as he lifted her to sit on the table.

"Darling," he murmured against her lips before trailing tender pecks down her neck, her delicate scent intoxicating his senses. "I will do anything you desire as long as I can have you in my arms."

"Charles." She was breathless. "Charles, did you feel the fire in your veins as you struck her, as you caused the blush to rise on her cheek?"

"I felt the fire of lust coursing through my entire body." The very same fire scorching him now. "But not for Lydia. No." He slid his hands over the curves of her tightly bound bodice. "For you. I can perform the act knowing the reward is you."

He fumbled with her skirt, trying to drag it up, the sheath gown too close-fitting around her legs, frustrating enough for him to long for the fashions of two decades ago. A ridiculous hoop skirt was easier than this.

She grabbed his hands. "Charles, darling." She smiled as she ran a finger along a tuck at the side of her skirt, revealing a row of buttons all the way to the hem.

"You little minx."

She laughed as he worked frantically on unfastening the buttons. The underskirts were easier to push up. He slid his hands up her calves, over her knees, hesitating when he reached her thighs, the creamy flesh visible through the split in her drawers.

God he wanted to fuck her.

"Rosamund," he said through ragged breaths, "will you mind much if I don't attend to your needs at the moment? If I'm selfishly indulgent in my own?"

She palmed the bulge straining against his trousers, her warm hand almost inciting him to spend. "Please be as selfish as you wish."

He tore at his clothing, loosening and unfastening only as much as he needed to take his satisfaction. Anticipation heated his brow when the room's humid air enveloped his prick. He grabbed her left leg and lifted it to rest on his shoulder. Rosamund gasped and adjusted herself to the strained position, the split in her drawers widening, revealing the glorious thatch of dark hair. He grabbed his cock and leaned in, sliding against slick and heated flesh, the scratch of wiry pubic hair shooting a shiver down his spine.

In his hastiness he had misjudged his aim and had slid along the furrow between the cheeks of her lovely arse, the path slick with her excitement. He paused momentarily, letting the cleft cradle him. One day he would explore the depths of her forbidden passage, a rite sure to raise her passions to excess.

But at the moment he just needed a proper fuck.

He repositioned his cock, a sigh from her lips confirming he had found his mark. He pushed through, groaning at her cunt's welcoming squeeze, which did not relent even upon his retreat. She clutched at his shoulders, gripping harshly as he began thrusting and jostling her on the table. He steadied her with an arm around her waist and a hand under her bottom.

He was on the edge, about to spend despite the brevity of their union. Rosamund was excitement personified, her charismatic sensuality prodding him further into erotic oblivion. His groin clenched, the harbinger of release, but should he—

"Fill me, Charles. Stay inside."

He erupted, his stones emptying as his body convulsed and shook. Utterly spent, he slumped forward, his lungs burning for want of air, as if he had run full speed down a hillside in Scotland.

Rosamund's grip relaxed as she sagged backward. His cock slipped from her, dripping and sated.

Jesus Christ. Is this what Jeremy experienced every damn time?

"Rosamund, my God, that was…that was…"

"Marvelously refreshing," she said coolly.

He grinned and fished out his handkerchief, offering it first to her. She shook her head with a sly smile and went about righting her skirts.

Furtive encounters with a magnificent woman? That was just one of the wonders to look forward to in his unusual arrangement.

Rosamund breathed in Sunday morning's warm air, damp with the fragrance of blossoms and flowers in bloom. London in spring was lovely. Sharing a serene amble along the Flower Walk in Kensington Gardens arm-in-arm with one's husband was lovelier still.

She and Jeremy both seemed somehow settled in their respective hearts. Whatever had distressed Jeremy the previous autumn had been resolved. He had stopped overindulging in drink—to Rosamund's great relief—and lately had been attentive and solicitous to her needs. He'd even accompanied her to the milliner's the week before to pick out a new spring bonnet. While there, he'd expounded on current fashions rather convincingly and Rosamund left with the sophisticated and elegant coppery-brown poke bonnet she wore proudly in the Gardens.

As for Rosamund's heart, she was eagerly anticipating her new life with Charles. He had sent roses—little pink buds—that morning with a brief note of endearment surreptitiously mentioning his new pastime. Which meant he was amenable to honing his new erotic métier. She had feared he would express discomfort, but had he done so, she would have sought another sort of relationship. She wanted Charles in her life regardless.

Rosamund squeezed Jeremy's arm, and he patted her hand in return. He was smiling about something, perhaps some fantasy playing in his head. He smiled easily these days.

All around, the park was lively with couples strolling, nannies pushing perambulators, children giggling and running, old men chatting. The moment could only be more perfect if Charles were with them. Would she walk arm-in-arm with both men? She laughed softly.

"And what do you find so amusing, Lady Threxton?"

"What if I had a handsome man flanking me on either side?"

He leaned over, his breath on her cheek. "Is one of them your husband?"

She turned her head only slightly, finding her lips almost touching his. "Always, darling."

"Hmm, perhaps we should turn around and head home?"

She nudged him with her elbow. "Darling, you said you needed to get out of the house and see some scenery. You needed to provoke some fresh ideas for your work."

"I did say that, didn't I? Ah, well. I'll have to hold on to this feeling for a while, then. It won't be difficult. I can never get enough of you, my bride."

Rosamund lowered her head to hide her blush from any passersby. After twenty years, Jeremy could still make her feel like a schoolgirl.

They turned, taking a diversion from the Flower Walk that would eventually lead them to Round Pond. Jeremy suddenly slowed, holding Rosamund back.

She followed his gaze to a group standing a few steps away on the path. A pretty young woman in a simple dress was gently taking a baby as a nanny cradled it in her arms. A man stood by and watched. It was a typical familial scene replicated all across the parks of London. But this scenario was a bit different.

The man was African, the young woman English, and the baby looked to be a mixture of both.

The young woman looked up, catching a glimpse of her and Jeremy, then smiled.

Good God. Lisette LaFleur.

Jeremy's arm tensed under hers. Rosamund certainly did not want to greet the woman, yet her genuinely happy demeanor, her atypically modest dress, and her sheer joy at the babe in her arms were compelling. Perhaps she had changed from the selfish brat of the previous year.

"Lord Threxton! Good morning!" Lisette called.

The African man waved them over. He shook Jeremy's hand like an old friend.

"Lord Threxton, so good to see you." He seemed genuinely pleased.

"Mr. Ndoye," Jeremy responded, "the pleasure is mine." Jeremy hesitated a moment. "You've not met my wife, Lady Threxton, have you?"

"No, my lord," Mr. Ndoye said, his London accent vaguely tinged with French. "A pleasure, Lady Threxton." He bowed. "I am Malachias Ndoye. Your husband created the glorious sets for our production of *The Tempest* last year."

"Yes, of course, Mr. Ndoye. I remember. Jeremy was so delighted to be able to work on something other than portraiture."

The baby gurgled. *Ah, yes, the baby.* A woman should always say something about a baby.

"And who is this?" she asked with a saccharine sweetness.

Lisette beamed. "Our daughter, Rebecca." She angled the child toward Rosamund. "She's almost four months old."

Rebecca was quite possibly the prettiest child Rosamund had ever seen, her skin a healthy sun-kissed brown, her dark eyes rimmed with thick black lashes. "Oh, she's a darling," she said unaffectedly. The infant gurgled again with innocent joy.

"Thank you." Lisette blushed. "Would you like to hold her?"

It had been a very long time since she had held a baby in her arms. Would it be like slipping on an old glove? "Yes, I think I would like that."

Lisette passed Rebecca to Rosamund. The weight of the child sparked a surge of emotion. "Ah, yes, now I remember."

"My lady?" Lisette gave her a questioning look.

Rosamund rocked Rebecca, to the infant's great delight. "I lost two children. I have not held a babe since."

Lisette's mouth dropped open. "Oh, my lady, my apologies. I had absolutely no idea."

Of course you didn't. You were fucking my husband, not having deep, meaningful conversations with him. "We don't often discuss such sad memories." She carefully passed the child back to Lisette.

Lisette held Rebecca out to Jeremy with wide eyes. "Would you like to hold her, my lord?"

An expression of horror flitted almost imperceptibly across his face. "I think I'd best not, Miss LaFleur," he said curtly. "I am ill prepared for such things."

Her husband's reaction was rude but understandable. "It has been a long time," Rosamund explained.

Lisette nodded with a smile and cradled her daughter.

"Will you continue to work in the theater, Miss LaFleur?" Rosamund inquired. "Or has motherhood changed the path of your pursuits?"

"Oh, heavens, no more plays for a while." Lisette laughed.

"We've only returned to London to pack what we left behind," said Mr. Ndoye. "Including Lord Threxton's fabulous sets."

Jeremy was uncharacteristically unresponsive to the compliment.

"And where will you live?" Rosamund inquired.

"France, my lady," said Mr. Ndoye. "I have family outside Paris."

"Darling," blurted Jeremy, "remember, I have a sitting this afternoon for which I must prepare."

There was no sitting. Jeremy was desperate to remove himself.

"Of course," Rosamund said calmly. "So nice to see you again, Miss LaFleur, and to meet you, Mr. Ndoye. You have a precious daughter. If I do not see you again, I wish you well in your new life in France."

Jeremy tugged on her arm a bit too forcibly. They turned around in the direction of home.

Jeremy walked at a clipped pace toward Kensington Road to hail a cab, Rosamund clinging to his side. Once settled in a carriage, he seethed, unable to say a word to the woman who deserved so much more than his tight-lipped mortification and restrained regret. But she endured the ride back to Belgravia. She had been witness to his moods long enough to know to keep silent and simply watch London pass by.

Once home, he stormed through the door, shoving his hat and gloves at Higgins before stomping to his study. Rosamund followed close behind.

Jeremy grabbed a glass and a decanter of brandy and poured out a good measure. He stared at the glass, then raised it to his lips.

What the hell was he doing? Getting drunk wasn't going to solve anything. He'd still be the same corrupt scoundrel when he awoke from his stupor.

He set the glass down with a heavy sigh and paced the carpet before the hearth.

Rosamund took a seat on the sofa and folded her hands in her lap. She gave him a quizzical look, as if waiting for an explanation.

"Damn, damn, damn," he muttered. His bad behavior warranted an explanation.

He plopped down in a chair opposite her. "Rosie, darling, I did something terrible to you and to our marriage. I am the worst villain."

She stiffened. "Go on."

He drew in a breath. "I was incautious during my affair with Lisette. I always pull out, or ensure the woman has taken precautions of her own." He looked her in the eye. "You've trusted me to do so."

"I have, Jeremy." Her voice was calm.

"There were several times—" No. That was a lie, wasn't it? "I mean, quite often—" *Bollocks*. "Rarely. I rarely pulled out with Lisette. I was caught up in her charms and reveling in my own success, absolutely certain nothing undesired would ever happen." He eyed the glass of brandy, wishing for the feeling of obliviousness it could bring. "Lisette and I parted on good terms. The affair simply ended. I thought no more of her until the Hammonds' hunting ball."

Rosamund paled. "The Hammonds? Miss LaFleur wasn't there, was she?"

"No, no. Of course not. She was in France and would not have been invited with that crowd anyway." Jeremy stood and resumed pacing the carpet. "But one night I overheard gossip about her."

"Gossip? About Lisette? At the Hammonds'?" Rosamund was right to be incredulous. Lisette certainly did not have enough fame to be fodder for gossip amongst the aristocracy.

"One of the girls at the party had taken a disliking to her as an overbearing actress—"

Rosamund snorted.

"Yes, well, the gossip was that she was pregnant." Jeremy sat next to his wife and took her hands in his. "My God, Rosie, I went mad, certain it was mine."

Now it was Rosamund who eyed the brandy. "You took up drinking," she murmured.

He fell to his knees before her. "Darling, I am so very sorry for my behavior. I was lost. I just couldn't bring myself to talk to you about it. I feared your reaction. I feared your contempt."

"I don't know how I would have reacted to such news," she said quietly.

"You would have hated me."

She met his gaze. "No…well, yes. I suppose it would have been difficult to separate the transgression from the man."

"And then I saw Charles at the Museion. After having ended his engagement to Annalee, he lived among the artistic set in Paris. He saw Lisette and the child and assured me the child was not mine."

"Yes. I can see that now." She smoothed her thumb over his fingers. "It must have been a great relief to hear such news."

"It was, darling. And a revelation." He stood and paced. "Once I heard the gossip about Lisette, I stopped all my affairs. All the anxiety made the pursuit, the game, the acts, simply not worth it. And…" He stared at his hands, the gold wedding band catching the light from the windows. "And I couldn't perform. I could barely perform with you."

Rosamund cleared her throat. "Well…"

"You noticed. I stupidly tried to dismiss it as the effects of age."

"And I also assumed it was because you were too numb from drinking."

He sat beside her and took her left hand, tracing his fingers around her wedding ring. "Rosie, love, I do not want to have affairs anymore." He kissed the palm of her hand. "I just want to be with you." Tears fell down his cheeks, catching in his beard. "I need you."

The moment his body wracked with sobs, she embraced him, tentatively, perhaps taken aback by his flood of emotion, then holding him more tightly.

"I need you, too, Jeremy."

Her voice held despondency, understandably so. He had just revealed the depths of his despair for the last six months. His private hell unknown to her.

But now he was ready to give Rosamund and their marriage his full attention. He would never let her down again.

CHAPTER FIFTEEN

Rosamund crumpled Madame Laperne's note and tossed it in her grate, staring into the fire as the thick paper twisted and burned slowly.

Charles had done well, Madame had written. He had learned how to administer services with the paddle and understood the reasons and emotions behind the act. He was, in short, prepared for servicing Rosamund. Any barriers for proceeding would be if Rosamund herself harbored lingering reservations.

Rosamund sat on the edge of her bed, confusion roiling her insides. At the very moment she had found the perfect lover, Jeremy wanted to revert their lives to their old ways. It wasn't fair. He had already had his fun. Years of it. He wasn't thinking a whit about her.

He knew she had certain sensual needs, physical urgencies that he had said he would attend to dutifully—if he had to. Together they had worked out how to satisfy her cravings by using others who were more inclined to perform the act.

And Charles was inclined to perform the act.

And now she had to give him up?

Charles had made a great effort for her, above his own predilections, taking part in an activity that was meaningful only to her, thereby showing his genuine devotion, his desire to proceed with the affair.

Had he just wasted his time? His emotions?

Had she?

Panic tore at her gut. She needed to see him. Right that moment.

It was just before six in the evening. Jeremy was at his club. She penned a note for him to have dinner there as she was going to visit an ill friend in Richmond. She rang for Gretchen.

Her lady's maid appeared promptly.

"Gretchen, please see that this note is delivered to my husband's club. Then please pack an overnight bag for me. I've a friend who has fallen ill, and I need to attend to her."

The subterfuge should work. As far as Gretchen was concerned, Rosamund had just received a hand-delivered note from an unknown correspondent.

Gretchen helped her pack simple day clothes, no dinner wear, no jewelry. Appropriate attire for an ill friend. Rosamund changed into a drab gown, no ruffles, no lace.

She donned a dark hooded cloak, perhaps too somber for the lovely spring evening. A cab was called. The drive there and back was too far for their own coachman, she explained to Higgins. As the carriage skirted around Hyde Park heading north toward Charles's house in St. John's Wood, sudden disquietude descended. What if he wasn't home? She'd wait outside in the cab. She'd pay the cabman extra. She'd ask Charles's butler to send a note around to wherever he was.

But what if he wasn't expected home?

She'd take that chance when she got there. Right now all she wanted was to see Charles, *her* Charles. To touch him, hold him.

An hour later, as the gray of dusk dusted the evening sky, the cab pulled up to his address.

The house was a modest, semidetached, three-story brick-and-stucco building, a dim light already burning in the bay window of the front room. A stucco wall with a wrought iron gate separated the house from the quiet, suburban street and pavement. Nothing about the house indicated a famous artist lived there. No, it was all quite ordinary.

Which was good for her circumstances at that very moment. No need for the cabman to know who the occupant of the house was.

"Please, wait here," she said to the driver as she let herself out. "I'm not certain the lady is at home yet."

Rosamund opened the iron entrance gate and clutched her cloak around her as she clicked along the brick path to the front door. She rang the bell.

A well-dressed older man answered. His brow quirked upward briefly before melting into a bland countenance. "Madame?"

"Is Mr. Westerman in?"

"He is. He is not expecting visitors. Whom may I say is here to see him?"

"Lady Threxton."

The man left the door ajar. Several minutes later, voices, then quick heavy steps came from inside the house.

Charles yanked the door open, breathless from running, his clothing dabbed with paint, a smile brightening his face. The moment he saw her his expression twisted in concern. "Lady Threxton?"

"I have a bag." She pointed to the cab.

Charles waved to the cabdriver. The man brought the small carpetbag. Rosamund paid him handsomely.

Charles pulled her inside, then pushed the front door closed.

She fell into his arms.

Charles let Rosamund cling to him. Something was terribly wrong. But he would be patient and let her tell him.

"Tyler, take Lady Threxton's bag to the guest room. Then bring us tea in the parlor."

He supported her as he guided her into the parlor. He removed her cloak and sat her down on the sofa.

He paced before her. "Rosamund, I'm in the middle of touching up a canvas. I need—"

"You need to work while the paint is wet and the light is good."

He exhaled relief. So astute. Such a comfort to have a lover who understood his life. "I need the evening light for the effect I'm seeking."

"Yes, of course."

He knelt at her side. "You look troubled, darling. Tyler will bring you tea. Come up to the studio when you've settled." He caressed her cheek, its usual glow dimmed with pallor. "Or come to the studio now. We'll have tea there."

She smiled, her bloodshot eyes still dry. "I would like to see your studio."

In the corridor he called to Tyler to bring tea to the studio. He led her up the two flights of stairs to the top floor atelier. The space had not been cleaned for visitors. He tore off the canvas cloth covering the sofa and brushed the worn cushioned seat with his hand. He gestured for her to take a seat.

"I apologize for the mess. But the sofa is clean. Tyler will bring the tea soon."

She sat and he resumed coloring the sky in hues of peach and gray.

"Is this a commission for a client?"

"Yes. For Lord Somerford."

"How very prestigious." She stood and went to the bank of windows. "So much light. What a fabulous space."

A knock presaged Tyler's entry. He uncovered a draped side table and set down the tray.

"Thank you, Tyler. That will be all. We're not to be disturbed."

"Very good, sir," Tyler said with a nod, then clicked the door shut behind him.

Charles took Rosamund's hand. Side by side they looked out the window.

"Darling, sit, have tea, tell me what's upsetting you. Or not. Just be here with me. I'm honored by your presence."

She leaned her head against his shoulder. "Thank you, Charles. I need to collect my thoughts."

She sat and attended to the tea. He resumed painting the sky. The evening was a perfect model, its pose the glow of the setting sun against clouds streaking the sky. And the studio conditions couldn't be more perfect with Rosamund at his side.

Except something was clearly wrong, especially since she had brought a traveling bag. Perhaps she and Jeremy had argued. As friend to them both, that would be an awkward situation to navigate.

He dabbed a bit of blue alongside the peach, blending them together. "Did you wish to test my newly acquired skills tonight? Is that why you brought a bag with you?"

The spoon rattled on her saucer. "I suppose that was very bold of me, wasn't it?" The rosy hue of her blush matched the paint he was adding to the canvas.

He chuckled. "Yes, it was. I could have been out dining with the prince. We'll need to plan our affair a bit more. I am a working man, you know."

"Yes, yes, of course. How selfish of me. Jeremy's affairs seem to be with young ladies who have all the time in the world."

She sipped her tea. Charles added a bit of white to the clouds.

He worked as quickly as he could to catch the impressions of the changing sky. He could work on refining and perfecting another day. Rosamund's presence ensured he would remember the colors of the sunset. She heightened his senses, all of them.

"There," he said. "I can stop here. I have enough to work with." He set down his palette, wiped his brush, then went to the tea table.

"Shall I pour you a cup?" she asked.

"Please."

"Sugar?"

"No, thank you." He grabbed the canvas cloth cover and laid it on half of the sofa. "I really should wash up and change." He sat on the cover.

She handed him a cup. "You are very precise and exacting, aren't you? I don't mean that as an insult. Just an observation."

"I suppose many of my colleagues are flighty and careless."

She laughed with an honesty that sent a sparkle to her sorrow-filled eyes. She sipped her tea with that expression for a moment. When she put her cup down, the somber cast to her visage had returned.

"What if you had something you greatly desired within your grasp," she said, "and then it was taken away from you? What would you do?"

So something had happened recently. Was it about their relationship? Or her and Jeremy? "I would be greatly disappointed."

"But would you seek to regain it?"

He thought for a moment. "It would depend on the circumstances."

"How so?"

Did he want to reveal to Rosamund the depth of his feeling for another? Perhaps he should, to test what they hoped—what they thought—they had. "Well," Charles began, "when I was engaged to Annalee, I thought I had something I wanted. I thought I wanted a wife, perhaps children, a life every man strives for. But then I lost Annalee. Another man might have fought to get Annalee back, but, in losing her, I realized my desires had changed. Not only did I no longer want Annalee, I no longer wanted a wife and children."

She stared at him, her eyes wide in incredulity. "Yes, I see. You lost the thing you desired and by losing realized you no longer wanted it. I hadn't thought of that." Her gaze fell to her empty teacup on the table. "But I want it. I really do want it."

He took her hand. "Rosamund, darling, what is it? Something has been bothering you since before you set foot on my doorstep. Something that drove you here in the first place."

She met his gaze, tears forming in her eyes. "I think I've done a bad thing."

"What? What have you done?"

"Wanted you."

A chill crept up his neck. "Darling, I don't understand."

"I…I'm not certain I understand either." She looked askance, then out the window at the fading sunlight. Tears slid down her cheeks. "I just need to be with you tonight."

"Of course. You are welcome in my home anytime. I'll tell Tyler to let you in whether I'm here or not."

She faced him. "Don't you have secrets?"

He gave her a questioning look.

"If I were to be let into your home, you would trust me?"

"I might have documents regarding commissions and payments, possibly a work that was private in nature. I trust you would not betray any professional confidences. As far as any personal secrets, if you discovered something you wanted to know I would tell you. One should not have secrets from a lover."

"No, one shouldn't." Melancholia imbued her words. She stood and walked to the window. "It's getting dark. Should you light a lamp?"

He did so, bathing the studio in a soft golden glow to contrast with the deepening blue outside the window.

"Charles, do you feel you mastered the arts Madame Laperne taught you?"

"I would not say 'mastered'," he snorted darkly.

"Are competent enough in them, then?"

"I think." If she were asking if he would want to pleasure her, he was certainly prepared to do that.

"I need you to..." She looked out the window again, the twilight almost completely faded. "I need you to strike me."

The request was not said with a seductive tone. Instead it was tinged with pleading, almost desperation.

"Why do you want me to do this?" he asked.

She faced him. "I'm numb. I need you to make me feel."

She was hurt, pained. He did not want to cause more misery. "Darling, I don't understand."

"Charles, do this for me." She gathered her skirts in her hand, lifting them to expose an ankle. "Now."

He looked around the studio. He had nothing with which to swat her. Nothing.

He had to think. Paint brushes? His easel? The damn tea tray?

His gaze fell to the palette still wet with oil paint, colors he needed to recreate the next time he worked on the canvas. But he had clean palettes somewhere…

On the wall, hung up like the paddles and floggers at Madame Laperne's.

The similarity was eerie.

He drew in a long breath and moved the tea table, setting it far away from the sofa, then grabbed a clean palette, a heavy one, the wood the same heft as the paddle he had used several days ago.

"On the sofa, my lady."

She started, wide-eyed, then moved to the sofa and began to sit. He grabbed her arm to stop her. She gave a timid yelp.

"Not like that, my lady. How will I be able to perform if you sit?"

He bent her over the stuffed arm of the sofa, then lifted her skirts, bunching them at her waist. She wore the most beautiful drawers he had ever seen. Lace edged the knees and decorated the seat. Row upon row of delicate lace covered the buttocks, making the area more prominent, and more lovely. He was tempted to spank her through the fabric, yet did not want to damage the garment. The unmarred cambric would be a fine covering to a sore bottom.

He reached around her waist and untied her drawers, then slid them down to her knees.

The milky globes of her backside sparked lust in his loins. Every night he dreamed of having her bared flesh so close, of having the soft roundness of her bottom, the creamy femininity of her thighs within his grasp. The sight in the soft glow of a single lamp shot arousal to every pore of his body, ricocheting to pool in his crotch. He stared, disbelieving there was so much beauty in the world still to be discovered.

He clutched the palette, unsure just how to hold it. He tapped her right cheek, then her left, testing out the usefulness of the thing, and the best grip. With his free hand he touched her bottom, feeling for the bones he should not hit and the flesh he very definitely should.

He pulled back a little and swatted her right cheek. The flesh jiggled a moment, but did not flush. He would have to try harder. He hit again.

She gasped. He was moving toward perfection.

He smoothed his hand over the spot he had just struck. The skin was warmer there than the surrounding flesh. Warmed flesh grew to be aroused flesh. He pulled back once again and hit below the warmth.

"Yes," she cried softly

The mark left behind was dark and oblong, an odd shape because of the palette and his precarious grip on it. What if he used another implement? Yet he'd already determined he had none.

What if he used his hand? What shape would mar her backside then? Would he imprint her with his palm?

He dropped the palette to the floor, then rubbed his hands together, priming them. He should switch sides so he could compare marks. He stepped to the left a little, then drew back his hand.

Hesitation stilled him for a moment. He had never hit a woman with his bare hand in his life. No gentleman would ever do such a thing. Perhaps that was why deviants created paddles and floggers.

The act had to be done somehow. He sucked in a breath and struck her with his right hand. She lurched forward, emitting a yelping sigh.

With his left hand he touched the reddening spot. Did the burn on his right mirror the burn on her cheek? Did she experience the burn on her cheek as delicious excitement, as he did?

He hit again, smacking a softer, more pillowy area. It felt good on his palm.

He struck again. She moved forward against the sofa, emitting a breathy moan. Relief. She was feeling relief. He had reached a level of force that benefited her.

He returned to her right cheek, trying to duplicate what he had just done. She wriggled for him, enticing him.

"More."

He couldn't do much more, his palm wouldn't be able to handle it; but his brain urged him forward. He hit the same spot with the same force, then watched as the redness grew.

Her left buttock would need relief, too. He hit with equal force. She groaned an oath.

It was not rosy enough, the sides needed to match. He pulled back and let loose, slamming on her flesh with the flat of his palm, his fingers flicking into the moist folds of her sex.

She was aroused. She was wet. His cock was hard. It would be so easy.

And yet, it would be wrong. She wasn't asking for a fuck. She was asking for something else. She wanted him to give her a satisfaction he barely understood, but was growing to understand.

She needed to feel, to feel an excitement beyond sexual ecstasy, to feel a sensual release for her mind, her emotions, as well as her body.

He leaned over her, his heart throbbing with joy and confusion.

"Did I satisfy you, darling?" He needed to know.

"Oh, Charles. My sweet. Yes. Thank you."

He picked her up, her lacy drawers falling to the floor, and moved them both back to sitting on the sofa.

"Rosamund, what next?"

"Just hold me."

He did, wrapping his arms around her tightly. She would stay the night in his bed, naked at his side. The thought swelled his heart. Whether they made love did not matter. He just wanted to be with her, exist with her, know that they had shared something deeper than sexual congress.

He still did not know what troubled her. Perhaps she would tell him later that night over dinner. Or tomorrow morning. Or never. Perhaps he had resolved the issue with a release of pent-up emotion.

R osamund turned over in bed and drew in her first inhale of awakening, the faint scent of a new masculinity imbuing her senses. Charles stirred at her side, naked and disheveled, the gray streaks in his blond hair more obvious in morning's bright sunlight.

They had stayed in all night, enjoying a simple supper and a cozy evening by the fire, he reading a short story aloud as they sipped warmed cognac. He had kissed her deeply before inviting her to his bed, giving her the option of staying in the guest room if she so chose.

His tender concern for her was sweet and gentlemanly, but she wanted—no, *needed* to be with him. They slept together in his large, comfortable bed, both naked, limbs entwined. But they did not make love. They had reached a new level of intimacy in their affair, an intimacy that needed to be cherished and celebrated in its own right.

Charles's glorious chastisement of the previous evening no longer burned on her body, yet the freeing release remained etched in her memory. He was perfect for her, a combination of the intimacy of Jeremy with the eagerness of Adam. She would not, could not give him up.

Charles awoke and stretched his limbs, nudging her legs under the covers. She giggled. He grabbed her and drew her against him, wrapping a muscled arm around her shoulders.

He kissed her hair. "Darling, last night was wonderful."

She nuzzled against him. "You know, I've never spent the night with a lover."

He pulled back a little. "No?"

"No," she said. "Never. They've always been furtive encounters. Like what you and I shared at Creslow's and in my husband's studio."

"I'm happy to be your first."

She laid her palm flat on his warm belly. "You may be my last."

He gave her a squeeze. "Hmm. It was that wonderful, was it?"

She drew her finger up his abdomen to trace circles through the hair on his chest. "It was." She inhaled his presence. "But that's not what I meant."

"Oh?"

She sighed heavily. "Darling, Jeremy no longer wants me to be with you."

Charles pulled back again, then lifted her chin with his index finger. He held her gaze, his blue eyes intense. "Are you certain about this?"

"He said he doesn't want us to have any more affairs."

Charles stroked her cheek before pulling her more closely against him. "Tell me what happened to make him have a sudden change of heart."

"We were walking in Kensington Gardens and came across the actress Lisette LaFleur." Charles's comforting scent was distractingly intoxicating. "She has a child now."

"Yes, I know."

"She had been his paramour, and Jeremy had feared the child was his."

"I know that as well." He traced circles on her shoulder. "I told him it was not. I had seen Miss LaFleur and her child in Paris."

"He explained all of that to me, but only yesterday." She nestled her cheek against his chest. "He had never revealed any of this until yesterday."

"For a couple whose marriage must rely on a great deal of trust, I'm surprised he never told you."

Rosamund's eyes burned. "The whole incident has soured his desire for our unusual way of life."

Charles drew back. "But darling, Jeremy himself told me I should pursue a relationship with you. He *wants* us to be together. I was the one who had qualms."

Tears dewed her lashes. "I'm so confused. I don't know what to think anymore."

He hugged her. "Rosamund, Jeremy is not a fickle man. He would not go to extremes to get me to bed his wife only to suddenly renege." He kissed the crown of her head. "Perhaps he meant *he* no longer wanted to have affairs, especially if children are a risk. Have you asked him expressly if you, too, are meant to stop your affairs?"

She hadn't considered that. "It all happened too quickly." She wiped her tears with the edge of the sheet. "One minute we were in the park, the next we were on our way home. Then he was sobbing in my arms. When he recovered, he left for his club. He said he needed to be distracted by men for a spell."

"Does he know you are here?"

"No. I left a note saying I was visiting an ill friend in Richmond."

"What?" he yelped. He sighed heavily with a shake of his head. "Bollocks," he muttered. "Rosamund, please don't lie when it comes to us. I already feel uncomfortable with the mere idea of an affair with a married woman. I do not want to be caught up in a lie."

A flush of shame tingled her scalp. "Yes, you're right. I should not have used you like that." She slid her hand down his abdomen, stopping at the wiry curls above his sex.

There was another lie she had yet to confess. It had been weighing on her since they began their new arrangement.

"Charles, do you remember the review of your exhibition at Moulton Gallery written by my father in *Kallitechnis*?"

He chuckled. "I'll never forget it. That review changed my life. One day I should thank Rutford." He squeezed her shoulders.

She tensed under his touch. "My father didn't write the review."

His breath hitched. "He didn't?"

"No." She closed her eyes against the dread of admission. Would the praise lose meaning if he knew the words were written by a woman?

"Do you know who did?"

"Yes." She swallowed emotion. "It was I."

He stilled.

The lingering silence was distressing.

She wanted to look at him, to gauge his reaction. She remained pressed against his chest. "Charles?"

"It's always been you," he whispered hoarsely. "My muse, my patron, and now my lover." He kissed her head. "It's as if our connection was meant to be."

"You must think I arranged all of this. Believe me, I hadn't meant to seduce you. I wrote the review from the heart. I didn't even know you."

"Obviously. Else you would have recognized me in Creslow's library."

She laughed nervously. "Do you still want to be with such a wicked deceiver?"

He nuzzled his nose in her hair. "I want to be with you. You know I do."

"Then come home with me today. Talk to Jeremy with me. Be at my side."

A groan rumbled in his chest. "Rosamund, I can't get in the way of your marriage."

"It is not my marriage I have concerns about. That is solid." She raised herself on an elbow. "It's the other part of my life. The part that includes you."

"A discussion of such a unique arrangement should be between husband and wife."

"And having you there will prove to him I have a stake in his sudden change of heart. That his new proposal is simply not fair."

"I don't want to get in the way of an honest and open discussion." Charles gave her a hug. "Rosamund, darling, after you and Jeremy have a discussion, I will be happy to join in the conversation. There are things a married couple need to discuss first before anyone else gets involved."

Rosamund sighed. Charles was absolutely right. She needed to be strong before Jeremy. He was her husband and her friend. They had survived emotional hell together. They could surely work this out.

"All right," she said, burrowing against him. "After breakfast."

CHAPTER SIXTEEN

Jeremy paced the carpet in his study, his fists balled at his sides. He stopped and sucked air through his teeth.

An ill friend, she had said. In Richmond. The problem was Rosamund did not have any close friends in Richmond that he knew about.

A new affair? Unlikely. She was head over heels for Charles Westerman. And if it was a new beau, who could it possibly be?

Who could satisfy her like he and Charles?

Jeremy stared at the brandy decanter still full from when Higgins had last refilled it the other day. The amber liquor beckoned.

Christ! It wasn't even noon. He turned on his heel and paced in the other direction.

A fuss in the foyer drew his attention. Rosamund? He held himself back from running out to greet her. He closed his eyes and drew in a deep breath before calmly walking out of his study.

Rosamund looked up at him as she mounted the stairs.

He kept his cool. "Rosie, darling, I didn't expect you home so soon. Is everything all right? I mean with your friend?"

She remained in her position on the stairs. Her eyes flicked to the foyer where Higgins was giving orders to a new maid to gather her lady's coat and bag. "It was so very sudden. Shall we discuss it in the study?"

She led the way and he followed, closing the study door behind him. She clasped her hands together, then flung them apart. She faced him, her forehead wrinkled, her lips pursed.

"It's not fair, Jeremy."

Clearly they were not discussing an ill friend. Or were they? "What's not fair?"

"Your proscription against affairs."

"My…what?" Had he said that? He had been quite upset the other day. He probably said a great many things he did not mean. And he said them completely sober, so really he should remember that he had said such a preposterous thing.

She thinned her lips. "We've only just started, and now, because you've had your fill of women, I have to be content with what little I've had. It's not fair. I can't give him up, Jer. I just can't."

Charles Westerman, then. "Is this about Charles?" She must be talking about Charles. "I'm not asking you to give him up, Rosie."

She stared at him hard, red veins in the whites of her eyes. "You're not? But you said…"

"I said what?"

"After you saw Lisette LaFleur in the park and you were terribly upset you said you didn't want to have any more affairs."

Ah. "That's right. I did. What I meant was *I* did not want to have any more affairs. They drive me to drink and away from you. You, on the other hand, may have all the affairs you wish, as long as they do not drive you away or me to drink."

She paled and stood stock still. Tears formed in the corners of her eyes and slowly traversed down her cheeks.

He went to her, wrapped his arms around her, waiting for the deluge.

After a beat of silence, it came. Rosamund bawled in his arms, sobbing the name *Charles*.

Rosamund sniffled and burrowed farther into the cocoon of Jeremy's embrace. Being in his arms was so comfortable, so cozy, so familiar. And, even after twenty years, being in his arms was still so thrilling.

She was lucky to have a husband who loved her so much he allowed her the freedom to satisfy needs he himself could not adequately assuage. A husband who was not so proud he did not comprehend his limits. A husband who was generous and caring and helped her find release, even if it was by the hand of another man.

She pulled back a little, her hands still wrapped around his waist. "I'm a lucky woman, Jer," she said with a sniffle.

He handed her his handkerchief. "Lucky that you have Charles?" His expression resembled that of a sad puppy.

She laughed softly. "No, silly. Lucky that I have you. You are the best husband a woman could hope for."

He turned her around and drew her against him, her buttocks nestled against his groin. He wrapped his arms around her. "I was almost the worst."

She sighed. "I would have been resentful and hated Lisette LaFleur even more, but I would have insisted we had a hand in raising your child."

He rocked their bodies side to side. "I'm the luckiest man in the world, you know," he murmured before nipping her earlobe.

She relished in his playfulness. She and Charles had not engaged in coitus that morning, yet he had riled up her senses to a point just before frustration. She had left his house wet and aroused. Jeremy would be amenable to completing the task.

"Hmmm, how so, Lord Threxton?" She turned her head to look at him. "Flattery may produce results."

He chuckled into her shoulder then bit her gently, shooting tingling shards of desire down her spine. "I have a wife, who even in her forties is considered one of the most beautiful women in London—"

"Oh, pshaw. Flattery, not half-truths and mockery."

Over the high collar of her dress his teeth wrapped around the tendon along her lower neck, the bite piquing her nipples under her corset. "So beautiful, in fact, complete strangers find her compelling."

"Compelling does not mean attractive, my lord."

He sucked on the skin of her neck. "A woman who is so passionate it takes three men to satisfy her."

She melted into him with a moan. "I hope you sent Adam away with a handsome bonus."

His tongue flicked wet and hot inside her ear. "A woman who still deigns to take her husband to her bed despite the torrent of suitors." He cupped her breasts, rubbing his thumbs across the mounds, tormenting her nipples.

"Shall we even bother with the bed, my lord?"

He growled as he kissed her neck, his hands grabbing and fondling freely. "Shall I bend you over the sofa and have my way with you?"

"Whatever will the servants think?"

"They will scurry away and exclaim 'good God, hide the virgin maidservants, there goes Lord Threxton and his wife at it again'. At least I imagine that's what they say."

She laughed. Jeremy was so damned charming.

He pawed at her in his attempt to divest her of her clothing.

"Where on earth did you get this dress? I don't think I've ever seen it." He picked at the buttons down the back. "It's horrid."

"I wear it for charity work. It's rude to flaunt one's wealth to the poor."

"Charles Westerman is anything but poor. I cannot believe you let him see you in this."

She laughed. "I will have to let Gretchen know to make sure I wear only the finest silks when I visit my lover."

The buttons undone, Jeremy tugged at her sleeves. "We'll just have to dispense with it. The sooner, the better."

He pulled it down over her simple petticoat and made her step out of it. He tossed the dress on a chair, then stood staring at her in her underclothes.

"My, my, Lady Threxton. A man would be a fool to not take what was offered him." He picked her up in his arms. "Even if that man was her fool husband."

He carried her to the sofa and laid her down. He took off his jacket and waistcoat and stretched himself over her, trailing kisses from her neck to the lace edging of her chemise as he fumbled with the buttons of his fly. His trousers undone, he pulled off his braces.

He knelt between her legs and placed his hands on her knees. He slid his hands up her thighs until he reached the waistband of her drawers. He loosened the tie and grabbed the garment, wrenching it down, exposing her quim.

He licked his lips like a wolf before prey. "Did he fuck you?" he asked with a gravelly rumble.

Poor Jeremy. He would not get the satisfaction of one of his favorite letches. "No."

He stared at her, incredulous. "No?"

"It wasn't that sort of tryst."

He gazed at her, a flicker of despondency in his depths. "Ah. Has he learned how to satisfy you, then? In the other way."

"He's a quick learner. He learned from the best."

Jeremy quirked a brow. "Adam?"

She laughed. "Madame Laperne herself."

Jeremy reached between her legs. "You must have been left thoroughly frustrated when you left his house this morning." He grinned as he twisted a finger in the damp curls of her motte.

He knew her too well. He would know that she would need release very soon. He teased her sticky folds with his fingers, avoiding her clitoris, grunting a chortle as she groaned too readily. She rocked her hips against his hand, hoping he would find his way to the tender nub.

But it was not to be. Instead he grabbed her hips and tilted her up. He bent over and took her sex in his mouth, sliding his hot tongue through her wetness before he thrust it inside her cunt.

It was exactly what she needed. Relief flowed outward to calm every limb, to soothe her frayed nerves, to fill her heart with contentment and her sex with more lust.

Jeremy lapped at her like a hungry man, deep-throated moans reverberating through her as he feasted. His long-standing fantasy was to delve his tongue into the spendings left by a previous lover. It was a shame she could not truly satisfy his letch this time. But she could rile him up.

She tucked her hips and pressed herself against him. "Lick it, all of it, leave nothing behind."

He came up for air briefly, his breath hot and humid on her aching pearl.

Rosamund grabbed fistfuls of his hair. "There's not much; his was a weak showing, a mere dribble."

Jeremy resumed, working vigorously, the wiry strands of his beard scratching and tangling with her pubic hair.

"Your cock will gush oceans inside me, filling me, deluging what little spunk his pathetic prick was able to produce."

With a snarling oath, Jeremy rose up and grabbed her at the waist. He slammed inside her with his iron-hard cock, holding himself there as he gazed down at her. His eyes were black with lust, his forehead furrowed and wrinkled in determination.

"Is his cock as hard as mine?" He shoved in deeper.

"No."

He began his slow slide out. "Does his cock fill your cunt like mine?"

"No."

He thrust with an even cadence. "Can he satisfy you as I can?"

"Never."

He clutched her to him and commanded her with the rhythm of his lust, fucking her with resolve, a man needing to take his pleasure. Sweat sheened on his face, his ragged breaths puffing in clipped grunts near her ear, signs he was at the edge. He would not need any encouragement. Still—

"He says he's saving all his spunk to spend inside your arse."

"*Fuck!*"

Jeremy slammed inside her, holding himself there as he sputtered and shuddered, his nails digging deliciously into her waist.

Moments later he loosened his hold and fell on top of her, panting, his heart pounding with every exhalation.

He laughed. "My God, woman, what has gotten into you?"

"My wondrously tolerant husband, who loves and trusts me so very much."

"And lets you cuckold him."

"And who enjoys that I cuckold him."

Jeremy chortled and nuzzled his nose in her hair. "God, Rosie, I love you so much. Words cannot express how much I love you."

Tears pooled in her eyes. She stroked his arm. "I love you, Jer. Thank you for being my husband."

"Gemma, fix your bonnet."

"Yes, Mama."

"And keep hold of Matilda's hand until you reach the park."

"Yes, Mama."

Charles leaned against the wall at the edge of Francesca's foyer and observed the charming familial scene. Francesca fussed with the collar of Lottie's coat before moving to Bobby's boot laces. Matilda hovered by, waiting patiently. When Francesca gave her the nod, Matilda gathered up the children and ushered them out the front door.

Francesca let out a heavy sigh. "They grow so quickly."

Charles draped an arm around her shoulders and led her down the corridor to the parlor. While Francesca called for tea, he settled in a pale rose velvet armchair, sinking into the thick, deeply tufted cushions. She flitted about, straightening objects in the well-ordered, tidy room, until the maid brought in the tray.

It was their usual Tuesday afternoon tea, shared by brother and sister alone. Except this time, Charles still felt the glow of Rosamund's presence from having been in his bed that morning and in his fantasies when he had frigged himself after she had left.

Francesca perched on the sofa and poured his cup. "How was your evening with Lady Threxton?"

Charles stared at his sister as the sting of suspicion stabbed his chest. "How the devil did you know I saw her last night?"

Francesca smothered a smile. "You look"—the smile broke through—"refreshed."

His cheeks heated. "Damn," he muttered.

"It's meant to be a compliment, dear brother. And, watch your language in my house." She handed him his tea.

Charles took the cup and quickly gulped a swallow, the hot liquid a balm to his mortification.

"I take it, then, the affair is progressing smoothly?"

He set his cup and saucer down. "Honestly? I'm not quite sure."

"Oh?" The teaspoon clinked against porcelain as Francesca stirred her tea.

"It seems Threxton is suddenly having second thoughts. Although I can scarcely believe that. He's the one who suggested it."

"Perhaps he feels threatened. You are more successful than he is, as an artist I mean." She grinned against the rim of her cup. "I don't know about your other talents."

Charles burst out laughing. Francesca's perspicuity surprised him sometimes. "I'm fairly certain we two men are well matched, if you must know."

"I really don't want to know, Charles."

He wiped a tear from the corner of his eye. "Well, the way Rosamund tells it, it's because Threxton saw an old lover. Their affair had gone miserably. I suppose Threxton could be trying to protect his wife from a similar outcome." *Damn.* What if Jeremy had decided to renege on his agreement? "Rosamund wants me to meet with the both of them and have a talk."

Francesca shook her head slowly. "Sounds dreadful. And complicated."

Charles grunted his agreement and sighed into the armchair.

"Charles," Francesca drawled as she put down her teacup, "what about a wife of your very own? Not one that you share with another man?"

"Did Father tell you to ask that?"

"No. I'm asking. I just suppose I'm old-fashioned in that regard."

Charles slumped in the chair. "Annalee soured me on the whole idea, I must admit."

"It's not all bad. You have many friends who have solid marriages. Including the Thrextons."

"True. But why do I require a wife?"

"Children, perhaps? You're so good with them."

"Frannie, I love your children, and will be as a father to them as needed. But I've never felt the urge to have any of my own."

"All right. How about companionship?"

"I have that with Rosamund now." An especial kind of companionship that lacked the trials and tribulations of a woman inexperienced in life and love, such as was Annalee.

"And for those occasions when Rosamund needs to be Lord Threxton's companion? What then?"

"I have you." Francesca had proved to be a rock where matters of his heart were concerned. If she never married again—for love, as it should be—then he would be there for her as an escort to society's affairs, and as an adviser and patron when she needed a man to navigate the vicissitudes of a man's world.

Francesca blushed. "Yes, well, dear brother, I'll have you know I might not be always available at your beck and call."

"How's that?"

She blushed deeply and glanced away.

Charles grinned. "Has Harbough proposed?"

"No," she said quietly. "But I think…I mean to say…well, I hope so. Maybe one day."

She deserved it. His wonderful sister deserved love and everything else that came with a connection to an honorable and handsome man.

Damn. He also deserved love and all its appurtenances. Rosamund fulfilled that for him. Maybe one day he'd find a woman who would be his wife. But right now he had Rosamund. And whatever the hell game Jeremy was playing with them had to stop.

CHAPTER SEVENTEEN

Charles stood on the doorstep of the Threxton residence, his stomach churning, his legs threatening to buckle. He had almost given in to nerves and not shown up.

It had been several days since Rosamund had spent the night at his house. Days filled with waiting, wondering, wanting. Had he done something wrong? They'd have told him, wouldn't they? Rosamund and Jeremy were his friends. What the hell did he have to worry about?

Jeremy's wrath, perhaps? Had Rosamund's reputation somehow been tarnished? Did they need time away from him to reconsider the whole affair?

Rosamund had written him, saying she cherished their time together, but that social obligations had got in the way, and she hoped he was progressing on his canvas for the Earl of Somerford in the meantime. She had said nothing about Jeremy, whether he knew or not, whether he cared or not.

Her restraint was somewhat off-putting, a little annoying.

Then, suddenly, there was a note from Jeremy requesting Charles's presence at the Thrextons' house for a private conference with Jeremy and Rosamund. The note wasn't completely impersonal, but it wasn't a jovial missive from a friend either. And it did not allude to what might be the topic of conversation.

Charles drew in a deep inhalation and pressed the doorbell. Mr. Higgins answered, stepping aside to allow Charles inside. The butler took his hat, then requested Charles follow him to the study. At the study door, Higgins knocked twice, then opened the door and waved Charles through.

The instant the door closed behind him Rosamund was in his arms, her delicate fragrance of roses swirling in his already agitated senses.

"Oh, Charles. It's so good to see you."

She had been sitting at a chair alongside a grand desk behind which sat Jeremy, grinning ear to ear.

So they weren't angry. Still, why the days of silence?

Jeremy rose and went to him. "I'm glad you've come, Charles." They shook hands. He gestured to a chair next to the one Rosamund had vacated. "Please."

Charles took his place, an elegant and ancient silver tea service before him on the desk. Rosamund sat and grabbed the teapot.

"Shall I pour you a cup?" she asked, the ornate pot poised above an equally exquisite teacup with Rococo gilding and flowers.

"Yes, please." Tea would add a measure of normalcy to the occasion.

"No sugar," she said with a wink.

Jeremy folded his hands and placed them on the desk. "You seem a bit nervous, Charles. I suppose you must be wondering why I called you here."

Charles gulped his tea. "I am."

"Right. Well, I'll get to the point."

About damn time.

Jeremy cleared his throat. "You know Rosamund and I grant each other a great many freedoms in our marriage with regard to lovers. My lovers have all been somewhat transient, and Rosie's have been furtive encounters or hired." Jeremy held his gaze. "What we have yet to try is having a lover be a more permanent part of our marriage. Another partner, if you will."

"A partner?" The word made his love affair sound like an outlandish business proposal.

"Yes," Jeremy continued, "and along with that we'd like to suggest some arrangements." He steepled his fingers. "When you're here at the London house, you'll stay in Rosamund's room. We'll alert the staff to your presence—"

Good God. Was this really happening? Charles gave a slight shake to his head, aghast.

"They are used to our unusual affairs and have been sworn to secrecy regarding such matters. We have yet to have a member of our staff spread gossip or rumors, so you needn't worry about your career."

His career? Charles was more concerned for his heart.

Jeremy drew in a breath. "At the country house, Langley Heights, you will be given your own set of rooms."

Like a guest? Or a kept man?

"It's a grand estate. We can set you up with a studio there, if you like."

Well, there was his answer. It seemed the aristocratic and privileged Thrextons had arranged everything for him, telling him what to expect, rather than letting him have a say in the matter. Keeping him at their country estate like hired staff, as Brockhurst had done.

The Thrextons weren't suggesting an affair of the heart, an exploration of the senses with a wonderful woman. Instead, their arrangement held an unpalatable suggestion of commerce.

"This is preposterous!" Charles stood. He turned his back to the couple, a part of him just wanting to leave, another part filled with a morbid curiosity, wanting to know how they would react.

No. He couldn't leave. He had to stay and fight. He couldn't give her up. He'd tried for over a year. He wanted Rosamund. Desperately. Admittedly the Thrextons had that hold over him. And, he had already given up so much in the face of Rosamund's seductive wiles, taking on her letch as his own. But now they were asking him to give up even more. Become a plaything in their house. In *both* their houses.

Charles turned to face the couple. "And what about that little viewing room, Threxton? Will I be expected to perform with your wife for your pleasure?"

Jeremy paled, his expression tightening into mortification. "Good God, Westerman," he said, his voice barely above a whisper. "On my word, no. I would never want such a thing."

Rosamund eyed Charles intensely, her lips twisting in thought before they pulled into a wry smile. "You don't understand the power you have in our relationship, Charles, do you?"

Charles started. "Power? How the hell do I have any power when you're planning my life out for me?"

Rosamund shifted in her chair. "I apologize that we seem so exacting and formal." She reached across the desk and took Jeremy's hand in hers. "My husband is more used to negotiating with Madame Laperne and her staff. We've never wanted a close friend to be part of our lives in this way. It is new to us as well." She leaned forward. "I am utterly under your spell, Charles. It is you who has power over me. And as for Jeremy, your effect on me has profoundly affected him."

Charles narrowed his eyes at Jeremy.

The viscount glanced away, coloring under his beard. He sucked in a breath. "I didn't mean to make you feel uncomfortable in any way, Charles. I think I became too excited myself with the potential of the proposition. I know the excitement of being with someone new, someone who is not my wife, and I know the disappointment that comes upon the realization that the pairing no longer works. Rosamund is in the throes of the initial excitement, except this time she—and I—feel there is the possibility of something permanent. Truth be told, I should bow down to you and thank you."

"Thank me?"

Jeremy beamed. "It's like she's—like we're young again. In that fresh excitement of youthful romance. If you don't mind me saying, the sex is fantastic."

Charles stood stock-still, unable to move. He blinked his eyes.

Jeremy colored again. "You do realize I still sleep with my own wife?"

Incredible. "Of course. Why wouldn't you?" Charles said vacantly.

"Just not while you're here."

"Not while—" Charles stopped. Threxton would give up sleeping with his wife if Charles were under the same roof? "What about at this country estate of yours? Will you not bed your wife while I am there for an extended holiday?"

Jeremy gaped. "I…" He threw a panicked glance at Rosamund. "We haven't really discussed that."

"Charles," Rosamund said quietly, "please. I want this to work." Her eyes pleaded above her quivering smile, the intensity of her emotion hitting him right in the gut.

The reality was he was sharing Rosamund with this man. Sharing the love and friendship of a remarkable woman with a man who wanted to share her. He was being pig-headed. Jeremy and Rosamund weren't trying to control him, they were navigating a new way of life in the only way they knew how—by using the methods they had used in the past for a similar sharing.

"But this time the relationship is so different," Charles muttered aloud.

Jeremy offered a quizzical expression. "Sorry? What was that?"

Charles snorted. "I'm the one who should apologize. I'm the one being selfish." He sat down. "Let's start this off again. As friends. It's not a business arrangement, it's an amicable arrangement."

Charles took his seat, and poured fresh tea to warm his cup. "I have no illusions and accept I am something of a lesser partner in this relationship."

Rosamund laid her palm on his knee, the touch livening, arousing. "Charles, darling, don't say that."

"No, hear me out. You two are married. That has a depth of meaning. You are bonded legally, bonded by your past together, by your memories. Amongst the permutations of the three of us you two are primary." He sipped his tea. "But I wouldn't call my status here secondary, as I suppose I have some importance. Perhaps affiliate is a more proper designation. Or associate."

Jeremy chuckled.

Rosamund smiled. "Our associate. All right. I think I like the sound of that."

"Concerning where all of this will take place, of course Rosamund is welcome at my house whenever she chooses." Charles met her gaze. "But staying overnight is risky for your reputation, my lady. I suggest you do not do it again."

"It was foolhardy of me. Still, I want to see you."

"Here, at Wilton Place," Charles suggested. "And only when Jeremy is present. Although I cannot think why I would not return to my own house."

"We've become best mates and drinking companions," Jeremy offered.

Charles grinned. "Perfect. How about we get drunk at the club one evening, you and I?"

"Darling," Rosamund said to Jeremy, "*your* reputation." She turned to Charles. "Yours, as well."

"Oh, pshaw, Rosie," Jeremy said. "We'll appear tipsy and friendly in public once and never again. As long as our work does not suffer, no one will take notice. They'll forget everything at the next exhibition, where we'll be on our best behavior."

"It's an excellent pretense for my staying here, and my joining you at Langley Heights." Charles pursed his lips. The next was going to be an awkward point of discussion. "Now, Jeremy, about your letch for voyeurism."

Jeremy flushed crimson.

"I need time to think about that."

"Charles, I'm not asking you to agree to such acts."

"I know. I'm willing to contemplate the idea, but I reserve the right to refuse."

Jeremy exhaled. "Absolutely."

"Gentlemen," Rosamund said. "We are forgetting something very important here."

Both turned to her. "Which is?" Jeremy said.

She once again laid her hand on Charles's knee, giving a little squeeze. "Charles," she said softly, "what about other women? I mean, for you."

"A wife, Westerman?"

Charles laughed softly at Jeremy's notion. He took Rosamund's hand. "Don't worry about me, darling. I think I have all I need right now."

All I need, he had said.

Rosamund relaxed in her bathtub, warm water gently lapping at her shoulders and breasts. She let out a sigh of contentment and fulfillment. The discussion earlier that afternoon had solidified her relationship with the two most important men in her life. Two men who loved and cared about her, each in his own way, each man uniquely satisfying a need, and, together, both men satisfying all her needs.

She inhaled the lavender-scented steam and closed her eyes, sliding farther down the porcelain into the deliciously sensuous heat. The moment could only be more perfect if Charles or Jeremy were at her side, ogling her, reading to her…

"You look so vulnerable when you're naked."

Rosamund jolted up, splashing water onto the tile floor.

"Charles!"

He laughed as he dragged a chair to the side of the tub and sat down.

"How did you get in here?"

He leaned his elbows on his knees, rolled-up shirtsleeves revealing the light-brown hair on his arms. "I gave Gretchen the evening off."

Which meant he was staying the night. Her nipples betrayed her excitement at the prospect.

He gazed at her lasciviously, tugging his lower lip with his teeth. "Do you realize how beautiful you are, Lady Threxton?"

A flush crept across her face. "Perhaps."

He stood and strolled casually around the tub, occasionally dipping his fingers through the water, humming throatily.

She chilled despite the warm water. He was up to something.

He knelt down alongside, staring at her breasts. He cupped one, then the other, before sliding his hand along her midriff and around her waist.

In one sudden movement, he pulled her up, lifting her out of the tub and into his arms. He grabbed a towel and carried her, dripping wet, down the hall to her bedroom, she too stunned and chilled to struggle. Once inside, he kicked the door closed and deposited her on the daybed.

"We never finished what we started the other night, my lady."

She shivered, her cold flesh prickling further from his words. He tossed the towel to her. She wrapped it around her shoulders.

"And now with our new arrangement, I have a desire of my own." He sat beside her, his warmth permeating her flesh. "A letch, if you will, that I wish to pursue."

He enveloped her in his arms, taking her in a deep kiss, the scruff of his cheeks scraping against her trembling lips. He tightened his hold as he hauled her over his lap, her hips bent against a strong masculine thigh.

Excitement plumped her sex. She tried to calm her pounding heart with steady breaths.

He teased her butt cheeks with gentle grazes of his fingernails, spiking gooseflesh on her damp skin. "So perfect."

The tenderness of his touch soothed her. She let tension slip away and melted against his legs.

"That's right. Let go. Just feel." The grazes stopped.

The slap of his palm on her still-damp flesh stung. She yelped.

"It hurts more when you're wet and chilled, my lady, does it not?"

She whimpered.

"I thought so." He slapped the other cheek.

Her cunt squeezed in reaction. He stroked her inner thighs, tantalizingly close to her quim. Surely he would know she was aroused.

"This glorious arse is mine." He kissed one cheek. "I can do what I want with this magnificence." He bit the other cheek.

Rosamund flinched. He held her fast, then swatted her with exhilarating firmness, raising a glorious heat and eliciting a satisfied sigh.

His fingers played in her slick sex, drawing the wetness up to her anus, lubricating the rosette. The intense intimacy sent shivers up her spine.

"Shall I lay my claim to your arse in a different way?" He pressed the tip of a finger into the tight hole.

Pain startled her. Rosamund tensed around him.

"I quite enjoy possessing a woman in this way. Have you ever done such a thing before, my lady?"

She had once. With Jeremy. It had been more thrilling for him than for her.

"Ah. Silence. Well, whatever memory of the act you have, I shall erase it."

He drew more of her dew to the orifice, once again slipping the tip of his finger inside, then, ever so slowly, more of his finger. Rosamund gasped and clutched Charles's ankles, her body tensing, her jaw clenching. He slithered his other hand between their bodies, questing until he found her clitoris, and began to massage the little nub.

Absolute pleasure was tempered by the agony of farther invasion into her forbidden depths. Rosamund tried to ignore the searing torment, tried to concentrate on the luscious ecstasy.

Suddenly, Charles stopped his erotic ministrations. He pulled his finger out of her bum, leaving burning discomfort in its wake, and got up. Rosamund tumbled to the carpet.

"Hands and knees," he said.

His forceful tone ignited an incredible surge of fiery lust, sparking every nerve with sensual need.

She positioned herself as commanded. Behind her came the rhythmic sputter of Charles tearing open the flies of his trousers and drawers. Her eyes drifted closed, waiting for his cock to fill her, her rosette unexpectedly flexing in anticipation.

But he was taking too long to undress.

The scent of lavender flared her nostrils. The cold cream from her dressing table. Rosamund's eyes flew open as he slathered the substance on her anus, working it deeply inside. She recoiled at his roughness, but he grabbed her and held her steady.

"Tonight you're mine, my lady, in a new way."

His cock poked at the tight entrance. She braced herself.

"Relax," he murmured. He reached around and found her excited nub, massaging with determination.

He entered her, his invasion excruciatingly slow while his attention to her clit was gloriously assiduous. Her eyes watered as she tried to temper her uneven breaths, tried to focus on the pleasure. Grunting enough blasphemies for the both of them, Charles slid in farther, deeper, shoving forward until he was fully embedded to the root.

"Oh, God." His attentions to her clit stopped as he grasped her hips. He dug his nails into her, adding piquancy to her now burning arsehole.

His slide out was as torturous as his return to her depths. Unwittingly, she let out a plaintive whimper. He chortled and resumed attention to her clit.

"Think of the rapturous release, my lady, while I claim what is mine."

He fucked her arse slowly, all the while steadily working her pearl of pleasure, pressing a finger harder against the slippery, sticky wetness. He tickled the dripping opening to her cunt, taking her to such a frenzy she wanted him to fuck her harder, wanting him to plunder her dark passage. She matched his cadence with an encouraging syncopated beat. He growled as he increased his pace, his stones slapping against her quaint.

Suddenly, he stopped his ministrations. She held on to the lingering ecstasy as he gripped her haunches to pound into her, the locus of pleasure now their taboo connection, his ragged breathing the symphonic accompaniment to their erotic dance. Pleasure and pain merged, taking her on an unexplored journey toward bliss.

He slammed against her with a clipped howl and emptied himself, each juddering jerk stretching her. He calmed and stayed poised for a moment, panting. His hold on her hips slackened, and he bent over her to envelope her in his arms.

"You're mine, Rosamund. Part of you anyway. I possess your bottom, do you understand? That husband of yours has no claim there."

She flexed around his waning cock in response. He chuckled darkly as his hand strayed once again to her clit, massaging relentlessly, this time concentrating only on her pleasure. The ascent to orgasm recommenced, his growing presence inside her hastening the climb to the peak. She held on to that luscious moment before climax, reveling at the tightness of his now fully erect cock. She let go, contracting as she came, pushing him out of her body.

She released a long exhalation. "Yes, Charles. I am yours."

CHAPTER EIGHTEEN

Langley Heights, Norfolk, August 1881

A graying ancient oak stretched its gnarled branches over a glassy stream edged by long grasses and faded wildflowers. Above, the white blue of the sky was tinted with the pale yellow of late summer.

Charles dabbed a bit more green on the canvas. A yellow green, the color of a lime he'd once seen in Spain. It set off the blue and white of her dress quite nicely and complemented the golden brown of her hair peeking out from under her straw bonnet.

He had never before included figures in his landscapes. Sheep, cows, and birds were not uncommon, but their existence was always dominated by the hills and fields. There had been a dog once or twice, a cat in at least one of them. But never a person.

Rosamund had changed all that for him. He felt compelled to include something of her in his work now. A composition she suggested, a color she wore, a feeling she instilled.

Even her very presence.

That day at the Summer Exhibition, seeing her standing before his large canvas had first given him the idea. He did not need to show her face; no one would know who she was, no one would gossip about who she might be. Just a woman from behind, sitting in a woven wicker chair, her head bent as she read a book.

Except in reality she was reading the newspaper out loud to him. The society column no less.

"Oh, my. Lady Hammond must be in a seventh heaven of delight. Her supposedly unmarriageable daughter just got engaged. I didn't foresee that."

Charles chuckled. He did not understand the appeal of such topics, but apparently Rosamund found it necessary to keep abreast of them.

The steady crunch of boots on the gravel path leading to the bucolic setting made him turn around. Jeremy approached, dressed in the casual walking attire he sported while in residence at his country estate. He, too, would be a good model one day, elegant, lanky, and bearded. The quintessential artist. Perhaps Charles and Jeremy would exchange portraits of each other. Charles's art had changed, reflecting the changes in his life. Delving into portraiture after having added figures to his landscapes would not be so remarkable.

Jeremy stood behind him. "You capture her well."

"Thank you," Charles replied.

A year ago he wouldn't have believed he would be so deeply involved with the couple. But the last few months had proved to be illuminating. Rosamund needed him. He saw a different side of her than what Jeremy saw. But she also needed Jeremy to complete her.

For the moment, Charles was content with their affair. The most surprising aspect was the relationship he was developing with Jeremy. They had begun critiquing each other's work, had begun influencing each other, had begun to talk of collaboration. The Summer Exhibition of 1882 would prove to be an interesting one for the both of them. Would art critics remark upon the influence?

Jeremy breathed in the late summer air. "You discern a side of her that escapes me."

Charles smiled. "And you allow her the freedom to explore that. Not many husbands are so gracious and understanding."

"I suppose not." Jeremy grinned as he stared at his wife.

Rosamund laughed softly. "I imagine not many husbands have wives that need such freedom."

"You underestimate your sex, my lady."

She turned and flashed a smile to the both of them.

Jeremy moved a matching wicker chair next to Charles, positioning it for a view of the easel. "Ours is a fine association, wouldn't you agree, Charles?"

Association. What they had started calling the relationship amongst the three of them.

"Yes, it is, Jeremy. A very fine association."

About the Author

Regina Kammer is a librarian, an art historian, and an award-winning, international best-selling, multi-published writer of provocative historical romance and contemporary romance with a touch of history. Her short stories and novels make history sexier, whether the era is Roman, Byzantine, Viking, American Revolution, or Victorian. She's even sexed up contemporary settings, Steampunk, and Greco-Roman mythology. She has been published by Cleis Press, Go Deeper Press, Ellora's Cave, House of Erotica, Story Ink, Loose Id, The Naughty Literati, and her own imprint, Viridium Press. She began writing historical fiction with romantic elements during National Novel Writing Month 2006, switching to erotica when all her characters suddenly demanded to have sex.

Keep up with Regina

Check out her website: https://reginakammer.com/
Never miss a new release! Subscribe to *Kammerotica News*:
https://reginakammer.com/newsletter/

Historical erotic romance by Regina

Victorian

The Pleasure Device (Harwell Heirs Book 1)
Disobedience By Design (Harwell Heirs Book 2)
Where Destiny Plays (Harwell Heirs Book 3)
The Westerman Affair (Art & Discipline Book 1)
The Demonstration
The Invitation
Disputed Boundaries (Stories from the San Juan Islands)

American Revolution

The General's Wife: An American Revolutionary Tale
Winter Interlude: An American Revolutionary Novelette
On the Eighteenth of January, '78; or, A Night At Valley Forge

Ancient World

Hadrian and Sabina: A Love Story
Ancient Shorts: An Ancient World Romance Collection

Steampunk

One Cheek Or Two? (Ockham Steam-Works Laboratory Chronicles 1)
Delia's Heartthrob (Ockham Steam-Works Laboratory Chronicles 2)
Swing Follies (Ockham Steam-Works Laboratory Chronicles 3)